Must Love Flowers

"A testament to the power of new beginnings. Wise, warm, witty, and charmingly full of hope, this story celebrates the surprising and unexpected ways that family, friendship, and love can lift us up."
—KRISTIN HANNAH,
bestselling author of *The Nightingale*

"Uplifting, warm, and hopeful. With her signature charm and wit, Debbie Macomber proves that the best relationships, like the perfect blooms, are always worth the wait. . . . This can't-miss novel is Macomber at the height of her storytelling prowess. I absolutely adored it!"
—KRISTY WOODSON HARVEY, *New York Times*
bestselling author of *The Summer of Songbirds*

"Debbie Macomber never fails to deliver an uplifting, heart-warming story. Whether you're just starting out, just starting over, or anything in between, *Must Love Flowers* should be at the top of your summer reading list!"
—BRENDA NOVAK, *New York Times*
bestselling author of *Before We Were Strangers*

The Best Is Yet to Come

"Macomber's latest is a wonderful inspirational read that has just enough romance as the characters heal their painful emotional wounds." —*Library Journal*

"This tale of redemption and kindness is a gift to Macomber's many readers and all who love tales of sweet and healing romance." —*Booklist*

It's Better This Way

"Macomber has a firm grasp on issues that will resonate with readers of domestic fiction. Well-drawn characters and plotting—coupled with strong romantic subplots and striking coincidences—will keep readers rooting for forgiveness, hope and true love to conquer all."
—KATHLEEN GERARD,
blogger at *Reading Between the Lines*

"Macomber keeps her well-shaded, believable characters at the heart of this seamlessly plotted novel as she probes the nuances of familial relationships and the agelessness of romance. This deeply emotional tale proves it's never too late for love." —*Publishers Weekly* (starred review)

A Walk Along the Beach

"Macomber scores another home run with this surprisingly heavy but uplifting contemporary romance between a café owner and a photographer. Eloquent prose . . . along with [a] charming supporting cast adds a welcome dose of light and hope. With this stirring romance, Macomber demonstrates her mastery of the genre."
—*Publishers Weekly* (starred review)

"Highly emotional . . . a hard-to-put-down page-turner, yet, throughout all the heartache, the strength and love of family shines through." —*New York Journal of Books*

Window on the Bay

"This heartwarming story sweetly balances friendship and mother-child bonding with romantic love."
—*Kirkus Reviews*

"Macomber's work is as comforting as ever." —*Booklist*

Cottage by the Sea

"Romantic, warm, and a breeze to read—one of Macomber's best." —*Kirkus Reviews*

"Macomber never disappoints. Tears and laughter abound in this story of loss and healing that will wrap you up and pull you in; readers will finish it in one sitting."
—*Library Journal* (starred review)

"Macomber's story of tragedy and triumph is emotionally engaging from the outset and ends with a satisfying conclusion. Readers will be most taken by the characters, particularly Annie, a heartwarming lead who bolsters the novel."
—*Publishers Weekly*

Any Dream Will Do

"*Any Dream Will Do* is . . . so realistic, it's hard to believe it's fiction through the end. Even then, it's hard to say goodbye to these characters. This standalone novel will make you hope it becomes a Hallmark movie, or gets a sequel. It's an inspiring, hard-to-put-down tale. . . . You need to read it."
—*The Free Lance–Star*

"*Any Dream Will Do* by Debbie Macomber is a study in human tolerance and friendship. Macomber masterfully shows how all people have value." —*Fresh Fiction*

If Not for You

"A heartwarming story of forgiveness and unexpected love."
—*Harlequin Junkie*

"A fun, sweet read." —*Publishers Weekly*

A Girl's Guide to Moving On

"Beloved author Debbie Macomber reaches new heights in this wise and beautiful novel. It's the kind of reading experience that comes along only rarely, bearing the hallmarks of a classic. The timeless wisdom in these pages will stay with you long after the book is closed."
—Susan Wiggs, #1 *New York Times* bestselling author of *Starlight on Willow Lake*

"Debbie dazzles! A wonderful story of friendship, forgiveness, and the power of love. I devoured every page!"
—Susan Mallery, #1 *New York Times* bestselling author of *The Friends We Keep*

Last One Home

"Fans of bestselling author Macomber will not be disappointed by this compelling stand-alone novel."
—*Library Journal*

ROSE HARBOR

Sweet Tomorrows

"Macomber fans will leave the Rose Harbor Inn with warm memories of healing, hope, and enduring love."
—*Kirkus Reviews*

"Overflowing with the poignancy, sweetness, conflicts and romance for which Debbie Macomber is famous, *Sweet Tomorrows* captivates from beginning to end."
—*Bookreporter*

"Fans will enjoy this final installment of the Rose Harbor series as they see Jo Marie's story finally come to an end."
—*Library Journal*

Silver Linings

"Macomber's homespun storytelling style makes reading an easy venture. . . . She also tosses in some hidden twists and turns that will delight her many longtime fans."
—*Bookreporter*

"Reading Macomber's novels is like being with good friends, talking and sharing joys and sorrows."
—*New York Journal of Books*

Love Letters

"Macomber's mastery of women's fiction is evident in her latest. . . . [She] breathes life into each plotline, carefully intertwining her characters' stories to ensure that none of them overshadow the others. Yet it is her ability to capture different facets of emotion which will entrance fans and newcomers alike." —*Publishers Weekly*

"Romance and a little mystery abound in this third installment of Macomber's series set at Cedar Cove's Rose Harbor Inn. . . . Readers of Robyn Carr and Sherryl Woods will enjoy Macomber's latest, which will have them flipping pages until the end and eagerly anticipating the next installment." —*Library Journal* (starred review)

"Uplifting . . . a cliffhanger ending for Jo Marie begs for a swift resolution in the next book." —*Kirkus Reviews*

Rose Harbor in Bloom

"[Debbie Macomber] draws in threads of her earlier book in this series, *The Inn at Rose Harbor,* in what is likely to be just as comfortable a place for Macomber fans as for Jo Marie's guests at the inn." —*The Seattle Times*

"Macomber's legions of fans will embrace this cozy, heartwarming read." —*Booklist*

"Readers will find the emotionally impactful storylines and sweet, redemptive character arcs for which the author is famous. Classic Macomber, which will please fans and keep them coming back for more." —*Kirkus Reviews*

"The storybook scenery of lighthouses, cozy bed and breakfast inns dotting the coastline, and seagulls flying above takes readers on personal journeys of first love, lost love and recaptured love [presenting] love in its purest and most personal forms." —*Bookreporter*

The Inn at Rose Harbor

"Debbie Macomber's Cedar Cove romance novels have a warm, comfy feel to them. Perhaps that's why they've sold millions." —*USA Today*

"Debbie Macomber has written a charming, cathartic romance full of tasteful passion and good sense. Reading it is a lot like enjoying comfort food, as you know the book will end well and leave you feeling pleasant and content. The tone is warm and serene, and the characters are likable yet realistic. . . . *The Inn at Rose Harbor* is a wonderful novel that will keep the reader's undivided attention."
—*Bookreporter*

"The prolific Macomber introduces a spin-off of sorts from her popular Cedar Cove series, still set in that fictional small town but centered on Jo Marie Rose, a youngish widow who buys and operates the bed-and-breakfast of the title. This clever premise allows Macomber to craft stories around the B&B's guests, Abby and Josh in this inaugural effort, while using Jo Marie and her ongoing recovery from the death of her husband Paul in Afghanistan as the series' anchor. . . . With her characteristic optimism, Macomber provides fresh starts for both." —*Booklist*

"Emotionally charged romance." —*Kirkus Reviews*

"Macomber's writing and storytelling deliver what she's famous for—a smooth, satisfying tale with characters her fans will cheer for and an arc that is cozy, heartwarming and ends with the expected happily-ever-after."
—*Kirkus Reviews*

CHRISTMAS NOVELS

The Christmas Spirit

"Exactly what readers want from a Macomber holiday outing." —*Publishers Weekly*

"With almost all of Debbie Macomber's novels, the reader is not only given a captivating story, but also a lesson in life."
—*New York Journal of Books*

Dear Santa

"[Dear Santa] is a quick and fun tale offering surprises and blessings and an all-around feel-good read."
—*New York Journal of Books*

Jingle All the Way

"[*Jingle All the Way*] will leave readers feeling merry and bright." —*Publishers Weekly*

"This delightful Christmas story can be enjoyed any time of the year." —*New York Journal of Books*

A Mrs. Miracle Christmas

"This sweet, inspirational story . . . has enough dramatic surprises to keep pages turning."
—*Library Journal* (starred review)

"Anyone who enjoys Christmas will appreciate this sparkling snow globe of a story." —*Publishers Weekly*

Alaskan Holiday

"Picture-perfect . . . this charmer will please Macomber fans and newcomers alike." —*Publishers Weekly*

"[A] tender romance lightly brushed with holiday magic."
—*Library Journal*

Merry and Bright

"Heartfelt, cheerful . . . Readers looking for a light and sweet holiday treat will find it here." —*Publishers Weekly*

Twelve Days of Christmas

"Another heartwarming seasonal Macomber tale, which fans will find as bright and cozy as a blazing fire on Christmas Eve." —*Kirkus Reviews*

"*Twelve Days of Christmas* is a charming, heartwarming holiday tale. With poignant characters and an enchanting plot, Macomber again burrows into the fragility of human emotions to arrive at a delightful conclusion."
—*New York Journal of Books*

Dashing Through the Snow

"This Christmas romance from Macomber is both sweet and sincere." —*Library Journal*

Mr. Miracle

"Macomber spins another sweet, warmhearted holiday tale that will be as comforting to her fans as hot chocolate on Christmas morning." —*Kirkus Reviews*

"This gentle, inspiring romance will be a sought-after read."
—*Library Journal*

Starry Night

"Contemporary romance queen Macomber (*Rose Harbor in Bloom*) hits the sweet spot with this tender tale of impractical love. . . . A delicious Christmas miracle well worth waiting for." —*Publishers Weekly* (starred review)

"[A] holiday confection . . . as much a part of the season for some readers as cookies and candy canes."
—*Kirkus Reviews*

Angels at the Table

"Rings in Christmas in tried-and-true Macomber style, with romance and a touch of heavenly magic."
—*Kirkus Reviews*

"[A] sweetly charming holiday romance." —*Library Journal*

Dear Friends,

After writing *The Best Is Yet to Come,* I honestly thought my writing days were over. After forty years as a published author, it was time to rest on my laurels and retire. Many of you cried, "You can't, you simply can't." Others wrote to congratulate me and thank me for my stories.

To be fair, I gave retirement the old college try. First thing I did was compile a list of all the projects I intended to tackle. Certainly, it was time to downsize, clean closets, and clear out drawers, as it seemed every single one had somehow evolved into a junk drawer. I eagerly looked forward to working in and organizing my yarn room. I had projects just waiting for me to get on my knitting needles. I even considered going back to school.

Alas, four months later I was bored, restless, and hadn't accomplished a single item on the list. Okay, one closet. You see, there was this story about a widow that pestered me to the point I finally sat down at the computer and went to work. And guess what? I was myself again.

It shouldn't have taken four months to realize I'm happiest when I'm writing. This doesn't mean I'll return to the same publishing schedule as in previous years, but it means I'll continue to write because the bottom line is this: I was created to write, and it makes me happy.

Your support is everything, and I thank you for your faith in me. Your feedback has and always will continue to be the guiding force of my stories.

I can't close this without thanking the wonderful

publishing team behind me. I am blessed every single day by your belief in me and your wisdom when it comes to shaping each book.

As I said earlier, your feedback is always welcome. You can reach me on all the social media platforms. If you prefer to write, my mailing address is: P.O. Box 1458, Port Orchard, WA 98366.

Warmly,

Debbie Macomber

Must Love Flowers

DEBBIE MACOMBER

Must Love Flowers

A Novel

BALLANTINE BOOKS
NEW YORK

Must Love Flowers is a work of fiction.
Names, characters, places, and incidents are the products
of the author's imagination or are used fictitiously.
Any resemblance to actual events, locales, or persons,
living or dead, is entirely coincidental.

2024 Ballantine Books Mass Market Edition

Published in the United States by Ballantine Books,
an imprint of Random House, a division of
Penguin Random House LLC, New York.

BALLANTINE BOOKS & colophon are registered trademarks of
Penguin Random House LLC.

Originally published in hardcover in the United States by
Ballantine Books, an imprint of Random House, a division of
Penguin Random House LLC, in 2023.

ISBN 978-0-593-60057-3
Ebook ISBN 978-0-593-60056-6

Cover design: Belina Huey
Cover images: Moyo Studio/Getty Images (woman),
Floral Deco/Shutterstock (flowers)

Printed in the United States of America

randomhousebooks.com

2 4 6 8 9 7 5 3 1

Ballantine Books mass market edition: April 2024

Must Love Flowers

Chapter 1

For the third time in as many minutes, Joan Sample glanced toward the kitchen clock. She'd expected to hear from her youngest son by now. She'd invited Nick to dinner, and prepared his favorite dish, even though it was *her* birthday. He hadn't responded, and she wasn't sure if he'd show or not. The dining room table was set, and the chicken enchiladas were warming in the oven, along with Spanish rice and refried beans. Joan wasn't fond of chicken enchiladas. So this was what it had come to—she had to bribe her son to visit. Steve, her eldest, had a good excuse, seeing that he lived in the Phoenix area. He did call, at least.

Slumping down in her favorite overstuffed chair in the family room, she reached for the television remote. The program was one of the Sunday weekly news reviews that she routinely watched. Talking heads. Only Joan didn't hear a word of what they were saying, and furthermore, she didn't much care. Rarely was there anything good to report.

Mother's Day had been the week before, and her sons had sent a floral bouquet of calla lilies and white roses along with a box of chocolates. At least they'd remembered how much she enjoyed flowers. It was bad luck that her birthday fell a mere seven days later. Steve and Nick seemed to feel they'd done their duty with the flowers and chocolates and covered both Mother's Day and her birthday.

Her sons' lack of caring, showing little love or appreciation, wouldn't bother her if only Jared was alive. Her husband never forgot her on Mother's Day and tried to make her birthday extra-special. Even after four years, she grieved. Her entire life went up in flames the minute Jared was pronounced dead.

She'd recently heard that the dentist who purchased Jared's practice was doing well. That should have pleased her, because it assured her that Jared's patients had made a smooth transition. Many had been with Jared for years, and since she'd worked in his office as his receptionist and bookkeeper, she was on a first-name basis with several of them.

Joan had loved working with her husband. It would be difficult for some couples to spend 24/7 together, but not them. They'd made a great team. They'd always been close and were each other's soulmates. Her life was empty without Jared. Stark. Void. Dark. With him gone, it felt as though she had no purpose, no incentive, no reason to get out of bed in the morning.

Shaking her head, Joan refused to allow his loss to bury her in grief as it had so often. It'd been four years. Four long, torturous years. The pandemic certainly hadn't helped. Jared hadn't been gone more than six months when the entire country had closed down. The first few months she'd remained sequestered, afraid to open her front door for fear of catching the virus. As the weeks progressed and time lagged on, Joan had grown comfortable with the isolation. Living in a cocoon became welcome. Familiar. Routine.

As the restrictions eased, she gradually ventured out a few times a week. Not for any extended length of time, and always with a mask, being cautious. She managed whatever was on her list—she always had a list—and didn't dawdle longer than necessary before rushing home to safety. More often than not, when possible, she ordered what she needed online, something she'd grown accustomed to doing during the pandemic. Living in isolation became the norm, and she discovered she preferred it. Life beyond her front door could be risky. Something to be avoided.

Deep in her thoughts, Joan was startled when her phone rang. For a millisecond she didn't even recognize the sound. Leaping from the chair, she hurried back into the kitchen, searching the counter, which was the last place she remembered putting the phone. She swore she spent half her day searching for the device. She'd do away with it completely if the nuisance wasn't necessary.

Without bothering to see who it was, she grabbed it on the fourth ring. "Hello." Her greeting sounded breathless after a near-frantic search.

"Happy birthday" came the singsong voice of her older sister, Emmie.

"Thanks," Joan said, grateful to her sister, who had become her greatest encourager. Emmie had sent a lovely card earlier in the week, along with a gift certificate to the

Cutting Edge, Joan's favorite hair salon. Emmie was friends with the owner, Charlene Royce, who had worked as a hairdresser for years at Cutting Edge before purchasing the salon. The two had gone to high school together.

Emmie was her usual cheerful self, her voice light, as though she was on the verge of laughing. The two were close, even with the distance that separated them physically.

"Are you doing anything special to celebrate your day?"

Joan shrugged, although her sister couldn't see her response. "Not particularly. It isn't necessary for someone my age."

"You're how old?" Emmie teased.

Her sister knew good and well exactly what birthday this was. "Fifty-four. Please don't remind me."

"You make it sound like you're seventy."

That was the way she felt. "I will be soon enough."

"But not yet. You have a lot of life to live, little sister," Emmie chastised. "What you need is an attitude adjustment. Do something fun for once. Get outside and enjoy life, breathe in the fresh air. Take a walk around Green Lake. Go shopping and buy yourself a new outfit. Take in a boarder."

"A boarder?" What a crazy idea. She couldn't imagine what her sister was thinking.

"I'll get right on that." Her sister was full of good ideas, none of which Joan intended to do anytime soon.

"I'm serious. You need to break out of that shell, and the best way, little sister, is to do something for someone else. I promise you'd feel better about life in general if you found a way to give to others. I talked to Charlene when I ordered your gift card; she is taking in a boarder and is excited."

Joan rolled her eyes toward the ceiling. "You're not serious."

"Maybe, maybe not. Still, it's something to think about. By taking in a boarder, you'd be helping someone, and that someone just might help you. Jared has been gone four years. It's time you lived again."

Joan didn't need to be reminded how long it'd been since she'd lost her husband. You don't spend more than twenty-five years with a man, living together, working together, sharing everything with each other, and then simply get over the loss of him because *it's time*.

"In some ways it feels like yesterday." Even now there were days when she wanted to tell Jared a joke she found on the Internet or something she'd read. She caught herself recently wanting to share an idea she had about painting the kitchen, only to realize he was gone. More than gone. He was dead and buried.

"I know how hard this time has been for you." Emmie's voice softened. "I've mentioned it before and you've always blown me off, but Joan, sweetie, you need to reconsider talking to a counselor."

Nearly every conversation with her sister landed on the same topic. Each time, Joan had dismissed it out of hand, unwilling to consider discussing the pain in her heart with a stranger. It was hard to talk about Jared to anyone without tears instantly flooding her eyes. She'd be mortified to break down in front of a stranger. It went without saying that she'd become an emotional mess because she wouldn't be able to stop herself.

"If not a counselor," Emmie continued, apparently

unwilling to drop the subject, "then a grief therapy group. I've heard they can be helpful."

"No thanks."

"Joan, think about it. What can it hurt? You'd meet others like yourself who have lost someone they loved as much as you loved Jared. You'd get the support you need and find a way to lean in to the future."

Joan automatically shook her head. "It isn't that easy."

"Why not?"

"I'll cry, and you know how much I would hate that." She could see herself sitting in a circle, bawling her head off, to the point that she wouldn't be able to speak. Then she'd need to blow her nose, and when she did, she'd sound like a honking goose. *Nope, not happening.*

"You're being silly. So what if you get emotional— don't you think everyone there would understand? My guess is each person in the group has shed buckets of tears themselves."

"I'll think about it," Joan offered, hoping that would appease her sister.

"Will you?"

Joan briefly closed her eyes. Emmie wasn't letting up. Her sister refused to leave this subject alone, no matter how uncomfortable it was for Joan. "Why is this so important to you?" she demanded.

"Why?" Emmie repeated. "Because you're my sister, and I'm concerned about you, which is why I think taking in a boarder would help you get back to living again. You've become a recluse."

"That's not true. I get out . . . Okay, not a lot, but I'm not an agoraphobic."

"That's something, at least," Emmie said, and then

changed the subject, apparently not wanting to belabor the point. "It was good to catch up with Charlene when I called to order the gift certificate. She bought the Cutting Edge during the pandemic and is doing well."

Charlene had been styling Joan's hair for years and had become her friend, too. "I heard that," Joan said, proud of their friend's step of faith.

"Tell me, when was the last time that you were in to see Charlene for a cut and style?"

It was a kindness not to mention that Joan needed more than a haircut. In the last four years, her hair had become salt-and-pepper, the gray dominating. Perhaps she should consider coloring it again, as she once had.

"It's been a while," Joan reluctantly admitted.

"A while?"

"Okay, two years."

"As I expected!" Emmie had never been one to hold back on the *I told you so*'s. "Promise me you'll make an appointment."

"Promise." A haircut would do her good. Her dark hair had grown long and unruly and was badly in need of a cut. Jared had liked her with shorter hair, and she'd grown accustomed to the easy-care style. It took her only a few minutes to fiddle with it to look presentable before leaving for the office each morning. Now her hair grazed the top of her shoulders. Unaccustomed to the length, she fussed with it, tying it back, as it often fell against her face. This length aged her, and not in a flattering way. The only person she saw, most days, was her own reflection in the mirror, so what did it matter?

"After the appointment, I want you to text me a photo so I can see the results," Emmie said.

"I will." Joan intended to follow through with the promise. All she needed was the incentive to make the appointment with Charlene.

"How are the boys?" Emmie asked next.

"Good. They sent me a beautiful floral bouquet for Mother's Day." She didn't mention the chocolates, which she'd immediately stuck in the freezer. She seldom indulged in sweets or kept them around the house. As a dentist, Jared had frowned on anything that might contribute to developing cavities.

"What about your birthday?"

"Steve phoned earlier. He was excited; he got the recommendation for a promotion he wanted." Their conversation had been brief and weighed on Joan's mind. Steve had often mentioned Zoe, a woman he was dating. Their relationship had sounded serious, and Joan had been waiting for her son to announce their engagement. When she'd asked about Zoe, her son had quickly changed the subject and made an excuse to end the call. Rather than mention how brief the call had been, she said, "Steve's the new assistant manager at the distribution center." Her son enjoyed his job and had excelled, rising quickly, working for Dick's Sporting Goods. At twenty-seven, he was being fast-tracked to take over as the center's manager within the next few years. Joan was proud of Steve and his strong work ethic. Despite her concerns about his relationship, she was pleased with how both her sons had matured.

"That's great. Is he still dating . . . What was her name again?"

"Zoe," Joan supplied.

"Right. They've been together awhile now."

"They have," Joan agreed, without adding anything else. In some ways, their short conversations were obligatory, as if he felt he should let her know he remembered her birthday but was otherwise too busy for more than a few minutes.

"What's Nick up to these days?" Emmie asked next.

"Nick always has three or four irons in the fire," Joan said. "He's working on a huge construction project, an apartment complex in Seattle." Even as a youngster, Nick was happiest when he had a hammer, nails, and a piece of wood in his hands. He was a born carpenter.

Jared had never seemed to mind that neither of his sons had chosen to follow him into the medical field. Steve had graduated college with a degree in supply chain management, and Nick had become an apprentice carpenter directly out of high school. Her husband had been good like that, not putting pressure on their boys, allowing them to follow their own paths. Joan was the one who had hoped either Steve or Nick would one day take over Jared's practice, but that was not to be.

Her phone buzzed, indicating she had an incoming text.

"I think that's Nick now," she said, her heart leaping with appreciation that he would soon stop by for dinner. "I'll talk to you later."

"Don't forget to send a photo after Charlene finishes with your hair."

"Will do. Gotta scoot."

Joan quickly ended the call with Emmie and checked the incoming text.

It was Nick, who preferred to text over making a

Chapter 2

Joan stared at the computer screen as she pondered which letters to choose for Wordle. This was how she routinely started each morning. The word game helped keep her mind fresh, along with the thousand-piece jigsaw puzzle of the Eiffel Tower that she was currently working on. Impossibly small pieces were spread across the top of the kitchen table. At one time this oak table was where she served her family meals. These days it was used for multiple purposes, none of which included family or eating.

It used to be . . .

That was what her life had become: a series of all the things that once were but were no longer.

Joan scooted her chair away from the computer and wandered into the kitchen to pour herself another cup of coffee when she heard the front door open. For just an instant, a spark of fear shot down her spine, until she remembered the deadbolt was in place. Only someone with a key could gain entry.

"Mom?" Nick shouted, as though he expected her to be standing by the front door, awaiting his arrival.

"In here." She came out of the kitchen, holding the coffee mug as she met him in the foyer. He stood in front of the staircase that led to the two large upstairs bedrooms. It was those bedrooms that had sold Jared on the house in this community. The master bedroom was on the main floor, away from the boys, who tended, especially in their teen years, to stay up until all hours of the night.

Her son stared at her for a minute before his dark brown eyes, so like his father's, narrowed into a frown.

Immediately concerned, she asked, "Everything okay?"

A multitude of problems tumbled through her mind like a rockslide racing down the side of a hill. Had her son lost his job? Did he get into a car accident? Had Nick received a concerning medical diagnosis?

"Yeah, everything's fine," he returned, sounding distracted.

"That's good," she said, sighing with relief. She had enough troubles of her own and felt unable to cope with anything more. "The thing is, you usually don't show up first thing in the morning. What's up?" She let him follow her into the kitchen, where she automatically got him a cup of coffee. Like his father, Nick was addicted to caffeine.

"We're getting a later start this morning, waiting on an inspection," Nick said. He sat down at the table and stared at the puzzle, which was about three-fourths completed. He picked up a piece, examined it, and then set it in place.

It was all Joan could do not to stop him. This was her

puzzle, and she preferred to work it herself. The satisfaction she gained, the sense of accomplishment, was why she diligently spent hours poring over it. She didn't need help and, furthermore, didn't want it.

"I'm sorry I wasn't here for your birthday," Nick stated matter-of-factly.

"You sent me a text." But he hadn't given her a reason why he'd been unable to come. She suspected he opted to spend the day with his friends and watch the Seahawks game. The pan of chicken enchiladas remained untouched in the refrigerator. Before he left, she'd make sure he took it with him, otherwise she'd end up tossing them in the garbage.

Nick shifted his gaze away from her. "Sorry, I was working."

"On a Sunday?"

"Mom, we're on a tight schedule with this project. If we don't finish our part on time, then we hold up the other trades. Let me tell you, those electricians can get downright cranky if we aren't done when they're ready to run the wiring."

"I hope they're paying you overtime."

Glancing up from the puzzle, Nick grinned boyishly. "Yup, which brings me to the reason for my visit."

"Oh?"

"Yeah, seeing that I missed dinner with you, how about I take you out to eat?"

The invite surprised her in a pleasant way. Joan couldn't remember the last time she dined out. She ordered DoorDash on occasion, and Uber Eats, too. It seemed nonsensical to leave the house to dine alone. *It used to be* . . . There it was again, like yeast bubbling up in dough. She and Jared had had a routine date night.

At one time, she'd kept in touch with friends. A group of classmates from college had routinely gotten together for lunch three or four times a year. That hadn't happened since the pandemic. It seemed everyone had gone their separate ways since the lockdown.

After Jared's sudden death from a massive brain aneurysm, Joan had been bombarded with sympathy and support from family and friends. That, however, had quickly died off, and then with COVID there was almost complete silence. It'd remained that way.

"Well, what do you think?" Nick asked, breaking into her thoughts.

For one wild moment, she struggled, thinking it best, safer, to decline, but then she changed her mind. Dinner out shouldn't intimidate her. Becoming familiar again with leaving the house was what she needed, if she was going to move forward in life. Emmie would be pleased to know Joan was making an effort.

"Ah, sure. Where would you like to go?"

"Mom," he said, grinning. "It's your birthday; you decide."

"You want me to decide?" Crazy as it sounded for a woman who managed a busy office, handled everything outside of the actual dentistry, she suddenly found it difficult to make even the smallest decision.

"Yup, I've got money to burn," he said, looking well pleased with himself. "Any restaurant in town."

"What if I say I want to dine at Canlis?" The iconic Seattle restaurant often had a several-weeks waiting list. Jared and Joan had dined there on their twenty-fifth wedding anniversary. It was a meal she would long treasure. The staff at Canlis had made it special.

Nick didn't even blink. "Doubtful I could get a reservation, but I'll try."

Joan enjoyed teasing her son. "Do you think Il Lucano survived the lockdown?" The family-owned Italian restaurant had been one of her and Jared's favorites. Joan had never tasted a better Eggplant Parmesan anywhere.

"I don't know," Nick said, and grabbed his phone from his pocket. He connected with Siri and within half a second had the information he wanted. Looking up, he smiled and nodded. "Looks like they're in business, and so are we. I'll call and make reservations for tomorrow night at six thirty. Sound good?"

"It sounds perfect." It astonished her how much this invitation excited her. It'd been ages since she'd had something special to look forward to. Seeing that the invitation had come from her son made it even more special.

"I better head to work," Nick said, as he stood from the table and delivered his empty coffee cup to the kitchen sink. "I'll come by tomorrow at six. Be ready, okay?"

"Of course, and after dinner you can take home those enchiladas."

His eyes lit up. "My favorite. Thanks, Mom." Nick kissed her cheek before he headed out the door.

Both excited and hesitant, Joan went straight to her bedroom closet to check what she had to wear for a night out. As she passed the full-length mirror on the closet door, she did a double take. No wonder her son had given her that strange look when he'd first arrived. She looked dreadful. She hadn't combed her hair and had dressed in old jeans and a Seahawks sweatshirt that had faded from multiple washings. She wore slippers and hadn't so much as put on lipstick. The contrast was striking, even to her, from the days she'd gone into the office with Jared. It used to be that she took pride in her appearance.

It used to be with a lot of things, she admitted. So much had changed, and not for the good.

Rather than stare at her reflection, she hung her head, embarrassed by the lack of attention to herself and how much of her personal appearance she'd let slide. This was the third day in a row that she'd worn the same tattered jeans and the faded sweatshirt.

Other than to step onto the porch to collect the mail, it'd been a week since she'd ventured outside. It used to be she had the most beautiful yard on the block. She was known for her love of flowers. Now it was rare for her to venture outside the house. So much loss, so much grief. Even the pride she had in herself had fallen by the wayside. Little wonder Nick had looked at her as if he didn't recognize her as his mother. Joan barely recognized her own reflection, let alone the woman she'd become.

It was then that she remembered the birthday gift from Emmie. No better time for a hair appointment than before a dinner date with her son. Refusing to continue berating herself, Joan headed to the dresser, where she'd left Emmie's birthday card. Opening it, she reached for the gift certificate and felt almost giddy. She was going out, and when she did, she planned to be dressed to the nines, whatever that meant. First things first, she needed an appointment, and went in search of her phone. She had a bad habit of leaving it all over the house. It took several minutes to locate it on the en suite bathroom counter.

As she swept it up, her gaze fell on the unmade bed,

and it stopped her cold. While working, she'd never left the house unless the dishwasher was empty of clean dishes. And the bed made. Never. Somehow, without even realizing it, she'd let the little things that had at one time been important slide along with everything else, including her appearance.

With a vengeance, she set aside the phone and hurried around the king-size bed and put it to order, placing the decorator pillows in place. They'd been tucked in the corner for weeks, abandoned and forgotten, which was how Joan felt most days.

Once she was finished, she felt a small sense of accomplishment. She retrieved the phone and sat on the edge of the mattress while she went through her contact list for Cutting Edge salon. The receptionist answered, and Joan realized how ridiculous she was being. It was doubtful she'd get an appointment on such short notice. Charlene was often booked weeks ahead. How foolish of her to think her friend would alter her schedule at the last minute for her.

"Hello," the receptionist repeated.

"Oh, sorry," Joan said, realizing she hadn't spoken. "This is Joan Sample, and I'd like to make an appointment with Charlene for a cut and style." On the spur of the moment, she decided to leave the gray. She'd earned those silver hairs and she wasn't going to hide them. It was what it was.

"Charlene doesn't have anything available in the next two weeks. When would you like the appointment?"

Exactly what Joan suspected. "I thought that might be the case."

Apparently, she didn't hide her disappointment well,

because the receptionist continued, "We have a new girl, Bailey. She's very good and she has several openings, if you're looking for something sooner."

If she waited two weeks for Charlene, Joan feared she'd find an excuse to cancel. "I don't suppose Bailey has an opening for tomorrow afternoon?" It was almost too much to hope for.

"She had a cancellation just this morning. Would three o'clock work for you?"

"It would. Yes, that'd be perfect."

"Great. I'll put you down. We look forward to seeing you tomorrow at three for a cut and style, Joan."

"Thank you. Thank you so much."

"My pleasure," the pleasant young woman said before disconnecting the call.

Joan felt like skipping around her bedroom. Once and for all, she was going to get control of this dustmop that was her current hairstyle. Enough was enough. It was a small thing and yet it felt like a huge accomplishment.

Next, she checked out her closet and spent several minutes shuffling hangers from one side to the other before she chose a silk blouse with a flower pattern that had a simple tie at the neck. The navy-blue skirt had been one of Jared's favorites. He had never failed to compliment her when she wore it.

An unexpected wave of grief hit her, nearly swamped her with a profound sense of loss. The excitement she'd so recently enjoyed left her as quickly as it'd come, leaving her bereft. It was the little things she missed most about her life with Jared. The shared smiles, the jokes that meant nothing to anyone else but that would send them both into fits of laughter. His gentle touch before he turned out the light each night, his words of love and appreciation. All that had been taken from her, and she didn't know if she could find a future without him being part of it.

Jared was the love of her life. They met in college and from the day they'd been introduced there had been no one else. They were meant to be together. It wasn't half a life without him. It was no life. A mere existence.

Swallowing down the self-pity, Joan returned to the kitchen, determined not to allow herself to sink into the black hole of emotions. Tears threatened, which she furiously blinked back. Since Jared's death, Joan had wept buckets and often woke at night, even now, her cheeks wet as she stirred awake. She carried her grief like lead weights around her heart. Some days the pain was so intense, she wondered why his loss hadn't killed her.

It was noon before she was hungry. She turned on the local news, although she didn't know why. All that was reported was the weather, traffic difficulties, and updates on the continuous crime spree. While half-listening to the reporter, she studied the puzzle as she munched on an apple, which she dipped in peanut butter. That was the way Steve, her older son, preferred to eat his apples. Joan had to agree it was a good way to mix fruit and protein. Thinking about her older son brought to mind their last conversation. It'd felt as if he couldn't get off the phone fast enough. It disturbed her. At another time she would have asked what happened with him and Zoe. She'd been comfortable to let the conversation slide and regretted that now.

She heard the mailman on the porch, and, having nothing better to do, she opened the door and reached for the few items in the box, which was attached to the left side of the outside door. Most of her bills were paid online these days and almost everything that came through the post office was junk. She wasn't expecting anyone else to remember her birthday, but she couldn't keep from wishing.

Standing over the kitchen garbage can, she automatically tossed in the Safeway sales flyer along with several postcard advertisements. One for a hot tub sale and another wanting to replace her rain gutters. If she went so far as to call for a bid, she could receive a fifty-dollar Amazon gift card. Whoop-de-do.

The next piece of mail caught her attention. It was from the homeowners' association, and it was personally addressed to her. Joan tore open the envelope and read the letter.

Groaning, she squeezed her eyes shut and wanted to stomp her foot. According to the HOA board, she had gone against Section 104 of the homeowners' agreement, signed and dated by both Jared and her. Her yard maintenance was below standard and had become an eyesore to the community, lowering property values. They found this especially distressing, as she'd once had such a lovely yard. Immediate action was required. She was given fourteen days to comply before a heavy fine would be assessed.

Yard maintenance. Joan so rarely left the house that she hadn't noticed how badly the lawn needed mowing. Looking at the current condition of her flower beds depressed her, so she avoided noticing.

Jared had always taken care of the yard while she worked the flower beds. Nick had been by a few times last summer to mow the lawn, but only when she called to ask for his help. She knew yardwork wasn't his thing and she hated to ask. Nick viewed it as a chore and could be unreliable, as evidenced by his brief text on her birthday. Feeling the weight of being single, Joan slumped into a chair, wondering how best to resolve this issue.

Setting her jaw, she refused to be a helpless female, looking for someone else to solve her problems. She had a college degree and a level head. She'd do what others in her situation did: She'd hire a lawn service.

Chapter 3

Maggie Herbert grabbed her backpack as she quietly slipped out her bedroom door. The key was to leave the house before her father woke. She had the early shift at Starbucks, and the mornings were always crazy busy, which was good, because it helped to pass the time quickly before she headed to Seattle Central College for classes.

Leanne, who handled the cash register, was down with the flu, which just happened to coincide with a trip to the ocean with four friends. The manager had asked Maggie to fill in for her until Leanne was back. Maggie wasn't any expert on the flu, but she suspected the illness would last three days. Maggie was willing to take on any task given to her, as long as it didn't interfere with her afternoon nursing classes and her tutoring schedule at the elementary school. Finals were coming up soon, and she'd been awake studying until almost midnight and was operating on less than four hours' sleep.

She needed to do well on these tests, as she'd applied for several scholarships. Once classes were dismissed for the semester, Maggie would be able to take on extra hours, and heaven knew she needed them if she was ever going to get out on her own.

On that front, she had real hope and recently interviewed with Mrs. Royce, a shop owner who'd advertised for a boarder. Mrs. Royce's husband was working out of the country, and she was looking for company. The rent was fair, and Maggie had provided several letters of recommendation. The interview had been positive, and Mrs. Royce had promised to get back to her as soon as she checked out Maggie's references. Once she heard back from Mrs. Royce, Maggie would be ready to move. That time couldn't come fast enough.

"Maggie." Her name came from the living room, which told Maggie her father was on another alcoholic binge. Likely he'd been up most of the night drinking, which had become the norm these days.

Although it was four in the morning, Roy Herbert sat slouched in his dilapidated recliner, his head twisted to one side, as he stared at Maggie. Guess she wasn't going to escape unnoticed after all, despite tiptoeing down the hallway leading from her bedroom. It didn't take a soothsayer to realize her father was drunk.

Maggie's heart sank. She'd hoped to be long gone before her father discovered she'd left for the day. As much as she was able, she avoided interaction with him. With her mother out of the picture, along with the increased alcohol, his moods were often dark.

"Did you see the electric bill? It says we're behind. The notice from the city claims they're going to turn off the lights." He cast her a pleading glance. "Can you cover it for me?"

Maggie wanted to groan. Her father spent his disability checks on alcohol and then expected her to cover all the housing expenses. While working part-time and attending school, she couldn't afford to pay more than she already was.

Her father didn't seem to understand or appreciate how hard she worked to set aside funds for school expenses. She'd already given him money to cover the electric bill earlier. It seemed he'd used it to buy alcohol instead. She should have known that was what he'd do. More than ever, Maggie realized she needed to find somewhere else to live. Maybe, with her gone, her dad would stop using her as a crutch.

"What happened to the money I gave you earlier?" she asked, doing her best to hide her discouragement.

Her father shrugged. "Al and me . . ."

"You spent it at the Half Pint, didn't you?" She did her best to keep the accusation out of her voice. Her father's lack of responsibility had become a constant frustration. He relied on her for everything. It was too much when, as best she could tell, he made no effort to change.

"Don't start on me," Roy muttered. "I'm doing the best I can. You have no idea of the pain I'm in."

After suffering a back injury from a construction accident that prevented him from ever working again, Roy had collected government disability checks for years, even before her mother died. Her mother's death was all he needed as an excuse to drink. Beer helped him get through the day, he claimed, not seeming to realize his dependence had made him an alcoholic. Several times Maggie had tried to suggest he join Alcoholics Anonymous. She might as well have been talking to the wind. Roy insisted his drinking was under control; he could stop anytime he wanted.

"I need you to pay that bill, Mags, or the city will do what they say."

"I already gave you what I had." She noticed an empty six-pack of Bud Light rested next to his recliner along with a couple empty whiskey bottles.

"Dad, how could you be so irresponsible? If we lose power, it'll be your fault."

Even with limited income, they shouldn't have these money problems. The house was an inheritance from his mother and came without a mortgage. Roy, Maggie, and her mother had moved into it following her grandmother's death. Maggie had been ten, and this was the first real home she'd ever had. Until then, the family had lived in small apartments. Since inheriting the house, Roy had done little toward upkeep and care. The roof had started to leak, and several areas of the house were showing signs of water damage.

"Dad," Maggie tried one more time, "you can't go on drinking like this. It's killing you. I can't live here and watch you drink your life away. I want to move out, and you should know I'm looking for a place."

That got her father's notice. He sat up and glared at her. "You'd leave me?"

"Yes. I can't bear to see what you're doing to yourself, drinking day in and day out. You keep saying you can quit at any time, but you don't, and I can't keep picking up after you. You have a problem." Although she didn't say it, Maggie felt like her living at home was aiding and abetting him. He relied heavily on her, and the burden had become more than she could bear.

"You won't do it," he said, sounding confident. "We both know you could never afford to move into an apartment, with all those pricey classes. You'll just have to stick around if you're so hell-bent on wasting your money on schooling that you don't even need."

"I'm going to be a nurse," Maggie insisted. "It's what Mom would have wanted for me and I don't care how much it will cost."

He simply shook his head, silently scoffing at her.

Maggie did her best to ignore him. The minute she got word from Mrs. Royce, Maggie was moving. Her father was right about the cost of renting an apartment. As a financially struggling college student, she couldn't afford the rent, even if she shared the space with three others. Rent in the Seattle area was outrageous.

"You'll never leave me," Roy insisted. "I'm all you've got."

"You're wrong, Dad. I plan on moving out as soon as I find somewhere affordable to live."

He snickered as though he didn't believe her. "No, you won't. You need me just as much as I need you."

Maggie had heard it all before and did her best to block him out. "I need to get to work."

Maggie headed toward the front door, refusing to allow his words to taint her day. She let his negative attitude flow away from her like water off a duck's back, because it wasn't her father speaking, it was the alcohol.

"Don't you dare walk away from me, girl. I'm talking to you. We could afford to pay the bills if you gave up school and took on a full-time job."

The urge to argue was so strong she had to clamp down on her jaw to the point that her teeth ached. She was aware her dad wasn't thinking straight and tried not to let his words discourage her, but it was hard. "I'm going to be a nurse. It's what I want for my future, and you're not going to take that away from me." Despite her attempt to not let him get to her, Maggie's words came out like nine-millimeter bullets, each one hitting the target.

"Come on, Mags, let's not fight. I'll stop drinking, I promise."

Maggie had heard it all before.

"I need to go, or I'll be late for work."

"Okay, but when you finish your classes, would you bring me dinner? I could go for a Whopper."

"I'll see what I can do." Likely that would be the only food he'd eat all day.

Because her father had held her up, Maggie arrived at Starbucks with only minutes to spare. She cleared her mind, determined to make the best of her day with a positive attitude.

She took her place at the cash register. Several of the morning customers were regulars, and she'd gotten to know them by name. It took effort to leave the negativity behind. Disciplined as she was, Maggie had learned to smile despite how unsettled her father made her feel. For the first time since her mother's death, Maggie had hope of escaping him.

"Morning," she greeted, as she automatically reached for a cup to scribble down the order and the name.

His hard hat identified him as a construction worker and someone Maggie didn't automatically recognize.

There was a huge apartment complex going up down the street, and she suspected he was one of the crew currently on that project.

"Morning," he murmured, as his gaze lifted to the menu listed on the wall behind her. While he perused the selections, she couldn't help noticing his dark brown eyes that reminded her of the chocolate brownies that were her favorites. Her mother had baked them for her birthday every year rather than a birthday cake because Maggie enjoyed them so much, plus they were easy to share with her friends.

This guy wasn't hard on the eyes, either, and she guessed he was probably married. He didn't wear a wedding band, but few in the trades did, because of the potential risk of injury. Even if he was available, it wasn't like Maggie had time for relationships. It would be nice, though, one day.

"I'll take a double espresso, a bagel with cream cheese, and give me a slice of your lemon pound cake." His gaze left the menu long enough to smile in her direction. Yup, this guy was a charmer, and he knew it.

"You got it," she returned, ignoring his lazy grin. She gave him the total, which he paid for with cash and left a five-dollar tip. "Your name?" she asked, ready to write it down on the cup to give to Ashley, who was filling the orders. "Einstein," his friend answered for him.

That was clearly a nickname. "Thanks, Einstein, your order will be right up."

The guy behind him was apparently working on the same project. "A bunch of us are going out for a few beers after work, you coming?" he said, speaking to his friend.

"Your order?" Maggie asked, not wanting to hold up the line.

"Oh, sorry." He glanced up at the board. "Give me the double-smoked bacon, cheddar, egg sandwich and a Frappuccino."

Typing in the order, she heard Einstein respond, "I can't tonight. I'm taking my mother to dinner."

"Your mother?" The other guy laughed. "Man, are you that desperate for a date you need to take out your own mother?" He seemed to find this information highly amusing.

"Ha, ha, you're hilarious. It's not my idea of a fun night, trust me. She's been in this emotional slump since my dad passed, like she's got this dark cloud hanging over her head. It's hard to ignore."

"Man, that's not good."

Maggie gave him the total for his order and got his name. Kurt. He swiped his credit card across the machine.

"I know I should go by the house more often, but every time I do, I leave depressed."

"So why are you taking her out?"

The two moved down the line, and another customer, a regular, stepped up to the counter. While Maggie took his order, she couldn't help overhearing the conversation between the two previous men.

"I ghosted her on her birthday," Einstein continued.

This guy ditched his mother on her special day. That said everything.

"You ignored your mother on her birthday? Not cool, dude."

"I know, but I had a good excuse. We were working on

Sunday, remember?" Ashley handed Einstein his order. He took it and then waited with his friend.

Kurt leaned against the counter, as if that would hurry things along. "Ugh, that was annoying. I hate spending my Sunday on the job, but the money was good."

"Real good," Einstein returned.

"Sorry you can't make it tonight."

"Yeah, me, too. Trust me, I'd much rather be at Duke's with you and the rest of the crew."

Ashley handed Kurt his order and the men walked out the door. Maggie's gaze stayed with them long enough to see them step into a large truck, which was probably why they hadn't gone through the drive-through.

As she continued taking orders, Maggie occasionally glanced in the car lot, where Einstein and Kurt had parked. Interesting. Einstein dreaded spending time with his mother, when Maggie would have given anything to have even ten minutes with hers.

It'd been nearly five years since her mother's death. Not a day passed that Maggie didn't think about her and miss her. Elaine Herbert had gone into the hospital for a routine surgery and had gotten an infection that antibiotics couldn't seem to kick. It was while caring for her mother that Maggie decided to go into nursing. The infection had spread to her blood, and she was gone within a matter of days, too weak to fight any longer.

Following her mother's death, it felt as if Maggie's whole world had shattered. Her father, who occasionally drank, became an alcoholic, steadily drinking more. First thing in the morning, instead of coffee it was beer. His decline had accelerated to the point that Maggie could barely stand to watch. Sadly, alcohol brought out the worst in him.

In his eyes, Maggie couldn't seem to do anything right. With her mother gone, Maggie was expected to cook, clean, and keep a handy supply of alcohol at his disposal as he drank himself into oblivion. Oh, how she missed her mother.

At the end of her shift, Maggie gathered her back-pack, prepared to head off to her classes. Ashley finished at the same time.

"How did your interview go with Mrs. Royce?" Ashley asked, as Maggie tucked her bookbag over her shoulder.

Maggie had left feeling encouraged. "Really good, I think. She's lonely. It's more about having someone around, I think, than the need for extra cash. She said she'd call me sometime today with her decision."

"I hope it works out for you."

"Me, too. Thanks for letting me know about it." Ashley was the one who'd mentioned Mrs. Royce was looking for a boarder. Maggie had struggled not to break down after a particularly unpleasant exchange with her father, and this opportunity was an answer to her prayers of moving out.

"It was no big deal. Mrs. Royce is a friend of my mother's, and I was happy to mention you."

"It's a big deal to me," Maggie said.

"And how much schooling will you have left?" Ashley asked.

"Two years." Once Maggie was hired at the hospital, she should be able to move out on her own. That was her plan, anyway. If she enjoyed living with Mrs. Royce, then she might stay on. It all depended on how well the relationship worked, as this was a new experience for them both.

Maggie was getting ahead of herself, though, as she had yet to get the green light.

Her first class was over and her spirits high when Maggie saw that she'd gotten a voice mail from Mrs. Royce, who asked her to return the call.

Eager now, Maggie stepped outside and hit the button that would automatically dial the number.

"Hello, is this Maggie?" the woman asked. She was a businesswoman in her late fifties who often worked late and worried about her pets being cooped up so long every day. With her husband working out of the country, she found the nights lonely and was looking for some help with her animals.

"Yes, it's me. I'm sorry I couldn't take your call. I was in class."

"I figured as much," she said, and paused as if reluctant to continue. "Listen, Maggie, I'm afraid I don't have good news."

"You don't? I don't understand, everything sounded so positive yesterday when we met. Did any of my recommendations fall through?" A chill went down Maggie's spine at the same time her heart shot up to her throat. She didn't understand what could have gone wrong.

"It has nothing to do with you. I felt you would be perfect. I called your references and each one gave a glowing report. I was all ready to let you know you could have the room when I got a call from my brother. His daughter, my niece, is moving to Seattle and needs a place to live.

She's gone through a bad breakup, and Dean felt living with me would help her through this difficult time. I'm so sorry, Maggie."

Swallowing down her disappointment, Maggie squared her shoulders. "There's no need to apologize. I understand."

"I'll keep my ears open. And if I hear of anyone else looking for a boarder, I'll give them your phone number, if that's all right with you."

"That would be perfect. Thank you, Mrs. Royce."

"Things have a way of working out the way they are supposed to be," she said kindly. "I know you're discouraged now, but the right opportunity and the right person will turn up soon."

Maggie certainly hoped so. She didn't know how much longer she could endure living with her father.

Chapter 4

Joan sat at her desk and reread the letter from the HOA. The board president had seemed to take delight in chastising her for the condition of her yard. To mention the condition of her flower beds was a low blow. It wasn't enough to outline her neglect; he'd made a point of explaining that such disregard for upkeep affected the property values of the entire development.

Joan couldn't help but roll her eyes. The housing market in Seattle was booming. She sincerely doubted her unkempt lawn would dissuade anyone from purchasing a home in her area. Nevertheless, she needed to comply or be fined.

That letter had kept Joan awake most of the night. Crazy how a simple sheet of paper could unnerve her to the extent that she remained restless, tossing and turning, unsure how best to proceed. She felt overwhelmed, discombobulated, and unsure.

Something was terribly wrong with her. At one time, she'd handled the business dealings that went along with

Jared's practice and managed the office, and she'd dealt with situations far more threatening than this. That this chastisement should upset her this much was evidence of how unsettled her life had become, how far she'd allowed her self-confidence to slide.

What Emmie had been saying for the last few years was true. Joan had wrapped herself in a cocoon, insulating from the world to the point that any outside interference felt threatening. While inside her home, Joan felt safe and protected. Sheltered. After Jared's death, she needed that comfort. The world outside her front door was risky. A virus ran rampant. People died. One place, and one place only, could she be guaranteed protection, and that was behind the locked front door of her home.

The letter seemed to shake the foundation she had stood on. It was almost as if she could feel the floor start to crumble beneath her. She needed to take action, and the sooner she dealt with this unpleasantness, the sooner she could retreat once again to what was familiar.

Sitting at her computer, she wasted a good hour on word games. The avoidance relaxed her to the point that she could look up information on local yard service companies. Several offered additional landscaping, along with weekly, biweekly, or monthly maintenance. After visiting the websites for four of the companies listed, she did due diligence and read the reviews. Two of the four had several five-star ratings and glowing comments.

Checking the time, she felt both businesses should be open by now. The first call went directly to voice mail.

"Thank you for calling Harrison Lawn and Landscaping service. I am currently unavailable, but please leave your name and number and I'll get back to you at my earliest convenience." The greeting was followed by a loud beep.

"Ah, hi. I'm Joan Sample. My HOA said my lawn isn't up to par. Would it be . . . could you kindly give me a call back. Thank you." Not until she cut off the call did she realize she hadn't left her phone number.

Dialing again, she listened to the spiel a second time and waited for the beep before she said, "Sorry, I don't know what I was thinking. That's the problem, clearly. I was the one who called because of the letter I got from the HOA. I need you, if you would, to stop by and give me a quote, but I failed to leave my number for you to return my call. Silly of me, right? If I don't take care of this soon, I'll be fined, and no one wants a pay a fine, right? Oh, and if you want the job, you must love flowers. My number is 206-876- . . ."

Beep.

She didn't get to finish before she was cut off. She'd babbled on so long she didn't have time to leave her contact information.

How was it that she couldn't even manage to leave a voice mail without screwing it up? Tossing her phone down on her desk, she covered her face with both hands and felt the strongest urge to cry. At one time she'd been competent. Capable. Unflappable. Now she couldn't accomplish a phone call without making a fool of herself.

Joan bit into her lower lip as she struggled to acknowledge the truth of the woman she'd become. For the last few years, her sister had tried again and again to open Joan's eyes by suggesting counseling. On their last conversation, she mentioned Joan taking in a boarder. It was time—past time, really—that she faced the future instead of hiding behind closed doors. At the mere thought her heart raced, and she felt paralyzed about where to start.

Closing her eyes, breathing evenly, Joan pictured herself as a butterfly.

She knew that leaving the cocoon was painful and often difficult. It was the struggle that made the butterfly strong enough to break free and able to fly away.

As daunting as it felt, she needed to seriously consider finding a support group. That was certainly more overwhelming than contacting a landscaper. How would she even know where to start? She needed to remind herself she was a strong, capable woman, or she once was, and she would be again.

As she struggled to find the courage to seek out a counselor, a memory came to her. It happened shortly after Jared's services. Gennie Davis, a friend from college, had connected with Joan and offered condolences. Gennie had lost her husband two years earlier and had mentioned a counselor who had helped her deal with the loss and pain that followed Joe's death. They'd gotten together, Gennie and the counselor, for a couple meetings before Gennie had transferred to a grief therapy group.

Unlike Jared, Joe had died of cancer after fighting the disease for several years. Jared's death had come about suddenly and had been a complete shock. Joan barely had time to get to the hospital, following the ambulance, only to arrive and learn her husband had been declared dead. The shock of it, the suddenness, had hit her like running into a bulldozer. She'd been devastated. When she'd first heard the news, she'd been convinced there was some mistake; someone had gotten it wrong. Jared couldn't be dead. Surely the medical team should be able to do something to bring him back.

Remembering that dreadful day sent Joan's thoughts spiraling down a deep, dark hole. She had to shake herself to pull her mind back into the present. If she were to book an appointment with a counselor, Joan would need to relive all that again and she couldn't do it, couldn't go through the agony of that dreadful day one more time. Once had been bad enough.

She'd call a counselor later, Joan decided, another time when she was better able to deal with that pain. She had never been one to rush into things. She was methodical. Until then, she'd make the effort to get out more. When she started to feel more like herself again, she'd revisit the idea. It might take a while, but it was important that she be mentally ready to take the step that would help her move forward. That time wasn't now. Or anywhere close to it.

Phil Harrison listened to the voice mail and couldn't contain his smile. The only criteria the caller wanted was simple: He must love flowers. She sounded a bit distressed, as if this letter from the HOA had unsettled her.

He sat in his pickup and was ready to return the call, when another came in from his dad. Phil had taken over the family business a few years earlier when his father decided to retire. His dad had been shocked that Phil would give up a thriving law practice to mow lawns and weed flower beds.

It'd surprised Phil, too, but he'd badly needed the change, needed to get out of the office and the courtroom.

As a kid, he'd hated working for his dad and did everything he could think to avoid yardwork. Then the accident had happened, and everything had changed. His entire world had imploded. Afterward, Phil felt the urge to get back to basics, close to the earth, to nature. The desire burned in him, and he started helping his father the way he never had as a youth. Digging into the earth, planting flowers and trees, bringing color and life into a world that had felt ugly and dark, revived him. Soon he was spending more time doing yardwork than he was in the office. It was about the same time that his father suffered a heart attack, and the doctors advised him to retire. Phil knew taking over the business was what he wanted, what he needed.

His dad kept his hand in the business, but most of his time was spent at the senior center with his friends. He'd taken up woodworking in his spare time and had become a rather good cook, much to Phil's surprise.

"Hey, Dad."

"Hey," his father replied. "I got a call from the old lady Wilson. Do you have time to squeeze her in this afternoon? She needs her lawn fertilized."

"I'll make time, no problem." Mrs. Wilson was one of his father's friends from the senior center. While his dad might refer to Samantha Wilson as old, they were the same age.

"She seems to think I'll be the one to stop by. That woman couldn't be more blatant if she tried, making every excuse under the sun to spend time with me. I wouldn't want to encourage anything like that."

"You mean to say she's sweet on you? Dad, go for it."

His father chuckled. "If I want romance in my life, I'll watch the Hallmark Channel."

Phil grinned. Like him, Phil's dad was a one-woman man.

Joan went about her day, checking the clock every now and again for the time. Her hair appointment was coming up that afternoon, followed by dinner with Nick. This was more to do in one day than she'd had scheduled in months. That encouraged her and convinced her she was making progress.

She was sitting in front of the latest jigsaw puzzle when her phone buzzed. Thinking it might be Nick, she answered without looking.

"Hello." If it was Nick, she wouldn't be overly disappointed if he needed to cancel. She'd keep her hair appointment, though.

"Is this Joan Sample?" a man with a deep, rich voice asked.

"Yes. Who's this?"

"I'm Phil Harrison. You left me a voice mail earlier today."

Joan's cheeks instantly filled with color. "I . . . I didn't leave my number, how did you . . ." Unsettled, she left the rest unsaid.

"Your number showed up on my phone."

"Of course." How foolish of her to have forgotten about caller ID.

"I'm sorry to hear your HOA is giving you trouble." He sounded sincere, kind.

"Yes, I fear my lawn has become something of a jungle." She didn't mention the condition of her flower beds, as that felt like a personal failure.

"I'm here to help."

"I've never had a lawn service before. My husband always took care of such matters, but unfortunately, he died a few years back." She swallowed tightly and recovered quickly. This man seemed to inspire confidence, his voice soothing and caring. "I have a lawn mower. It's top of the line. Jared always insisted on buying the best."

"We have our own equipment, but thank you. I'm sorry to hear about your husband. It's hard, isn't it?"

"Very." Not wanting to discuss her grief, she quickly added, "My son was able to mow the yard a few times last year . . ." Joan kept speaking, knowing it wasn't a good idea. Everyone knew not to give out personal information to a stranger, and here she was blurting out the details of her life.

"I'd be happy to stop by and give you a quote, if you'd like."

"Yes, please, that would be appreciated."

"Are you available later this afternoon?"

"Ah . . ." She stopped herself from mentioning that she would be away from the house. No need to set herself up for a burglary. "Tomorrow would be more convenient."

"Sure thing. Let me check my schedule," he said, and was silent for several seconds. "I have several commitments tomorrow, but I can come around six, if that isn't too late."

"That would be perfect."

"Great, then I'll see you at six tomorrow. May eighteenth."

"May eighteenth," she repeated, and then remembered that was the anniversary of the date the Mount Saint Helens volcano erupted. She'd been just a kid back then, and she recalled watching the ash fall from the sky. She and Emmie had collected it and stored it for years in a mason jar. Funny how memories like that floated into her mind.

"See you then," Phil Harrison said.

"Thank you."

"My pleasure."

The call disconnected and a warm sensation came over Joan. Phil Harrison sounded like such a nice man. She'd be cautious and get more than one bid, although she already liked him and hoped he lived up to the image she had of him in her mind.

Chapter 5

Joan arrived ten minutes early for her hair appointment. The shop was abuzz with activity. Chatter hummed across the room as women and a couple men filled the stations, with stylists doing a variety of tasks involving hair. Joan couldn't keep from smiling. It was as if the pandemic had never happened. Life had returned to normal. It had felt anything but normal for so long that this small reminder was enough to boost her spirits to the point she could almost forget.

"I'm Joan Sample," she announced, as she stepped forward to the desk where the receptionist sat. "I'm a bit early."

The young woman greeted her with a welcoming smile. Her name tag identified her as Jordan. "No problem. Take a seat and Bailey will be with you in a few minutes. Would you care for something to drink while you wait?"

"I'm good, but thanks." Joan chose a comfortable chair and noticed the wide assortment of magazines on the coffee table in front of her. She reached for *People* and absently leafed through it, astonished that she didn't recognize a single celebrity. They were all so young.

"As I live and breathe, it's Joan Sample," Charlene said, walking toward Joan. Her smile was wide, and her eyes sparked with delight. While the salon owner had been Emmie's high school classmate, she'd been Joan's friend, too. They hadn't socialized much, but Joan had been a regular at the salon. The two had lunched whenever Charlene could get away from the shop and Joan was able to leave the office.

She stood to greet her old friend. The two women briefly hugged. Taking hold of her shoulders, Charlene leaned back as if to get a good look at Joan. "Other than needing a decent haircut, you haven't changed a bit."

Oh, but Joan had changed in myriad ways. She might resemble the old Joan on the outside, but inside she was a completely different woman, one she hardly recognized herself. One she wrestled with on a daily basis, struggling to navigate this unfamiliar world in which she'd found herself thrust.

Jordan approached them. "Bailey is ready for you now."

"It's good to see you," Charlene said, as she returned to her station.

"You, too," Joan replied, and she meant it. She shouldn't have waited so long to make an appointment. "When you have a minute, I'd like to ask you about your boarder."

Charlene's eyes revealed her surprise.

"Yes, of course. As soon as you're finished with Bailey, we'll chat."

"I hope that won't put you behind, I mean, I'm not sure this is anything that would interest me," she admitted, although the thought had darted through her mind a few times since her sister had mentioned it. She rarely saw her sons, and having someone living in the house might help her to break out of the protective shell she'd built around herself. That cocoon that she needed to break free from in order to fly again.

Jordan gestured toward the young woman who would be styling her hair.

"Hello," Bailey said as Joan took a seat at her station. The young woman was in her early twenties, with her shoulder length hair parted down the middle. One half was a pale, almost white blond and the second half was pitch black. She looked a little like a checkerboard or a harlequin, which made Joan smile.

After draping the cloth apron around her neck, Bailey ran her fingers through Joan's hair and frowned ever so slightly.

"It's been a while since I was last in a salon," Joan confessed.

"Well, you're here now, and we're going to have you walking out looking good as new."

The two exchanged pleasantries as Bailey led Joan to the shampoo bowl. Back at her chair afterward, Bailey asked Joan a few questions about how she styled her hair and what she wanted.

Joan realized she no longer knew. She'd always worn her hair short in an easy-to-wash-and-wear style. It was longer now than at any time since she'd attended middle school. She'd grown accustomed to seeing herself with this length and often wore it in a ponytail at the base of her neck.

Given a free hand, Bailey reached for her scissors and went to work, clipping here and there, working her magic. She used a blow dryer and a huge brush to shape the style and then handed Joan a mirror so she could review the back. Joan barely recognized herself. She looked good. Really good, even if she said so herself.

When Bailey was finished, Joan left the young stylist a larger-than-normal tip. Bailey had earned it.

Her eyes widened with appreciation when she noticed the bill. "Thank you."

"You did a great job."

"I hope you'll come back again."

"I will."

Joan stepped up to the receptionist's desk and waited until Jordan was off the phone. She paid with the gift certificate from Emmie and booked another appointment for a trim the following month.

Charlene had finished with her client at about the same time and waited while Joan paid before walking her to the door. "You look great," she said approvingly.

"Bailey worked a miracle." She hesitated for a moment, and then said, "Emmie said something recently about you taking in a boarder and suggested I might do the same. I wonder how that's working out for you."

"I did mention that to Emmie," Charlene confirmed. "With Evan away, the house was so quiet; it sort of spooked me. Both our children live out of state. A widow friend of mine was the one who suggested I consider renting out a room. Her children live in the Midwest somewhere and she has a large home but didn't want to downsize. I found a young woman who sounded perfect, Maggie. She's a nursing student, a hard worker and very bright. Her references assured me she was decent and honest, and I wouldn't go wrong if I decided to rent her a room."

"She sounds ideal. How's it going?"

Charlene sighed with obvious regret. "I was happy to offer Maggie the room, but then I heard from my brother. My niece took a job in Seattle and needs a place to stay, and a little TLC after a bad breakup. I'm Shelley's godmother and really couldn't refuse. I didn't feel I can take in two boarders, especially with Shelley in such a sad emotional place."

Joan listened intently and silently wondered if considering taking in Maggie herself was something she could do. It went without saying that Emmie would encourage her to give it some thought. Knowing Charlene had already vetted her was a bonus. She trusted that the savvy business owner wouldn't be easily deceived, which gave Joan confidence. The more Charlene went on about Maggie, the more enthused Joan felt. Maybe having someone move in with her wouldn't be such a bad idea after all. Joan had heard about renting out bedrooms but had always assumed people did that because they needed extra funds. Certainly, Charlene didn't need the money. With Evan, her husband, working out of the country, the hairdresser was lonely. Although Joan had never thought of herself as lonesome, she was. The silence, the lack of purpose, was one of the elements that had led to her isolation. The more she mulled over the idea, the more appealing she found it.

"Maggie seemed perfect," Charlene said again. "I felt terrible telling her the news."

Charlene held Joan's eye. "Do you think taking in a college student is something that might interest you?"

Slowly, Joan nodded. "I think it just might. I'll think about it."

"Wonderful." Charlene was clearly on board with the idea. "I have Maggie's contact information and would highly recommend you reach out to her. She seemed delightful. I got the impression things weren't great for her at home, which made me feel even worse that I had to refuse her."

Joan needed to think this through before deciding what would be best. "I'm seeing Nick tonight and will discuss it with him. There's no reason I couldn't rent out one of the bedrooms." With both her sons living on their own, their bedrooms had been empty for years.

"Then consider it, Joan. I think it would be good for you and for this young woman. You can decide for yourself after you talk to her."

Joan was thinking fast, her mind whirling with the possibilities. Having someone live with her wouldn't be a disruption. She'd welcome the company. While the house had become her sanctuary, it was also cold and silent. It had been meant for a family, for people, not a lonely woman, lost in her grief. Before she decided, however, she would get Nick's feedback. In the end, though, the decision would be hers.

Meeting Charlene's gaze, Joan nodded. "Yes, send me her contact information. I'll give her a call."

Charlene beamed. "I think that's a terrific idea."

The thing was, so did Joan.

Chapter 6

As Joan readied for dinner with Nick, her spirits were high. She'd heard back from Charlene with the contact information for the young nursing student and intended to call Maggie Herbert first thing in the morning. She dressed carefully in a blouse and skirt she'd picked out earlier. Because it remained chilly in the evenings, she added a thin sweater.

Nick arrived right on time. He let himself in and found Joan in the kitchen. When he saw her, he did a double take. His mouth sagged open for a moment before he recovered and closed it. "Mom? Wow. You look great." He walked a full circle around her, smiling all the while.

"Thanks."

"I like your hair."

Her hand automatically went to the side of her head. "I had it styled earlier today by a lovely young woman. I told her all about my handsome son, but she let me know she's already in a committed relationship."

"You didn't," he said and groaned.

"I did. It's a shame, because I think the two of you would do well together."

"Mom," Nick said, shaking his head. "I don't need you playing matchmaker."

"I don't know what it is with young people these days," she muttered to herself. By the time she was Nick's age, Joan was married and pregnant with Steve. From what she'd observed, so many young people tended to wait until their thirties to marry and even later to start a family.

"I appreciate the thought, but I prefer to find my own dates," Nick said, but not unkindly.

"As you wish."

"You ready?" Nick asked, jingling the car keys in his hand.

Joan reached for her purse, and Nick led her out of the house and down the stairs. He seemed to notice the condition of the yard and paused outside the door. "If I don't have to work Saturday, I'll stop by and mow the lawn."

"Thanks, but no thanks. I'm actually hiring a lawn service." She didn't mention the HOA letter, knowing it would irritate her son as much as it had her. Nor did she want to start their evening on a negative note. Her mind flittered back to the conversation with the man from the lawn service. He seemed friendly and helpful. She looked forward to meeting him and was grateful he hadn't teased her about the comment that anyone she hired must love flowers.

"You hired a service? When did you do that?" Nick seemed surprised.

"I should say I'm planning on hiring a company for yard maintenance. I'm getting a quote tomorrow from one and another the following day. I'll go over the cost and review the contract before I make the decision."

"Good. I wish I was more help than I have been. I know Dad would have wanted me to be available to do these sorts of things for you." His words were laced with guilt.

"Nonsense," Joan said, and placed a reassuring hand on his arm. "You have your own life." She knew early on, after laying Jared to rest, that she couldn't allow herself to rely on her children. She had to learn to stand on her own, as painful as that was.

He sighed as though relieved, and escorted her to his truck. Ever the gentleman, Nick opened and closed the passenger door and then walked around the front of the vehicle.

"I'm looking forward to Il Lucano," Nick mentioned as he started the engine.

"Wonderful. I'm happy to hear they survived the lockdown." From what the local news station had reported, Joan knew that many of the restaurants in the area hadn't been as fortunate. It pleased her to learn that her favorite restaurant, one where she had enjoyed many celebratory meals with Jared, was still in business.

After they arrived and were seated, Joan was relieved to see that little had changed. The tables were covered with red checkered tablecloths. An empty bottle of Chianti served as the base for a candle that had melted into small rivers down the bottleneck. Traditional atmosphere and traditional Italian recipes. Home cooking, Italian style.

Joan didn't need to peruse the menu; she ordered the same dish every visit, as the Eggplant Parmesan was her favorite. Jared hadn't been fond of the vegetable, so she never cooked it.

In contrast, Nick carefully analyzed the menu, as if tempted by a number of dishes. After several minutes, he set aside the menu and said, "I'm going to have the Pasta Bolognese."

Joan broke into a wide smile.

"What?" Nick asked, cocking his head to one side.

"That was your father's favorite dish."

"It was?" He seemed both surprised and delighted. "I guess the apple doesn't fall far from the tree."

The server arrived, a young man Joan didn't recognize, who took their drink orders. Nick asked for the wine list, and together they decided on the Sangiovese. The server left, and Nick leaned back in the chair to ask, "Is that the wine Dad would have ordered?"

"No, he preferred Brunello di Montalcino when he could find it. You know how your father enjoyed discovering new wines."

Nick shrugged. "I think Dad got into wine more after Steve and I left home."

Joan agreed as the waiter returned with the bottle and two stemware glasses. After opening and pouring the wine, he was ready to take their dinner orders. It wasn't long before their meals arrived.

The Eggplant Parmesan was as good as Joan remembered. The wine relaxed her, and for the first time in longer than she could remember she felt like her old self. "I have an idea I'd like your opinion on."

"Sure, what is it?"

Without going into a lot of detail, she relayed her short conversation with Charlene from that afternoon.

Nick listened intently. "You aren't really considering taking in a boarder, are you?"

"Actually, I am." Joan had been taken by the story Charlene told of the nursing student. All the poor girl needed was a hand up and a decent place to live.

Her son shook his head. "I don't think that's a good idea."

"Why not?" Joan wasn't defensive, only curious at how adamant Nick seemed to feel.

"It would be a mistake to let a stranger into the house, Mom."

"She has excellent references, or so I've heard. I plan to check them out myself, of course."

Nick listened intently. "I don't want to make a big deal out of this, Mom. The choice is yours."

"But you'd rather I didn't."

He nodded. "You wanted my opinion, and you got it. All I ask is that you carefully think this through before you decide."

She mulled over his words and then sighed. "I appreciate your input."

"Glad you asked. Anything else on your mind?"

Now that he mentioned it, there was. "Emmie thinks I should find a grief therapy group." The conversation with her sister had stayed in her mind, although she wasn't keen on the idea of spilling her heartache out to a group of strangers. Since her son was happy to share his thoughts, she might as well get his feedback on this.

"Aunt Emmie said that?" Nick asked. The wine seemed to relax him, too.

"Emmie feels that I've never dealt with the grief I have over the loss of your father."

Nick's look became solemn. "I'm going to tell you the truth, Mom. I think it's a good idea. It wasn't just Dad you lost. Everything changed, and it hit you hard."

He said this as though she hadn't been aware of the losses. Hanging her head, she agreed. "It did."

"I don't want to hurt your feelings, but we both know you've changed since Dad died. There've been more times than I can count that I wanted to talk to you and realized you weren't hearing me."

"When?" she asked, shocked that this could possibly be true.

"I was thinking about buying a house and have been saving up for one for the last couple years. With the housing market high, I worried if the time was right and wanted your advice, remember?"

"Vaguely," she said, and bit into her lower lip before she realized what she was doing. "I'm sorry."

"No worries, Mom, I decided to wait a bit anyway."

Joan felt bad for letting her son down. In order to not ruin their evening, she asked, "Do you remember Joe and Gennie Davis?"

"Sure. I used to hang with Sam, remember? What about them?"

Joan took in a breath before she answered. The wine had loosened her tongue, and after what Nick had mentioned, her mind was whirling.

"After the funeral, she told me that after Joe died she saw a counselor she highly recommended and gave me her name and phone number."

"You never made the call, did you?"

Joan shook her head. "No. I don't know what I did with it and doubt I could find it now."

"Then call Gennie. I bet she'd be happy to hear from you."

Still Joan hesitated.

"Mom," Nick said, shaking his head. "You need to do this."

His insistence surprised her. It seemed her son had strong opinions.

Nick closed his eyes and released a heavy sigh. "Mom, you mean the world to me and Steve. We love you, but we don't know how best to help you out of this slump. I think talking to a counselor will do you a world of good."

Leaning closer, he lowered his voice as if he didn't want anyone listening to their conversation. "The thing is . . . being around you is hard sometimes. You're so sad, and it makes me sad to see you like this."

Joan's eyes widened as she struggled to accept what her son was saying. She hadn't realized how her grief had affected her sons. Absorbed in her own misery, not once had she considered that her children had not only lost their father, but in many ways her as well.

"Steve and I have been worried about you for a long time and didn't know what to do or if we should say anything. We thought, you know, that all you needed was time to get over losing Dad, but it's been four years now and you're no better now than after Dad first died."

Joan opened and closed her mouth. Instinctively she wanted to argue how off-base her sons were and then realized they were right. She felt trapped in her grief, lost and floundering.

"I'm making progress," she said instead.

"I hope so, Mom, for your sake as much as for Steve and me."

Joan had no clue her sons had been overly concerned about her. "I'll admit I've been in the doldrums for a while now."

"Mom, it's more than a while. I'm so happy to see you making an effort to take care of yourself."

Although her throat had narrowed to the point she could barely speak, she said, "You're right."

"Then you'll get the name of that counselor?"

"I will," she promised.

Nick eased back in his seat and studied her for a long, tense moment. "We good?" he asked, as though he feared his honesty had bruised their once close relationship.

"More than good," she assured him, and while she wanted to close her eyes and lick her wounds, she forced a smile.

Nick's face revealed his relief. "It'll be great to have my mom back," he said.

It would be great for Joan, too.

Chapter 7

Maggie wasn't sure what her next move would be. She'd had such high hopes after the interview with Mrs. Royce.

It had all felt so positive. She needed to move, get some boundaries and distance from her father and his drinking. The house no longer felt like her home, and hadn't since her mother's death.

He wouldn't be able to pay the electric bill. It went without saying he'd blown his disability check on beer.

Avoiding the inevitable, Maggie remained at the library until it closed, studying for her finals, struggling against the uncertain future that filled her with dread.

With nowhere else to go, she finally headed to her father's house. Noticing that the mailbox was stuffed, Maggie pulled everything free and with a heavy heart headed inside. As was the norm, her father sat in his ratty-looking recliner, a beer bottle in his hand while staring at the television.

"You bring me dinner?" he asked.

"Sorry, I wasn't able to swing by." And she hadn't, discouraged as she was after hearing back from Mrs. Royce.

"But I'm hungry." Roy looked at her with pleading eyes.

"I am, too, but there are a couple cans of soup in the cupboard. I'll heat those up for dinner. Besides, eating out gets expensive."

"What about your tip money?"

"Dad, I needed gas. I've been putting off an oil change."

Her father grumbled under his breath, as if she had let him down and he was now deeply disappointed in her.

Maggie ignored him while she shuffled through the mail, much of which contained past-due notices. She tore open the one from the electric company and saw the date on which the lights would be shut off. Two days. The only way to keep that from happening was to pay the full bill. It had been in arrears for several months, and there was no way Maggie could make a payment that was nearly a thousand dollars. It was hard enough living with her father with electricity; she couldn't imagine what it would be like without it.

Maggie realized she had to get out of the house, even if she had to make the 1996 Ford she inherited from her mother into a condo. As she headed into her bedroom, her phone rang. She didn't recognize the number and she was in no mood to talk to a telemarketer.

"Hello." Her greeting was tentative, as she was half expecting it to be a nuisance call.

A slight hesitation followed. "Is this Maggie Herbert?"

"Yes."

"I hope you don't mind my calling you this late. I got

your contact information from Charlene Royce. My name is Joan Sample."

"Yes?" At the mention of the other woman's name, Maggie's heart leaped.

"I'm calling because Charlene mentioned that you're looking to rent a room. I have a spare bedroom, and I thought we could meet and discuss the possibility."

The anxiety that had weighed down Maggie ever since the call from Mrs. Royce lifted. She did her best to hide her enthusiasm. "That would be great . . . I'd like that. When can we meet? I mean, I'll make myself available anytime that's convenient for you."

"Would tomorrow afternoon at two work? I can text you my address." The woman on the line hesitated, as if suddenly she had second thoughts. Maggie feared she might have already changed her mind.

"Two would be perfect. Thank you."

"Good . . . I'm not an impulsive woman. I never have been. This evening, I had dinner with my son, and mentioned you moving in with me. To be frank, he was dead set against the idea. I left the restaurant, thinking his concerns were legitimate. I'm not the kind of woman who would normally bring a stranger into my home."

"Your son is against this?" The hope that had sparked to life inside her faded quickly and was in danger of being snuffed out before it even had a chance to light.

"Yes, and I understand where he's coming from. The thing is, I make my own decisions. Once I got home from dinner, I couldn't get you off my mind. I had the strongest urge to connect with you right away, which I know sounds strange. I tried to set my mind at ease, yet nothing worked.

I promised myself I'd reach out in the morning, but I still felt the need to call you this evening."

Then Joan asked, "Are you okay? I know that's a weird thing to ask, and I apologize for being this forward."

Unsure how best to answer, Maggie went with honesty. "I'm okay . . . mostly. Things with my dad aren't the best." Maggie was afraid to say too much. She didn't want to come across as desperate, although she was. The prospect of living in her car terrified her. Her choices were limited. She could couch-surf for a few days with friends, but that wasn't a viable solution, at least not for long.

"I had a feeling that might be the case. I think we could be good for each other. Anyway, I'm rambling. I look forward to seeing you tomorrow afternoon."

"Thank you again."

Maggie disconnected the call and held her phone against her chest as she breathed in a huge sigh of relief. She'd pinned all her hopes on Mrs. Royce. She needed to remind herself that this opportunity might turn out to be a bust, too. She had to be practical and do her best to convince Joan Sample that renting her a room was one of the best decisions she would ever make.

The following afternoon, Maggie arrived several minutes early at the address Joan had texted. She sat in her car, mentally preparing herself for the meeting. The white house with black shutters was in an upper-class neighborhood, was two stories, and had a wide, inviting front porch. The yard needed a bit of TLC, but otherwise the home seemed to be a newer one built in a colonial style.

At precisely two, she rang the doorbell and stepped back to rub her sweating hands down the front of her outfit. She wore her Sunday best, a dress she'd gotten for her high school graduation. It was the last time she had bought anything new, as her finances had been on a downward slide ever since she'd started school and was doing her best to balance her studies and her work schedule.

The door opened and an attractive woman stood on the other side of the threshold. Maggie had assumed Joan would be older. That wasn't the case. Joan was slim and attractive, with deep, dark chocolate-brown eyes and thick hair. She couldn't be more than forty, perhaps forty-five, although age was difficult to judge. Her hair had silver streaks, so she might be closer to mid-fifties.

"You must be Maggie." Joan held the door open for her. "Come in, please." She led Maggie past the foyer and down a short hallway to the kitchen. Maggie did her best to take in the atmosphere as she obediently followed. Everything was tidy and neat. The house was meticulously kept up. Nothing seemed to be out of place.

"I baked cookies this morning, something I haven't done in years." She indicated Maggie should take a seat at the table. The cookies smelled as if they had only recently come from the oven, and the sugar and cinnamon hung invitingly in the air. Snickerdoodles, one of her favorites.

"You didn't need to go to any trouble, Mrs. Sample."

"Please call me Joan."

"All right, Joan."

"I see you like jigsaw puzzles?" Maggie commented, noting the puzzle took up a large portion of the tabletop.

Joan nodded as she took a seat. "The challenge of putting them together occupied my mind after my husband died."

The other woman's voice trembled slightly, and Maggie recognized the subject of her husband was one to be avoided.

"And, of course, through the pandemic, too."

In order to be polite, Maggie reached for a cookie. If it was a long time since Joan had baked cookies, it was even longer since Maggie had enjoyed anything homemade. The stove at the house had only one working burner, and the oven no longer held any heat. As far as Maggie was concerned, it was a minor miracle that it worked at all. By tomorrow it would be a moot point, with no electrical power coming into the house.

She set down two cups of tea as she took the chair across from Maggie. The scent of orange spice tickled Maggie's nose. She wanted to wrap the feeling of comfort and home around her the way she'd once carried her favorite baby blanket as a toddler.

"I checked out your references," Joan said, before she raised the china cup to her lips and sipped the tea.

Maggie held her breath while she waited to hear the outcome.

Joan met her gaze and offered Maggie a reassuring smile. "Everyone had nothing but good things to say about you. Your teachers claim you're their star pupil, and your manager at Starbucks assured me you have a strong work ethic and were honest and dependable."

Maggie relaxed somewhat.

"Your pastor had a great deal to say about you and your mother. He assured me I couldn't go wrong if I decided to rent you the room. He was a talkative fellow and told me how much he admired you and how sadly your mother is missed."

"I was blessed with a wonderful mother. I miss her every single day."

Joan seemed to soak in her words. "I sympathize," she whispered. "I know what it is to miss someone, too." Then, as if she needed to change the subject, she went on, her voice stronger now. "As you can see, the house is too big for one person."

"You have a lovely home, and if you decide to rent me a room, I can help with the housework and the cooking and anything else you need. I have finals next week, but after that I'll have a short break before the next quarter and can make myself available."

"I appreciate the offer, Maggie, but that won't be necessary. I understand you work two jobs and rarely have free time."

So far, so good. "Do you have any questions for me?"

Joan shook her head and seemed comfortable after having met Maggie. "You're everything I hoped you would be."

Maggie's throat tightened and she struggled to speak. "Thank you."

"Would you care to see the room?"

Maggie didn't want to make any assumptions. "Does this mean . . . you're willing to let me live here?"

Joan grinned. "I think we'll get along nicely."

Spontaneous tears pooled in her eyes, which Maggie quickly blinked away.

Joan seemed to pretend not to notice. "The two spare bedrooms are upstairs. You can have your pick. We'll need to shuffle a few things around so you can make the space your own, but that shouldn't take much effort."

"Okay." This was the best news ever, more than she'd hoped, more than she felt was possible.

"Follow me," Joan said, as she headed up the stairway.

Maggie dutifully traipsed up the stairs after Joan. The two bedrooms shared a Jack-and-Jill bathroom. Even a glance into the rooms told Maggie they had once belonged to boys. The rooms were typically male, with high school memorabilia and trophies from sporting events.

Joan waited while Maggie examined each room, then chose the slightly smaller of the two.

"This one is perfect." It had a queen-size bed, which was much larger than the twin she currently slept in. What she liked best was the desk beneath the window, allowing in the light. She didn't have a desk at her father's house and balanced everything on her knees in bed when forced to study at home.

"That's Nick's old room," Joan mentioned.

"Is he the son who objected to you taking in a boarder?"

Joan answered with a wry grin. "He is. My other son lives in Arizona. Nick lives here locally."

"Will he be upset when he learns I'm living here, and in his bedroom?"

"Why should he be? Like I mentioned earlier, I make my own decisions. He hasn't slept in that room in years. As far as I'm concerned, the space is yours."

Maggie didn't want to start out on the wrong foot with Joan's son. "Perhaps I should take the other room, then."

"No, you've already made your choice, and I agree this room suits you. When would you like to move in?"

Once again tears came close to the surface. "Would later today be a problem?"

"None whatsoever. Go collect your things, and by the time you return I'll have dinner ready."

"I don't expect you to cook for me," Maggie was quick to tell the other woman. She was grateful beyond words Joan had agreed to take her in as a boarder. Anything else was far more than she'd hoped or expected. Nor did she want to give the impression she expected meals to be included.

"We can discuss those details over dinner," Joan told her.

"I'll need to know how much you want for rent." This was the last hurdle Maggie had to climb. If the fee was beyond what she could afford, she didn't know what she would do.

Joan seemed to need to think about this some. "Can we go over that at dinner?"

Maggie needed to be sure the other woman understood that her finances were limited. "I . . . I can't afford much . . . if it's more than I can afford, would it be possible to make payments later once I finish my classes and am fully employed?"

"We'll hash all that out later. No worries, Maggie, I can work with your budget."

Maggie's relief was instantaneous. "Thank you, but I won't feel right until I know what you plan to charge." As happy as she was to find a space to rent, Maggie needed to nail down the details before she packed up her belongings.

Joan shrugged, as if the rent was of little concern to her. "Is three hundred dollars a month fair?"

"Three hundred?" Her father charged her more.

"That isn't too much, is it?"

Maggie beamed a smile. "It's more than fair. I can easily pay that."

"Then it's settled. I have an appointment at six this evening. I'm hiring a lawn maintenance company. Dinner will be ready, and afterward we can finalize the details."

"That's perfect." Maggie resisted the urge to hug the other woman. "Thank you again."

"While you're away I'll move a few things around in Nick's old room."

"Oh, please, let me. I can—"

"Nonsense. Don't be late for dinner."

"I won't." As she walked back to her car, Maggie felt as if she was walking on air. One door had closed and a sliding glass one had opened. This was big. This was amazing. Only a day earlier she'd been fighting to keep her spirits up. Within less than twenty-four hours, everything had turned around. Joan was asking for a cheaper rent than Mrs. Royce wanted. It felt like a miracle, and perhaps it was. She couldn't discount that her mother had been behind this from heaven.

Now all that was left was letting her father know she was moving out.

And frankly, that was a task Maggie dreaded, knowing how much he counted on her to help with the bills and his daily supply of beer.

Chapter 8

Joan stood in the doorway as she watched Maggie drive away. What she'd told the young woman was true. Joan was rarely, if ever, impulsive. Reaching out to Maggie had been completely out of character.

Before she'd left the salon, Charlene had hinted about Maggie's unhappy home life, which had weighed on Joan's mind. Her heart had gone out to the girl. Now, after personally spending time with her, she couldn't imagine not helping the young woman.

After she'd spoken to the manager at Starbucks, Joan had been even more reassured. She'd learned Maggie was prompt, kind, and patient with the customers. The manager claimed she wished she had a dozen employees just like her.

Joan had also learned that following Maggie's nursing classes, she tutored children with reading disorders. Every minute of her day was taken up. All Maggie really needed was a hand-up.

Now, after meeting Maggie, Joan was so grateful to

Charlene and to her sister for suggesting Joan take in a boarder in the first place.

Joan found it difficult to admit how lonely she was. It had been easy to deny the silence. She'd always been more of an introvert and appreciated quiet times. For most of her life, she'd been a deep thinker, methodical, rarely acting rashly or on impulse.

She had that night. After talking to Charlene, as hard as Joan tried to put Maggie out of her head, she couldn't. For reasons she would likely never understand, Joan had made the call.

Their conversation didn't last long. The meeting time was set. The relief that followed was uncanny. As silly as it sounded, she recognized deep down with a certainty that she didn't question that she was meant to help Maggie Herbert. For whatever reason, God had put Maggie in her path.

Eventually Nick would discover what she'd done. For now, she'd keep the information to herself. Nick rarely stopped by the house, and if he did happen to drop in when Maggie was present, she'd introduce the two and let the chips fall as they might. As she'd told Maggie earlier, Joan made her own decisions.

After Maggie's ramshackle car had disappeared around the corner, Joan closed the front door and returned to the kitchen. She had taken a small roast out of the freezer for dinner. It'd been a long time since she'd cooked for someone other than family. She had a recipe Jared had especially liked: Mississippi pot roast. Seeing that it was years since she'd last cooked it, she opened the kitchen drawer where she stored papers she wanted to keep. Everything was neatly filed. It didn't take her long to find what she wanted.

As she pulled out the typed sheet, a small piece of paper was stuck to the backside. When she went to remove it, she realized it was a name and a phone number.

Not just any name or any phone number, though.

It was the grief counselor Gennie had recommended shortly after Jared had been laid to rest.

If this wasn't a sign from God, Joan didn't know what was.

Wow. Talk about getting hit over the head. She set the paper on the kitchen counter and stared at it, her mind abuzz.

Tomorrow. She'd make the call tomorrow. Better yet, she'd wait until Monday, get a fresh start to the week. Her limit for change had been reached. She'd stretched herself as far as she could go for now.

Contacted a lawn maintenance company.

A hair appointment.

Dinner out with Nick.

Taking in a boarder.

That was far and away more activity in the last three days than she'd had in years.

Something she couldn't name had taken hold of her on her birthday. The emptiness had hit her hard, and Joan realized she needed to make a change. She felt that God had just given her a giant shove in the right direction, and she had followed through. Next was meeting with Phil Harrison regarding her lawn. She looked forward to it, which was silly of her, really. He'd sounded friendly and kind. Human contact was something she'd been missing.

Now Maggie was moving in with her, and Joan felt almost giddy, eager to get to know this young woman. Knowing that she was helping Maggie filled her with a certain pride. Which reminded her of something Steve had once mentioned. It had felt like it was coming out of the blue when he suggested she do volunteer work, thinking that might help her. She'd blown off the idea but realized now her son had been right; already she felt better about life, about the future.

Earlier, following the recipe, Joan had put the roast in the Crock-Pot. Now it was time to add the potatoes. She'd just finished dumping the peelings into the garbage when her doorbell chimed. Checking her watch, she saw it was fifteen minutes before her scheduled appointment with Harrison Lawn and Landscaping. She didn't mind that he was early.

Wiping her hand on a kitchen towel, she headed to the front door. From force of habit, she checked the peephole first. A man stood on the other side. His shirt had his name embroidered on it: Phil Harrison.

Disengaging the deadbolt, Joan opened the door.

"Joan Sample?" he asked.

She nodded, warmed by his smile. "And you must be Phil Harrison."

He nodded in return. "I hope you don't mind that I'm a few minutes early."

"Not at all." Stepping outside so that she stood on the porch with him, she noticed that the sun had come out after a shower earlier in the day. Wide swings in the weather in the spring weren't uncommon in the Pacific Northwest.

Joan gestured toward the yard. "As you can see, the yard is in need of a little TLC."

"That's what we do," Phil assured her, as though he looked forward to mowing it into submission. He held a pencil and clipboard.

He was around her age, Joan guessed, early fifties, with salt-and-pepper hair. Average height and looks, but definitely attractive. He wasn't likely to make any fireman's calendar, but kindness emanated from him. Even this early in the year, he was deeply tanned, a testament to the time he spent outdoors. What she noticed right away were his eyes, compassionate and gentle, a piercing blue.

"It shouldn't take us more than a few hours to get this cleaned up. Are you interested in both the front and the backyard?" he asked.

"Yes, please."

"Would you mind if I took a look at the back?"

"Of course." Joan started to head through the house when Phil stopped her.

"I'm filthy." He glanced down at his boots, which were caked with dried mud. "Is there a side gate I can use?"

"Oh heavens, yes, I didn't think about that." Joan doubted she'd opened that gate once in all the time she'd lived in this house, and that was more years than she cared to remember.

"I'll meet you in the back," he said, and disappeared around the side of the house.

As he suggested, Joan went through the house and joined Phil in the backyard. At one time she'd grown a small garden there. Nothing much. Rhubarb on one side of the fence and tomato plants along the other. The flower beds where she'd once lavished her attention were in front of the house.

Volunteer tomatoes had sprung up last summer without Joan doing anything to care for them. The fruit was small, and the bushes flopped over from the weight of the bounty. Years before, Joan had proudly canned her produce. Perhaps she would again one day.

"We can manage the lawn, no problem."

"Good." She stood with her arms across her front, embarrassed that she'd let the maintenance of her yard deteriorate to this point.

"Would you like the beds cleared at the same time?"

"Yes, just for now. I'll take over after they are cleared and weeded." As for her garden, perhaps she should think about that, even if it was a little late in the spring. She'd start fresh with healthy plants from the local nursery.

"Front and back flower beds?"

"Yes, please."

"If you'd like, I can plant some low-maintenance bushes in the beds that would require minimum care and attention."

"I appreciate the offer, but I'd rather plant that area myself." She adored the calla lilies that sprang up each spring. The tulips had bloomed with her barely noticing. She'd planted the bulbs years earlier after a trip to Skagit County where the scene of fields of blooming tulips had taken her breath away. It depressed her how neglected the flower beds had become with the lawn encroaching.

Phil grinned. "I forgot. Must love flowers."

Joan's cheeks reddened with the reminder. "Forgive me for adding that—"

His smile widened. "Nothing to forgive. I found it

rather refreshing. As it happens, I'm rather fond of flowers myself."

Joan appreciated his effort to put her at ease.

Phil made a few additional marks on the clipboard. The woman was a surprise. He wasn't sure what he'd expected and was pleased to find her younger than he'd imagined. He recognized the very things in her that he'd felt years earlier—the pain, the loneliness. He felt immediate empathy, as he was well aware of what loss could do to a soul.

"How long have you been a widow?" he asked.

"How did you know . . ." Her eyes widened, as if Joan couldn't remember mentioning her marital status.

"You mentioned your husband had passed away when we first spoke on the phone."

"Ah, yes, I did say that, didn't I? It's been four years now." He remembered how frazzled she'd sounded when he'd listened to her voice mail. He suspected she hadn't reached out much since then. The isolation from COVID likely had only complicated her healing process. He didn't judge, seeing how long it had taken him to move forward.

"If you decide to hire me, I promise that I can whip your yard into shape in quick order and I'll be fair in my pricing." He wanted to reassure her that he was honest and would do a good job.

She nodded as if she believed him.

"I'll get an estimate from the nursery for any plants you would like, and I'll get back to you within a day or two with a bid."

"Would you be able to bid on regular maintenance at the same time?"

"Of course. Every two weeks? Or every week?"

"Every week for now."

"I'll be happy to do that." He'd taken notes as he'd surveyed her yard and was ready to leave when she stopped him.

"Would you mind if I asked you a few questions?" she said, as if she felt she should.

Phil didn't mind. He was happy to give her the reassurance she seemed to need.

"Of course. What would you like to know?" He lowered the clipboard and met her gaze.

"How long have you been in business?"

"My father started the company back in the early seventies. He's mostly retired now. I took over five years ago. I'm bonded and can offer references if you'd like."

"So you've always worked with your father, then?"

"Actually, no, I had another career before I decided to become a landscaper. Funny how life is," he said, without going into any details. "My dad needed me, and I realized the time was right for me to make a change. But Harrison Lawn and Landscaping has been in business for nearly fifty years."

"I think I remember reading that now."

"The fact is, I grew up pushing a lawn mower and learning just about everything there is to know about the local trees, bushes, and flowers. I never thought I'd end up following in Dad's footsteps."

"Why's that?"

"At sixteen I was more interested in girls and football. Yardwork was the last thing on my mind. Any other job was preferable to mowing lawns. I flipped hamburgers, parked cars, and carried out groceries. Anything that meant I didn't need to work for my dad."

"And yet here you are."

"Here I am," he admitted with a wry grin. "and I'm loving it. As a teenager I couldn't see what Dad found enjoyable in his work. It made no sense to me that he'd be out in the rain, day after day, and come home with a satisfied smile."

"What changed?" Joan asked.

He didn't answer her right away, wondering how much to reveal. He lowered his eyes, unwilling to let her read him. "Unexpected turns in the road, I suppose. Life can sometimes kick us to the curb, you know? After years of wearing a suit day in and day out, I had the inexplicable need to dig my hands into the soil, to get back to the basics. You probably understand that better than most."

Joan nodded. "I do."

He'd said more than he intended. He liked Joan Sample and understood her hesitation. "I'll get back to you in a day or two with the cost of the initial cleanup and clearing the flower beds for you to plant."

"Plus the weekly maintenance," she added.

"I'll add that to the bid." He had all the business he could handle as it was. Nevertheless, he hoped to get this job. This widow needed help, and if there was anything Phil understood, it was loss and heartache.

Chapter 9

Joan walked Phil to the gate and watched as he returned to his truck, which he'd parked at the curb. He didn't leave right away, and seemed to be going over the notes he'd made when assessing her property.

The most lighthearted feeling came over her. It wasn't meeting Phil, or Maggie moving into the house, or even finding the contact information for the counselor. It was all of it. For the first time since that awful day when she'd followed the ambulance to the hospital, praying Jared would be okay, she felt ready to deal with life again.

Joan remembered a quote from Winston Churchill she'd read years ago. *If you're going through hell, keep walking.*

She'd made her way out of the darkness that felt like it had nearly buried her. She'd stepped out of the oppressive night and into the early light of morning. Freed now, Joan felt as if she could breathe again.

Joan was just starting toward home when Maggie returned with her things from her father's house. As soon as Maggie climbed out of the car, Joan knew something was wrong. The girl's face was streaked with tears and her lower lip trembled.

Joan hurried across the yard to her. "What's happened?" she asked, immediately concerned.

Maggie's startled gaze met hers. Tears continued to rain down Maggie's cheeks. Attempting a small smile, which failed, Maggie sniffled. "I'm okay . . . It was harder leaving my dad than I thought it'd be; he never thought I'd actually leave. When I started packing up my things, he got kind of aggressive. He . . . wouldn't let me take anything out of the house. Thankfully, I had my laptop with me, or he'd have that, too, but all my clothes and toiletries . . . Everything that's important to me is there." With that, Maggie broke into sobs.

Joan wrapped her arms around her, wondering how best to help. Her first thought was to reach out to the authorities. Calling the police, she feared, would complicate matters and cause more hard feelings, creating an even bigger rift between father and daughter. Besides, who knew how long it would take for them to respond to a low-priority situation. Not knowing what to do, Joan looked to Phil, who remained parked outside her home. She was at a loss, and Maggie was too upset to think clearly.

The landscaper seemed to read the desperation in her eyes. He climbed out of the truck and asked, "Is everything okay here?"

"No," Joan said. "Maggie is moving in with me and

her father is preventing her from taking her belongings out of the house."

"He can't believe I am actually moving out. I've been telling him for weeks that as soon as I found a place, I was leaving. He refused to believe me. He . . . drinks," Maggie added between sniffles.

Phil didn't hesitate. "Come on, I'll go with you and do my best to distract him while you collect whatever you need."

Maggie didn't bother to hide her surprise. "You'd do that?"

Phil nodded. "No worries. I'm happy to help and make sure things don't get out of hand."

"I'm going, too," Joan insisted.

Maggie's watery eyes revealed her appreciation.

Offering reassurance, Joan squeezed Maggie's arm and was grateful Phil was willing to keep watch while Maggie and Joan collected Maggie's things.

Joan rode with Maggie, and Phil followed behind in his work truck. When they arrived at Maggie's home, Joan noticed the dilapidated condition of the house and yard. If her lawn was unkempt, this one was a wilderness. It looked as if there'd once been flower beds, but they had long disappeared behind weeds that reached halfway up the side of the porch. The lawn, what was left of it, was nearly knee-high. The steps to the porch had collapsed on one side and one window was broken and covered with cardboard. It was little wonder Maggie had been desperate to leave. The house was falling down upon itself.

Unsure whether he was doing the right thing, Phil left his truck and joined Maggie and Joan on the sidewalk outside the house. He took in the sight of the run-down property and frowned, glancing toward Maggie and then Joan.

"Dad's drunk," Maggie explained. "He's probably sitting in front of the television . . . The power is about to be turned off because he hasn't paid the electric bill. He didn't used to be like this, but then my mom died, and drinking became his coping mechanism."

With all the counseling he'd had through the years, Phil was fairly hopeful he could keep Maggie's father talking.

"No worries," he said. "I'll chat with him while you and Joan collect what you need."

Together the three of them entered the house. Just as Maggie had said, her father had situated himself in the recliner in front of the television. When he saw Maggie with Phil and Joan, the other man half rose from his chair, only to stumble and fall back into a sitting position.

"You can't come in here," he shouted. "This is my home. Get out."

"We'll only stay a few minutes," Phil assured him calmly. "Just long enough for Maggie to get what she needs. I'm Phil Harrison. What's your name?"

"Roy Herbert. Now leave. My daughter is no longer welcome in this house. She made her decision; as far as I'm concerned, good riddance."

While Maggie's father continued explaining what a thankless daughter he'd raised, Joan and Maggie went down the hallway to Maggie's bedroom.

Phil listened as Roy continued. "Ungrateful, she is, after all I've done for her. Selfish, too, only thinking of herself. She doesn't give a damn about me or what will happen to me once she's gone."

Phil let him speak without interrupting. As Roy's tirade continued, Phil noticed Joan and Maggie leaving with several boxes.

"It's hard to let go of our children, isn't it?" Phil said, after he was convinced the two women had finished collecting Maggie's items.

Roy snorted and shook his head.

"For some, but not for all of us. I remember when my daughter left for college, I was a basket case. I didn't want her to go, and at the same time, I realized she was an adult now and needed to find her own way in life."

Roy didn't say anything for several seconds. The anger seemed to have drained out of him. "My Maggie wants to be a nurse. I can't afford to help her with all those college expenses. She doesn't realize she's in over her head, taking out loans she'll spend years paying back."

Phil could appreciate Roy's concern. "Maggie has to make her own decisions, though, the same way my Amanda did."

"Maybe," he grumbled. "I never thought she'd abandon me."

"It feels that way, doesn't it?"

He huffed. "Told her if she leaves, then she's not welcome back."

Phil wasn't convinced Maggie would take his angry words to heart. "I'm sorry to hear that."

"She's stubborn, that one. Gets it from her mother." He paused and choked back tears. "Miss that woman every day. Nothing seems right with her gone." He sniffled and wiped his forearm under his nose.

Knowing well what the other man must be feeling, Phil

nodded in commiseration and said, "Looks like Maggie has her things. We won't be troubling you again," he said.

Roy shrugged with defeat.

"Nice meeting you, Roy."

He snickered. "Wish I could say the same."

Phil left the house. Both Joan and Maggie stood outside and seemed to be waiting for him.

"How'd it go?" Maggie asked, her forehead wrinkled with concern.

"Good," Phil said.

"I appreciate your help."

"No problem."

"I do my best to help him," Maggie said, glancing back toward the house, "but I just had to get away."

Phil held Maggie's gaze, letting her know he understood.

Maggie crossed her arms over her chest as though to hide the emotional pain she'd endured through the years.

"He talked about losing your mother."

Maggie lowered her eyes. "Everything went downhill after Mom died. He changed a lot. He used to keep up the house with Mom's encouragement, but after she died, he didn't even try."

Phil noticed Joan's reaction to his comment. Her eyes rounded and she looked down and folded her arms as if protecting herself. He wondered what she was thinking, and if she was comparing herself to Roy, who had let his yard and life deteriorate. Phil wanted to tell her she was nothing like Maggie's father, but he kept silent.

"My mother held everything together in our family," Maggie whispered. "And with her gone, all that was right and good fell apart."

Phil understood all too well what grief and heartache could do to a soul. He looked to each woman before he said, "I was happy to help, but I best head home." Dinner was likely waiting for him.

"Again, I can't thank you enough," Maggie said earnestly.

"Yes, thank you," Joan echoed. "You came to give me an estimate and went far and away beyond that."

He shrugged off their appreciation.

He started toward his truck and turned back. "I'll have that bid ready for you on Monday."

"No need. Consider yourself hired."

He nodded, grateful for the work and the opportunity to know both women better.

Chapter 10

On the drive back to the house, both Maggie and Joan grew quiet.

"A penny for your thoughts," Joan said, glancing Maggie's way. Her own musings were caught up in appreciation for Phil's help. How he'd been willing to step in, even not knowing what the situation was. She wasn't sure what might have happened if Phil hadn't distracted Maggie's father. Hearing what Maggie said about the changes in her father after her mother died had hit close to home. Everything seemed to have come to a head at once, and Joan realized she'd continued to carry her grief these last four years like a piece of luggage, hauling it with her through each day, refusing to release the burdensome weight.

"I'll help you take your things up the stairs," Joan offered, once they reached the house.

"Please, you've done so much already. I can handle this."

Joan was more than ready to help. "I'm sorry I didn't

get around to moving Nick's things out of the bedroom. I'll see to that while you unload the car."

"Okay." Maggie offered her a weak smile. She remained in the car, her look pensive.

"Maggie?"

"I think I should visit my dad from time to time," she murmured. "Just to see how he's doing. Without me there, I don't know what will happen to him."

"That's generous of you."

Maggie's eyes were sad. "He relied on me to take care of him, and I did my best. With me gone, he's going to need to look after himself now. He might need a little encouragement now and again."

Joan was impressed that Maggie, who had endured so much while dealing with her own grief over the death of her mother, would be so generous and compassionate toward her father, especially after the way he'd treated her.

"I understand now," Maggie continued, apparently deep in thought.

"Understand?"

"He didn't want me to become a nurse, always said it was too expensive, but deep down I think he knew that once I got my nursing degree I'd move away. I think he's scared of being alone, and now that I've moved out, he is."

Joan squeezed Maggie's shoulder, letting her know she understood. "Visiting your dad isn't a bad idea."

Maggie nodded before opening the driver's-side door.

They each carried a load as they approached the house. As soon as Joan unlocked the door, the scent of the roast in the Crock-Pot hit her, reminding her that dinner was ready. While working, she'd relied on that slow cooker for many a meal. Putting it to use again made her smile, as if this was yet another sign that she was on the right path, taking her own time to recover.

"Wow, that smells good."

"As soon as we're finished upstairs, we can eat."

Maggie gave her a look of appreciation. "I can't remember the last time I had a real home-cooked meal."

For that matter, neither could Joan.

While Maggie collected the rest of her items from the car, Joan transferred Nick's sports trophies into Steve's old room. He had a couple posters on the wall, which she took down, along with a few other personal items. His dresser drawers were mostly empty. She found his high school yearbooks and a few video games, which were easy enough to deliver to the second bedroom. All in all, it took only a few minutes to clear his things out of the bedroom.

Maggie immediately went about making the area her own. The first thing she did, Joan noticed, was put up the picture of her and her mother. As best she could calculate, it was taken when Maggie was about seven or eight.

She stared at the photo of the two of them. The resemblance wasn't hard to miss. Seeing his daughter must have been a constant reminder to Roy Herbert of the wife he had loved and lost. She'd never expected to feel sympathy for the man, and yet she did. He was weak, no doubt, and she suspected the loss of his wife had crippled him the same way losing Jared had done to her. Deep down, she believed that once he started pulling himself together, he would want Maggie to follow through on her dreams.

By the time Maggie had finished unpacking, Joan had

dinner on the table. She removed the jigsaw puzzle she'd been assembling for the last two weeks. She needed that space for their serving dishes. Spending mindless hours on the project no longer held appeal.

When they sat down to eat, Maggie said, "I hope you know I don't expect you to provide dinners for me."

Joan was convinced Maggie often skipped meals or ate on the run. "I don't mind. It will give me an excuse to cook again."

"I would like that." Her eyes lit up with appreciation. "But to be fair, I'll need to pay you more in rent."

"No, please, the price is more than fair."

It looked for a moment as though Maggie wanted to argue. "Okay," she conceded, "but only if you let me help around the house."

"We can discuss all that later." Joan handed her the platter with the roast for Maggie to help herself.

They were halfway through the meal and the conversation flowed smoothly. Although they didn't know each other well, they appeared to be at ease, comfortable, as if they'd known each other beyond this single day.

"What will your son say when he learns you've gone ahead and rented me the room? His room?"

Joan grinned, thinking what Nick's reaction would likely be. "He'll probably be upset at first."

"I'm sorry. I wish now I'd taken your other son's room."

"Nonsense. Nick hasn't lived at home in years. At one point I considered turning that room into a craft area." And perhaps one day she would if she ever decided to take painting classes or learned to knit. She'd look forward to the time she was comfortable enough to do those very things. Baby steps, she reminded herself. One thing at a time.

Thinking about the future was something else Joan hadn't done in a long while. It seemed pointless, but now it was an idea she'd entertain.

They finished their meal, and Maggie insisted on washing the dishes. Joan let her. It was a small concession, and it made Maggie feel like she'd contributed, which she did.

"My alarm goes off early," Maggie explained, as she finished with the dishes. "I work the morning shift. I hope I don't wake you."

"Don't worry about it. If you wake me, I'll go right back to sleep." Joan didn't sleep well most nights and wasn't overly concerned.

"I also tutor three days a week until the school breaks for the summer."

Joan remembered hearing about that. "I believe Charlene mentioned you helped young readers."

"It doesn't pay much. The school district only offers a small stipend, but I enjoy helping the second-graders. It makes me feel good when I see them making progress."

"How many students do you tutor?"

"Just two. Caleb has a minor case of dyslexia. All Victoria needs is someone patient and loving. She comes from a low-income family and didn't attend preschool, so she came into the classroom already behind, according to her teacher."

"Caleb and Victoria are fortunate to have you."

"I feel like the fortunate one. On the last day of school, I'm going to surprise them with a special treat."

When she finished the dishes, Maggie headed up the

stairs, explaining that she needed to study for finals, which were scheduled for the following week.

"Night, Joan, and thank you again for everything."

"You're most welcome. I hope you sleep well."

"I know I will."

Joan watched Maggie disappear up the stairs before returning to the kitchen. She found the slip of paper Gennie Davis had given her and looked at the name and the phone number. If she'd learned anything from the confrontation with Maggie's father, it was that she couldn't delay making this appointment.

"Well, Dr. O'Brien, I hope you're everything Gennie claims."

Joan stared at the paper for so long she had the phone number memorized. First thing tomorrow morning, she would make an appointment.

Chapter 11

Joan sat in the large reception area, waiting for her name to be called. She'd buried her face in a magazine, afraid, foolish as it was, that someone might recognize her. Dr. O'Brien's office housed three other counselors who shared a common receptionist. Joan had made the appointment first thing Thursday morning, thinking—hoping, actually—that the first available time slot wouldn't be for a week or longer. That would give her time to mentally prepare for this meeting. Oh no, that would have been too easy. Instead, she got a late-morning appointment on Monday.

Thursday to Monday had given Joan four full days to fret and worry. Far too many times to count, she'd toyed with the notion of canceling. When she spoke with the receptionist, she was informed she would be charged for the session if less than twenty-four-hours' notice was given. By Friday afternoon it was too late. The weekend spread before her like a yawning beast.

Something was drastically wrong with her. Joan had

never been an impulsive woman, and twice within the same week, she'd gone against her very nature. She used to feel that she knew herself. Not any longer.

When she woke that morning, dread filled her that she would need to face this unknown person and expose the deepest, most excruciating pains of her life. She'd never been a crier until the last four years. Already she could feel the tears welling in her eyes. Her hands trembled, and she felt both hot and cold at the same time. She needed to escape. It didn't matter that she would be required to pay for the session; it was worth it to break free while she had the chance.

She rose to her feet, intent on making a beeline for the door, when the receptionist called her name.

"Joan Sample. Dr. O'Brien will see you now." The woman stood and opened the door leading down a long hallway. "Dr. O'Brien's office is the third door on the left," she instructed, and gestured in that direction.

"Ah." Joan froze mid-step. Looking longingly toward the door that would lead to her escape and then the door that might possibly alter her life, she had a decision to make.

Fearing if she left, she'd never be able to heal, Joan hesitated. Indecision gripped her like a boa constrictor, defining her own efforts to negate and ignore the difficult changes in her own life.

She turned toward the door leading to Dr. O'Brien's office.

The woman stood as Joan entered the room. Dr. Lannie O'Brien was a young woman. Much younger than expected, for all the letters listed after her name.

"Welcome, Joan." Dr. O'Brien signaled for her to take

a seat on the sofa. The counselor sat in a chair directly in front of her but not so close as to make her uncomfortable. The room, small and inviting, was painted a pale blue. Several colorful pillows decorated the sofa. The paintings on the wall were soothing and familiar, with landscapes of the Pacific Northwest.

Joan sat and clenched her hands together. She didn't lean back and sat up straight as a fir tree.

Dr. O'Brien smiled encouragingly. "Tell me what brings you here."

The lump in Joan's throat felt as though it were the size of a goose egg. She swallowed several times before she could speak. "Gennie Davis recommended I talk to you."

For a moment Dr. O'Brien's face remained stoic, as if trying to remember who Gennie Davis was.

"She lost her husband . . . That was several years ago now, so you might not recall seeing her. I imagine you talk to a lot of people."

"I remember Gennie. How is she doing?"

"Good, I guess. I mean, I haven't talked to her in a while." Like years, but Joan didn't mention that.

"Can you tell me why she thought I might be of help to you?"

"My . . . My husband died."

"Was this recent, Joan?" Her eyes were sympathetic.

Joan looked down at her hands, reluctant to admit how long it had been. "Jared died four years ago."

"I see. Tell me about Jared."

For the next several minutes Joan spoke of her loving relationship with her husband. After she relayed the basic information, how they met, married, and raised their two sons, she hesitated and then spoke of the aneurysm that took his life.

When she finished, she added, "Many couples who spend as much time together as Jared and I did eventually have marriage difficulties. It took effort for us to separate our business life from the one at home. Somehow, we managed to do that and keep both relationships strong.

"We were good together, complementing each other. We raised our sons with love, and when it came time for them to make their own lives, we adjusted easily to an empty nest."

"You never argued?"

"Rarely." And that was true. In all the years of their marriage and their work, there were seldom any conflicts that couldn't be resolved with patience and love.

"I can understand why Jared's death was such a tremendous loss."

That goose egg was back, and once again Joan was forced to swallow it down. As she had earlier, she blinked away tears. "It feels like a part of me died along with my husband." Her vision was blurred by the moisture in her eyes.

Dr. O'Brien reached for a tissue box and handed it to Joan.

"Thank you," she whispered brokenly.

"It's been four years," Dr. O'Brien said. "I can imagine Jared's loss has been a major adjustment for you and your children."

Joan nodded.

"Tell me how you've made that adjustment."

That was the point of her visit. Joan really hadn't adjusted. She had an excuse and was more than ready to use it. "It wasn't long after Jared's passing that the pandemic hit," she said, as a way of explaining how isolated her life had become.

"And you holed up inside your home like the rest of the world."

"Yes." Another nod—a confession, really—an admission of guilt. "The problem is, I continued to falter, unsure of the direction my life needed to go after the pandemic. My home became my shelter as well as my prison. I need to know what to do next. I have no idea where to go from here. I don't need to work but feel like maybe I should." She made an empty gesture with her hands. "I'm lost, Dr. O'Brien, and I'm hoping you can help me find my way."

"And that's the reason you made this appointment?"

"Yes. That and other reasons."

"You should know that I don't give directions, Joan. That's not the way a counselor functions. My role is to help you find your own way. It will be painful at times and joyous at others. It isn't easy to break patterns that we fall into when our natural instinct is to steer toward what is familiar. Are you ready to make those changes?"

"I'm here." That should be answer enough.

Dr. O'Brien smiled. "That's a wonderful first step in the right direction, and I applaud you. Would you consider attending a grief therapy group?"

Joan automatically shook her head, vehemently rejecting the idea out of hand. "No."

Showing no outward sign of disapproval, Dr. O'Brien asked, "Can you tell me why you're so adamantly against the idea?"

Inhaling a calming breath, Joan lowered her gaze to

the floor. "The people in this group have all lost loved ones, right?"

"Yes, that's the reason they chose to join the group."

"Each one is grieving, the same way I am . . . I can't take on their grief, I can't sit and listen to all that they've lost when I'm dealing with my own pain. It would destroy me." Joan could only imagine how hard it would be to carry the weight of another's immense loss along with her own. She wasn't strong enough.

"It isn't like that, Joan. The sessions are affirming; it's about healing, leaning on one another with shared experiences. Many participants in this group have worked through their grief and come out the other side or are on their way there. They treasure their loved ones and always will. Like you, they lost their equilibrium in their pain but have found the courage to right themselves and move forward."

A group meeting was completely out of Joan's comfort zone. "Can't I just continue to see you?"

"Of course, if that's what you wish. I'd be happy to work with you. However, I wish you'd give the group at least one try. Afterward, if you decide it isn't for you, then the two of us can continue as we are now. Deal?"

Although reluctant to agree, Joan felt she didn't have anything to lose. "Deal."

"Wonderful."

"Will you be there?" Joan asked.

"Of course."

"How large is the group?" She had more questions, and while she'd agreed to attend a session, her mind was already made up; she wasn't interested in group therapy.

"We currently have eight members."

At least that number was manageable. She hoped she wouldn't feel too overwhelmed.

"We meet Wednesday night at seven in the conference room."

Joan made a mental note of the information. "I'll keep the commitment, but I don't really think this is for me."

Dr. O'Brien nodded, accepting her words. "I appreciate your willingness to give it a try." She looked at the time, silently letting Joan know the session was over.

She stood, and Joan did as well. They exchanged handshakes. "I'll see you Wednesday."

"Wednesday, at seven," Joan repeated. "Thank you."

"It was my pleasure. I appreciate how difficult it was for you to make this appointment, Joan. I'm proud of you."

For the third time that morning, Joan's eyes flooded with embarrassing tears. She lowered her head as she hurried toward the exit, keeping her gaze on the floor as she fled into the parking lot.

By the time she returned to the house, Joan was emotionally exhausted. The doctor was right. It had taken courage and fortitude to keep the appointment. Nevertheless, it was progress in the right direction. All she needed to do now was continue down this path to life, to recovery, to the future . . . whatever it might hold.

By the time she made herself a cup of her favorite tea, an orange spice combination, the front door opened, and Maggie came barreling in and raced up the stairs to her room. This was the week of her finals. Maggie had spent nearly the entire weekend in her room studying.

Joan met her at the foot of the stairwell as Maggie came racing down, clenching a bookbag.

"Everything okay?"

"I forgot my textbook. Sorry, I've got to run or I'll be late for class." She rushed out the door.

Smiling, Joan followed her onto the porch and shouted after her, "You're going to do great. Relax."

Maggie gave her a wave and a smile as she rushed to her car.

The young nursing student had been with Joan only a few days and it seemed that the house that had lain fallow for the last four years had come to life. Joan had insisted Maggie join her for dinner over the weekend and they had a lively discussion about the books they'd both read and politics on which they basically agreed, with some differences. Joan appreciated that they could share their opinions without those differences interfering in their genuine liking of each other.

After making herself a sandwich for lunch, Joan called her sister. Emmie seemed pleased to hear from her.

"You called me," her sister said approvingly. "Instead of me being the one to reach out to you."

"That's because I have news," Joan said, feeling almost giddy.

"Good news, I hope."

"Very good." Joan spent the next thirty minutes updating her sister on the positive changes she'd made since her birthday.

"Whoa," Emmie said, clearly overwhelmed. "You took in a boarder, and you've seen a counselor."

"Yup."

"Anything else you've tackled since we last talked, like the homeless situation in Seattle or world peace?"

"Very funny, but I did find a really good landscaper . . .

one with a heart." She explained how Phil had stepped in to help with the situation between Maggie and her father.

"Is he cute?"

"Oh, come on, Em, he's married." Although he hadn't mentioned a wife, she'd made the assumption. Before he'd left, he'd said it was time to head home, as dinner would be waiting.

"You're still young, you know. You could easily re-marry."

Her sister was right. Joan was still young enough to consider another relationship. The truth was, she didn't want to live the rest of her life alone. However, now wasn't the time to even think about dating again. She had to heal first, and she was a long way from that happening.

She was about to explain her feelings further when the doorbell rang. Still holding on to the phone, she went to the front door, thinking it might be Phil. He'd been early before and was due within the hour.

Only it wasn't Phil.

There, standing at her front door, was her son, Nick, with an adorable puppy in his hands.

"It's Nick," she told her sister. "I have to go." She opened the screen door for her son.

"Hey, Mom, I brought you a late birthday gift." Nick thrust the puppy in her direction.

"Nick, no." She automatically shook her head. No way did she want a dog, and especially not a puppy. They made messes, stinky ones, and chewed on expensive fur-niture and shoes. They demanded constant attention and love. She didn't have the time, the inclination, or the de-sire for a dog in her life.

"You can't turn down a gift, Mom," Nick protested.

"Yes, I can."

Nick was just as adamant. "You said you were thinking of taking in a boarder, remember?"

"Yes, well . . ."

"You're lonely and this dog is the perfect solution."

Joan continued to shake her head. "He's not a solution; he's a nuisance."

Her son refused to listen. "Look into his eyes and tell me you aren't smitten."

"I'm not smitten," she insisted, while avoiding looking at the dog, who whined softly.

"You can't resist this, can you?" Nick continued, sounding downright gleeful. "You might think you don't need a dog for a companion, but you do. I'm here to see that you don't have a reason to be lonely ever again."

"I don't need a dog for a companion," she repeated, and then added, "because—" She didn't get to finish as her son cut her off.

"You'll thank me later, I promise you."

"Nick," she pleaded again. "No."

"Here, take him." He placed the dog into her arms and hurried down the front steps.

"Where are you going?" Joan shouted after him, intent on giving the puppy back to her son.

"I have food, a crate, and a few toys to entertain him. They're in the truck. I'll be right back." He made a quick run from the truck to the house and set everything down in the small foyer. "Sorry, Mom, I've got to run. I'm on my lunch break and I gotta get back to work. Love you."

"Does he have a name?" she shouted.

Nick shook his head as he hopped inside his truck. "You get to name him."

Great. She looked down at the tiny dog in her hands and he looked back at her and licked her arm.

"Well, well," she muttered. "I guess we're stuck with each other."

The puppy looked up at her, and Joan had to agree with her son. He was adorable.

Just then he peed, as if he'd been holding it far too long. The warm liquid ran down the front of her silk blouse.

As she looked in horror at what he had done, Phil Harrison's truck turned the corner and pulled up to the front of the house.

Chapter 12

Joan rushed into her bedroom and quickly shucked off her wet blouse and wiped herself down with a washcloth. The puppy sat obediently at her feet as she shuffled through the hangers in her closet, seeking another top. After considering several, she chose a long-sleeved cotton pullover.

Phil had the lawn mower out of his truck and paused when she came onto the front porch. "I see you're ready to get to work."

He grinned. "Johnny-on-the-spot is what I like to tell my customers."

"I appreciate it. Listen, I . . . hope you don't mind, but I baked you something. I wanted to thank you for all your help the other day with Maggie and her father. I don't know what I was thinking, involving you the way I did." Even now she marveled at how Phil hadn't hesitated to step into what might have been a delicate situation with Roy Herbert. His insight into Roy's behavior spoke of a deep compassion and understanding. His wife was a lucky woman.

"It's fine, Joan. I was happy I was there to lend a helping hand."

She'd looked for a way to show her appreciation and felt a bit shy about mentioning it. "It's not much, but both Maggie and I wanted to let you know how much we appreciated what you did. I hope you like banana bread."

His eyes widened with appreciation. "How'd you know that's my favorite?"

"I didn't," she said, hiding a smile. "It just so happened I had several ripe bananas and I thought, you know, that I shouldn't let them go to waste."

"It's been a good long while since I had homemade banana bread. Thank you."

"When you're finished, I'll cut you a slice. Would you like a cup of coffee to go with it?"

His eyes brightened. "That sounds great."

Almost against her will, Joan noticed how lean and muscular Phil was. As she had before, she noted he was deeply tanned from his work outdoors. In fact, by all outward appearances, he seemed quite ordinary-looking, and yet despite their brief acquaintance, she viewed him in a completely different light. She returned to the house and cut off a slice from the loaf and wrapped up what remained.

When the sound of the mower died down, Joan stepped onto the porch with a plate and a fresh cup of coffee. He hadn't mentioned how he liked his brew, so she left it black. Seeing her lawn mowed, she was surprised at what a vast improvement it made. "The yard looks great."

"All it needed was a little TLC," Phil said, wiping the sweat from his brow as he headed up the steps.

Joan handed him the slice of banana bread and the coffee. "I hope you like your java black."

"I do," he said between bites of the banana bread. "Have there been any more threats from the HOA folks?"

"There shouldn't be. I'll let them know I've hired you, and that should satisfy their concerns."

"Good." He said the lone word with a nod.

The puppy cried from behind the screen door, and Joan collected him, still unsure what she was going to do with this dog. "Look what my son brought me this afternoon."

Phil's smile widened as he set aside the empty plate and the coffee cup. He took the pup from her hands and held him at eye level as he looked him over. "What a cute little fellow. Do you have a name for him yet?"

"No . . . I haven't even started to think about that. If you have any suggestions, I'm open to them."

Phil thought for a moment and then shook his head. "No need to rush into it. He'll show his personality soon enough. When the time is right, you'll figure out one that's perfect for him." He paused and then added, "Amanda had a dog when she was little. Oh, how she loved that silly dog. He followed her everywhere. She named him Cocoa." His eyes became sad. "Cocoa died shortly before she left for college. Losing him nearly broke Amanda's heart."

"I'm sorry." Joan felt bad for bringing up unhappy memories.

"That loss was a good life lesson for us both. A painful one for sure."

Feeling bad for him, she paid attention to the puppy and changed the subject. "Until he shows me his personality, I'll call him No Name."

Phil chuckled. "No Name," he repeated, and appeared to find that amusing. He waited a moment and then said, "It's time I headed out."

Joan hadn't wanted this dog, had never considered getting a pet. Having No Name thrust upon her was a shock, and yet she found herself warming to the idea.

Phil handed the puppy back to her. "Thanks for the banana bread."

"Oh, wait, I have the loaf ready for you." With the puppy still in her arms, she returned to the house and collected the loaf, handing it to him.

"Thanks." The warmth in his eyes revealed his appreciation. "The two of us are going to enjoy this immensely. I'll be back later in the week. Can we discuss the flower beds then? I know you want to work on those, but I have a few ideas I'd like to pass along, if you'd like."

"That sounds wonderful. Later in the week would be great."

Again, he hesitated. "Before I go, I wanted to check to see if everything was okay with Maggie."

"It's working out well. I've never had a boarder before, and the truth is I had a few qualms about taking one on. Once I heard the circumstances surrounding her home life, I felt the need to act quickly. I'm grateful I did. Maggie's a delight."

"From what little I've seen of her, I agree."

"Maggie's decided she wants to check in on her father now and again to be sure he's getting along okay without her."

"That alone says a lot about Maggie, doesn't it?"

"It does. I didn't mean to detain you, but I wanted to thank you again for your help."

"Like I said, no problem."

Phil left her then, and she watched him go.

As his truck disappeared around the corner, it came to Joan that she was moving forward. A few baby steps at a time. When Jared was alive, she had purpose, working together with her husband, day to day. Her routine was set. She knew who she was and was comfortable in the work she'd been given. For the first time she could feel that again.

The puppy whined, and, thinking he might need to do his business, she placed him on the freshly mowed lawn, where he smelled the grass and hopped—yes, hopped—like he was walking on hot coals, causing her to laugh. He raced back to her and stretched up, using her leg for balance.

Joan returned to the house and poured herself a cup of coffee, which she took to the front porch, taking No Name with her. With the sun on her face warming her, Joan sat on one of the Adirondack chairs Jared had purchased the year before his death.

She held No Name in her lap, and the puppy promptly fell asleep. For the first time she could remember in a long while, Joan felt perfectly content.

Chapter 13

Maggie checked in for the early shift at Starbucks and reached for her apron. She was scheduled to handle the cash register again this morning. The rush in the morning sometimes overwhelmed her as she did her best to keep up with the orders and keep the line moving. She looked forward to seeing the two guys from the construction crew who routinely stopped in before heading to the jobsite. The completion of the apartment complex was on schedule, if the chatter the men exchanged was anything to go by.

Einstein was a big tipper and had captured her attention. Because of work and school, Maggie didn't have time for relationships. High school was the last time she'd been out on a real date. That didn't mean she was blind to attractive men, though. It flustered her how much this one construction worker had taken hold of her imagination. She looked forward to seeing him, especially when they had the chance to exchange a few words. He'd flirted with her, and she'd flirted back. Today, working the register would give her the opportunity again. She could hardly wait.

"You seem to be in a good mood," Leanne said, as she put on the headset to take orders from the drive-through.

"I am," Maggie concurred. Since moving in with Joan, everything was looking up. Living with the widow had worked out far better than she could have ever hoped. Although it had been less than a week since Maggie had moved in, Joan had quickly become a trusted friend, almost like a second mother.

"How's the puppy?" Leanne asked.

The morning before, Maggie had arrived to work blurry-eyed because the dog had cried most of the night. She knew Joan had been up and down until dawn, caring for the distraught puppy.

"It was better last night." Maggie sympathized with the sweet dog. He was miserable without his siblings and his mother. Joan was infinitely patient with him. She hadn't asked for the dog and explained it was a gift from her son. Apparently, the puppy was Nick's way of persuading her not to take in a boarder. Since he knew nothing about her living at the house, the puppy was supposed to help with Joan's loneliness.

"Have you got a name for him yet?"

"Not yet. Joan is giving it serious thought. For now, we're calling him No Name."

"Clever," Leanne teased, and rolled her eyes.

"She'll settle on one soon." Maggie smiled, remembering how Joan had gone online for the list of the most popular dog names and hadn't found even one that caught her fancy.

The construction crew stopped off shortly before six.

Maggie lowered her gaze when Einstein walked toward the counter.

"Morning."

Maggie blushed and Einstein grinned. "Morning," she returned.

"You look happy this morning."

She blushed. "That's because I am. Now, what can I get you?" He was a charmer. She nearly melted when he smiled, which he seemed to do often. "Do you want your usual?" she asked again when he didn't immediately reply.

This guy definitely made her heart beat faster, and that smile of his was her kryptonite.

"Sure." He leaned closer to the cash register.

Building up her courage, she asked, "Do you mind if I ask you a question?" Distracting herself from looking at him, she wrote out his order on the cup and handed it to Ashley, who elbowed Maggie in her side. The entire morning crew knew she was attracted to him.

"Not at all," he returned with a sly grin, as though approving of her interest.

"Is your actual name Einstein?"

He snickered and rolled his eyes.

"Nah, it's a nickname because he's got a head for trivia," his friend offered. "This guy is good. We're on a team together, and he's our secret weapon."

Einstein thrust his hands up as if awaiting her applause, which made Maggie laugh out loud.

Kurt nudged his buddy and leaned toward the counter. "But he can be a real idiot when it comes to asking out a woman he's attracted to."

Einstein glared at his friend.

In an effort to get back to business, Maggie turned her attention to Kurt. "What can I get you?" she asked.

"My usual, same as Einstein here," Kurt said, as if testing her to see if she remembered his order the way she had his friend's. Her mind was whirling, and she had trouble concentrating. Kurt seemed to suggest that Einstein wanted to ask her out. She would enjoy that more than she was willing to admit.

"Did you really pawn that puppy off on your mother?" Kurt asked as they moved forward, waiting to collect their orders.

"I didn't have a choice. No one else wanted to take him in, and I couldn't continue to leave him all day and not expect to come home to a few messes."

"And she bought that this was just a generous gift?" Kurt shook his head.

Einstein sighed. "I left before she could say anything."

Maggie's gaze shot back to the two men. Joan had mentioned her son Nick worked in construction. She also knew Nick had dropped off the puppy, not giving his mother a chance to refuse. Could it possibly be that Einstein was Nick Sample? Her breath froze in her lungs. Could it be that this guy she'd found so attractive was Joan's son? It seemed too much of a coincidence that he not be. With her mind spinning, she tried to think of what would happen if Einstein was Nick Sample. He was bound to be furious once he learned she was living in his old bedroom.

She avoided eye contact and focused her attention on the next woman in line placing her order.

Maybe she should ask him. She quickly decided against that. What a mess. It was just her luck to find herself attracted to Joan's son, if indeed Einstein was her son, but it seemed highly likely that he was. Furthermore, this puppy wasn't the thoughtful gift she'd assumed.

The two men collected their orders and left. No sooner had Nick walked out the door when he returned. He got at the end of the line, as if he wanted to place another order.

When he approached the cash register, she asked, "Was there something else?"

"Yeah, are you available Friday night?"

Her eyes widened, afraid he was about to ask her out. "I . . . I'm sorry but I already have plans." This wasn't good. From their earlier conversation, she was afraid this would happen. If they were to date, he would discover his mother had gone against his wishes. There had to be a better way to break the news, and going out with him wasn't it.

"What about Saturday night?"

"Ah . . . then, too. Sorry."

Surprise filled his eyes and his easy smile disappeared. "Are you giving me a message here? Are you saying you'd rather not go out with me?"

She pinched her lips together, not knowing what else to do. "I'm sorry, I . . . don't think it's a good idea for me to date a customer . . . It's against company policy." She had no idea if that was true or not and hoped Einstein would accept the excuse without question.

He didn't easily accept her rejection. "That's ridiculous."

"It's best you don't ask me out again."

"If that's what you want." He shrugged as if it was no big deal and left. Maggie swallowed hard and was fairly certain she was destined to meet Einstein again soon. When they did, she had a feeling it wouldn't be pleasant for either of them.

Both Ashley and Leanne sent shocked looks her way when they heard Maggie turn down Nick's invitation. Maggie thought it best not to explain when they riled her about the company policy she'd quoted.

Maggie's mind wasn't on her chemistry final when she headed to Seattle Central College on Friday. This was an important exam and the last one for the day. Then and only then could she relax. Getting a top grade on this exam could be the difference between receiving a scholarship and needing to apply for a student loan. She should be thinking about this test. Instead, her mind was on Joan's son.

Thankfully, because Maggie had studied hard and was familiar with the material, she cruised through the final. It wasn't until after she finished and left the classroom that doubts assaulted her. She found herself second-guessing her answers. She so badly wanted to make the grade, but decided to put it out of her mind. She'd given it her all and had to trust that that was enough.

Although it was well past lunchtime, Maggie treated herself to a Whopper, her favorite fast food. It also happened to be her father's favorite as well. She hadn't had any contact with him since she'd moved. He hadn't reached out to her, either, although she didn't expect he would.

Her father's reaction to her moving weighed on her mind all afternoon. Her dad had relied on her heavily since she'd lost her mother. He would never openly admit that he needed her; that would show weakness. To Roy Herbert, weakness was unacceptable.

Although it didn't fit into her food budget, she ordered a second Whopper for him.

When she arrived at the house, the sight of it brought up a slew of unhappy memories. For a good five minutes she sat in her car, wondering if this was a good idea after all. By now the electricity would have been cut off and he was sure to be in a foul mood. The last person he'd want to see was her. Almost against her better judgment, she opened her car door and climbed out. Although she'd spent most of her life in this house, she knocked softly before letting herself inside.

Her father looked up when she entered. He was exactly where she'd left him: in his recliner. To her surprise, the television was on. Somehow he'd managed to avoid having the power cut off.

"Well, look who's here," he said with a satisfied smirk, as if he fully expected her to move back.

"I brought you a Whopper." She stepped farther into the room to hand him the brown bag.

"You think you can buy your way back into my good graces?" he asked, clearly pleased. "It's going to take a lot more than a hamburger."

"I'm sure it will," she said. Arguing with him wouldn't serve either of them well.

He tore open the bag and reached for the burger.

"You paid the electric bill?" Where he got the funds, she could only imagine.

He ignored the question as he wolfed down the Whopper. Without her there to see to his meals, she worried he'd survive solely on Bud Light.

It didn't look like he was in the most communicative mood. She'd done what she'd come for. This was her good deed for the day, and it was time she left.

"Where do you think you're going?" he asked, his mouth full of food.

"I tutor this afternoon. I only stopped by to see how you're doing."

He laughed, as though he found her excuse amusing. "Sure you did. You left me to fend for myself and now you feel bad. Surprise, surprise, I'm doing perfectly fine without you."

"I can see that," she said, again refusing to get into an angry exchange with him.

"I figured it wouldn't take you long to come to your senses."

"Dad," she said softly, so as not to arouse his anger. "I'm not coming back."

He frowned, as if he found it hard to believe.

"Is there anything you need before I go?" she asked.

He stared at her and shook his head.

"I'm glad you have electricity."

"Go, then," he snapped, and pointed toward the door, as if she didn't know where it was located. "Get out and don't come back. I've got news for you. I can take care of myself."

"So I see. I'm happy to know you can. It would have been miserable for you without power."

He sat up a bit straighter in his recliner. "You think I was going to fall apart without you. Well, I've got news for you. I talked to those people at the city and found a program that will keep the lights on."

Her father had tackled the problem on his own. Maggie wouldn't have believed he could solve anything by himself. This meant he either had to make a phone call or stop by the city office on his own. This was progress.

"I'm proud of you, Dad."

He snorted, as though he didn't believe her. "Didn't need you then, and I don't need you now."

"You'll do great without me," she said. "I'll stop by again next week."

"Don't bother," he called after her. "You aren't welcome here."

"Okay, I won't," she said, losing her cool.

She opened the door and was about to leave when she heard him speak again, almost under his breath.

"If you do come, bring another Whopper."

Maggie smiled as she headed back to where she'd parked her car.

Once she finished with her tutoring, she drove to Joan's, all the while silently debating if she should mention having met Nick. She noticed how nice the yard looked since Phil Harrison had taken over the maintenance.

Maggie found Joan sitting at the kitchen table with a sleeping puppy in her lap. She looked up when Maggie entered the room. "I think No Name has his days and nights mixed up. He sleeps most of the day and cries all night."

"Poor baby," Maggie cooed, as she gently patted his

head. At her touch, No Name opened his sleepy eyes and lifted his head to look at her.

"If anyone deserves sympathy, it's me," Joan said, yawning as she spoke. "I had no idea a puppy could be this much trouble."

Maggie pulled out a chair and sat. Her look must have been troubled, because Joan asked, "Is there something on your mind?"

She nodded. "I think I might have met Nick."

"My Nick? Silly question," she asked with a shake of her head, as if she realized what she'd said.

"I've seen him quite a bit in the last couple weeks, without knowing who he was. He comes by Starbucks before work with his friend Kurt. Kurt calls him Einstein, so I didn't make the connection until Kurt mentioned Einstein had given his mother a puppy."

"The work crew calls him Einstein?"

Maggie nodded. "From what Kurt said, it's because they're on a trivia team and Nick is their ace in the hole."

Joan studied her and frowned slightly. "Nick does play trivia. From your frown I'd say you don't have a good impression of my son."

"But I do," she corrected quickly. "I like him, but when he asked me out, I didn't know what to say and made up a ridiculous excuse about it being against company policy to date a customer."

"Oh Maggie, you didn't need to do that. Nick is going to find out I've taken in a boarder sooner or later."

What Joan said was true. In retrospect, Maggie should have handled this awkward situation differently. Now it was too late.

"From what Kurt said, Nick had tried to give the dog

to several other people first before he decided No Name would go to you."

Joan laughed. "That sounds like my son. As a kid he often got himself into messes he couldn't find his way out of."

"I liked him up to that point."

"Don't judge him too harshly, Maggie. Nick has a good heart."

Maggie wasn't sure she believed that.

Chapter 14

"Come on, No Name," Joan urged, as the puppy galloped across the front lawn. She swore he smelled every blade of grass before leaping forward to chase after a butterfly.

"This isn't time for fun and games," Joan chastised. She tried to sound stern, but the puppy's antics made her laugh. He was determined to discover this new world. "You're supposed to do your business, not chase butterflies."

No Name looked more like a kangaroo than a puppy as he galivanted across the grass, causing Joan to shake her head in defeat. She'd had limited success housebreaking him, which was why she spent more time in her yard than in the house. She hadn't been outside this much in years, and it felt good.

She'd read on the Internet that the best way to housebreak a puppy was to take the little one outside every two hours, as well as immediately upon waking and after eating. Which made sense. To be on the safe side, Joan had set a timer for every hour. No Name had yet to get the hint, though. What she didn't want was for him to assume the best spot to pee was beneath the dining room table, which he had already done more than once.

She would need patience and more patience. Sooner or later, God willing, he would understand why she'd brought him outside. All she could hope was that he caught on soon. To this point, No Name had far too much fun chasing butterflies and bees or anything else that captured his attention.

Although she'd protested that she hadn't wanted a dog, she could see the wisdom in having one. After living basically as a hermit for four years, she was making positive changes, and they all seemed to be coming at once.

She enjoyed having Maggie live with her, and the puppy kept her on her toes. Life had meaning and purpose for the first time in years.

The school bus stop was down the street and the big yellow bus pulled up to let the grade school kids out. It was a lovely afternoon, one of those rare sunny ones in May.

Joan watched as the kids raced down the sidewalk toward their homes, backpacks flapping as they ran. Her boys had once ridden that same bus to and from school and hurried home, knowing she would have a snack on the kitchen counter ready for them.

Two of the children headed in her direction and stopped when they saw No Name rolling around on his back.

"Is that your puppy?" the boy asked. He looked to be in first or second grade, with ruddy cheeks and a head full of red hair.

"He is."

"What's his name?" the girl with him asked. No question she was his older sister, possibly in fourth grade, with the same red hair and freckles.

"I haven't got a name for him yet," Joan confessed.

"Why not?"

Joan had tried out several, but none of them seemed to fit the adventurous little fellow. "I haven't found the right one yet."

"How about Floyd?" the boy suggested. His backpack had his name embroidered on the back. Todd. His sister had the same style of backpack, only in a different color. Her name was Ellie.

His sister slapped his arm. "That's an awful name."

"Do you have a better idea?"

"Yes," Ellie insisted with a tone of righteousness. Being older, she seemed to assume she was by far superior.

"Then what is it?" Todd challenged.

"Snicklefritz."

Joan hid a smile.

"What kind of name is that?" Shaking his head in disbelief, Todd looked to Joan for support. "I bet she just made that up."

"It's a good name," Ellie insisted.

"While it's clever, it's a bit of a mouthful." Joan credited Ellie for her imagination.

No Name noticed the two children and scurried toward them, seeing them as his next adventure.

"He's so cute," Ellie said, kneeling down on the grass. "Can I hold him?" She looked up to Joan for permission.

"Of course. Just be careful, he's still a baby."

"Can I hold him, too?" Todd asked.

"Sure. As soon as Ellie is finished."

Both children sat in the grass, sharing the puppy. No Name cherished the attention and repeatedly licked their hands.

"I wanted a dog and Dad said I could have one, but we have to get the backyard fenced first."

"You can come visit No Name anytime you want," Joan offered.

"Can we really?" Todd's eyes lit up like twin flares.

Ellie glared at her little brother. "She said we could, dummy."

"I'm not the dummy. You're the dummy."

Their bickering reminded Joan of when her own boys were children. They constantly harped on each other, too. She didn't remember this much sibling rivalry between her and Emmie, but then Emmie was several years older and had always looked after Joan. Come to think of it, she still did.

"Do you live here?" Todd questioned. "Because my mom said she thought the house was empty."

"I've lived here a long time," Joan explained. The neighborhood had been populated with young families when Jared and Joan first moved into the house. Several families had since sold and moved away. These days, her neighbors were strangers.

"We moved here last summer," Ellie said. "Dad said he thought your house might be for sale."

"I didn't get outside much," Joan admitted. Like hardly ever. No reason to venture out, certainly not during the pandemic. All that had changed since her birthday, and she was glad of it.

"What about naming him Oliver?" Todd said.

Joan considered his suggestion and then shook her head. "He doesn't look like an Oliver to me. I'll come up with a name soon." She'd need to; otherwise, the poor puppy would suffer an identity crisis.

"He's rowdy. You could name him that."

"Rowdy?" Joan mulled it over in her mind. That might work.

"That's what Mom calls me," Todd informed her.

"Well, you are," his sister concurred.

A harried-looking woman came down the sidewalk as if on a search. The baby on her hip gripped hold of the neckline of her blouse as if she needed to anchor herself. The woman paused when she saw Ellie and Todd sitting on the grass with Joan standing nearby.

"What are you doing here?" she asked her children, clearly frustrated. "You know you're supposed to come directly home from the bus stop."

"Mom, look. She has a puppy." Todd leaped to his feet and Ellie followed. No Name stretched his tiny body up against Todd's leg as if he wanted the boy to pick him up for more cuddling time.

Joan knew where the children got their red hair, although their mother's was more auburn than red. The baby on her hip sucked on a pacifier. "I apologize if they were bothering you."

"Not in the least," Joan assured her. "They're helping me name my dog. Your children are welcome to stop by anytime."

"That's more than kind of you. I'm Kylie Pursell and I can see you've already met Ellie and Todd."

"Joan Sample. I'm pleased to meet you, Kylie."

"I best get these ragamuffins home."

" 'Bye, Joan," Ellie said, as she left the yard. "Let me know what you decide to name No Name."

"Will do," she promised.

Once back inside the house, Joan set No Name in his crate. Maggie was due back anytime. The girl certainly lived a busy life between school and two jobs. Joan couldn't help but admire her determination to succeed. The day before, she'd gotten word that one of the scholarships she'd applied for had been awarded to a classmate. While discouraged, Maggie had been happy for her friend. When Joan questioned her about it, Maggie said there were still three other scholarships available that she had yet to receive word on. Instead of feeling depressed and unhappy, she looked at the bright side. Joan admired the young woman's positive attitude.

It was time to think about what to make for dinner. Joan retrieved her most trusted cookbook for ideas. Seeing what a lovely afternoon it'd turned out to be, she was thinking of something light. One of her favorite summertime meals had always been soup and/or a salad. She flipped to the soup recipe she had flagged. Homemade tomato soup. Incredible how simple the recipe was.

She'd assembled the ingredients on the kitchen counter when the front door opened.

"I'm back," Maggie said, unnecessarily. She joined Joan in the kitchen.

"How was your day?" Joan asked, as she brought out the kettle. "I hope you like tomato soup."

"I do."

"Toasted cheese?"

"Perfect. But you don't need—"

"Maggie," Joan chastised, "we've already been over this. I enjoy cooking, and sharing the meal with you gives me an excuse to do what I enjoy. I get no pleasure from eating alone. Besides, we make a good team. I cook and you clean up after me."

"It's the least I can do." Maggie opened the refrigerator and brought out a pitcher of iced tea. "Is your meeting tonight?"

Joan groaned inwardly. "Don't remind me." In a moment of weakness, she'd shared her reluctance to attend this grief therapy session with Maggie. She'd hoped Maggie would side with her. Instead, her boarder had encouraged her to make the most of it.

"It's just the one time," Maggie reminded her. "If you don't like it, then there's no obligation to return. Isn't that what you said?"

"Yes," Joan muttered, although she'd already made up her mind.

Taking a glass of the iced tea, Maggie went over to the crate to remove No Name. She set him in her lap, and the puppy licked her arm. "Have you decided on a name yet?"

"Not yet. A couple of the kids from the neighborhood stopped by and gave me a few ideas, but none of them seemed to fit."

"He's so darn cute."

"You know, I was dead set against having a dog. I didn't want him when Nick dropped him off. I tried to tell him to take him away, but Nick refused to listen. I'm grateful he didn't. That little puppy has added light to my life."

Maggie's head shot up. "Light," she repeated slowly, and then nibbled on her lower lip as if mulling over an idea. "What about naming him Edison, the inventor of the lightbulb."

Joan paused and set the can of crushed tomatoes down on the counter as she turned. "Edison," she repeated slowly. "I like it." Walking over to where Maggie sat with the puppy in her lap, Joan placed her hand on his head. "I hereby dub you Edison, companion of light to Joan Sample."

"And to Maggie Herbert," Maggie added.

Maggie went up to her room, and Joan started dinner. She was reading over the soup recipe again when the phone rang. Checking the caller ID, she saw that it was her son Steve.

"Steve," she greeted, more than pleased to hear from him.

"Hey, Mom," he replied, sounding cheerful as usual, "just checking in to see how you're doing."

"I'm good, really good." And for the first time in a long while, Joan meant it.

"I talked to Nick," Steve said, his upbeat tone changing, "and he said he'd pawned off a dog on you."

"A puppy, you mean." She glanced down at Edison, who was chewing on a toy, and smiled. Edison demanded a lot of patience and energy, but she'd quickly fallen in love with him.

Steve groaned with irritation. "A puppy?"

"It's fine. I wasn't keen on the idea at first, but I've come around. Edison adds light to my life."

"Nick said you were lonely, and this was supposed to be a help."

"His intentions were good. No worries, Steve."

"You sure about that?"

"Well, I wasn't in the beginning, but I am now. I'm happy with the puppy. Is that why you called?"

"Yeah, and to tell you I'm going to be in Seattle for some meetings in a week or so."

Joan's spirits rose. It'd been far too long since she'd last seen her son. "How long can you stay? I'll get your room ready and—"

"Mom, hold up. It's a two-day trip, and I'm going to be in meetings the entire time."

"You will stop by, right?" If he was in town and didn't come see her, she'd be devastated.

"I'll do my best. It sort of depends on what flights are available. If I can catch an early-morning flight, then I'll be by for sure."

"What about after the conference?"

Steve exhaled audibly. "I tried to arrange that, but the warehouse is scheduled to do inventory right afterward. When I realized I would be in Seattle and might not have time to visit my own mother, I booked a flight in September for a week."

Joan's heart leaped with excitement. "Oh Steve, that's wonderful. I can't wait to meet Zoe. Will she be with you?"

"No, Mom. It'll just be me."

"Oh." This disappointed Joan. She longed to ask what had changed between the two, but hesitated. The last time she'd brought up Zoe's name, Steve had been quick to change the subject. Not wanting to cut off the conversation, she kept her questions to herself.

His phone buzzed, indicating Steve had another call coming in. "I need to take this, Mom. It's work. We'll connect soon, okay?"

"Of course." With the call ended, Joan sighed. The conversation was far too short. She'd wanted to tell her son about the positive changes she'd made in the last few weeks, and that she'd taken in a boarder and gone to a therapist, but she hadn't had the chance.

Next time, for sure.

All too soon it was time for Joan to leave for the therapy group. She dragged her feet as long as she could, dreading this. She would keep her word to Dr. O'Brien and attend this one session, but that was it. Once her obligation was fulfilled, she wanted nothing more to do with this group. Her main goal was to get through the meeting without breaking down into a sobbing mess.

The reason she'd sought a therapist was to dig herself out of the dark hole she'd buried herself in for the last four years. What she didn't need was to meet others in the same pit and feel the weight of their grief along with her own. For the first time, she was making progress. She wanted to move forward, not backward, and she was convinced this group would impede her efforts rather than help.

"I shouldn't be long," she told Maggie, who'd taken to studying at the kitchen table. Joan was pleased that she chose not to spend all her time in her room. Maggie had one last final. Her plan, as she'd explained to Joan, was to work as many hours as she could over the summer months to save up for the next semester of schooling. She wouldn't hear about the scholarship for another few days. Joan sincerely hoped Maggie received the financial assistance she needed to continue her studies. From everything she'd seen, Joan believed Maggie would make a wonderful nurse.

The parking lot was filled with several cars when Joan pulled in. She was lucky to find a space. She waited in her car until the last minute before she headed toward the office. Dr. O'Brien was in the foyer area and appeared to be waiting for her.

She opened the door for Joan. "I'm so pleased you came."

"I said I would."

"You could have easily found an excuse."

Joan had come up with several. In the end she felt obligated to follow through, even if she had to grit her teeth the entire session.

"Is there anything you'd like to know before we go into the group?" Dr. O'Brien asked.

Joan shook her head, then reconsidered. "There are only eight members, right? That's what you told me earlier."

"Yes, and all eight are in the conference room already."

"There seems to be a lot of cars in the lot."

Dr. O'Brien nodded, confirming her observation. "Several of the counselors see clients after-hours. Not everyone is able to make a daytime appointment."

That made sense and eased her concerns of having to face a roomful of strangers.

"Are you sure you don't want to know anything about the other group members before we go in?" she asked, as she led the way down a long hallway.

"Seeing that I only intend to be here for this one session, I don't think that's necessary."

"As you wish." She stopped in front of the door marked CONFERENCE ROOM and pushed it open.

Joan walked into the room and noticed a circle of folding chairs. Several faces turned to look in her direction, but she avoided eye contact, keeping her gaze lowered.

"Good evening," Dr. O'Brien said. "We have a visitor tonight. I'd like you to welcome Joan Sample."

A chorus of greetings came, and Joan looked up for the first time.

Her breath froze in her lungs.

There in the group sat Phil Harrison, her landscaper.

Chapter 15

If Joan was shocked to see him, it was nothing compared to the way Phil felt. His emotions bounced from regret to relief and then to a sense of welcome. Knowing she was a widow, Phil had tossed around the idea of mentioning the grief counseling group himself. From personal experience, he knew being with others who had suffered significant losses would help Joan. Convinced the group might interest her, he'd tried to think of ways to bring it up in their conversations and never found the right opportunity. That Joan discovered the group on her own was a blessing, although he feared his being a group member might make her uncomfortable. He hoped that wouldn't be the case.

"Oh good," Mary Lou chirped in, breaking into his whirling thoughts. "Another woman. Welcome, Joan." Mary Lou patted the empty chair next to her, indicating that she wanted Joan to sit by her.

Joan offered Mary Lou a weak smile and claimed the seat, which relieved Phil. He was afraid she might sit next to him, as the only other empty chair was at his side. Having her close would be uncomfortable for them both.

His mind was racing, trying to decide if he should mention that they already knew each other or wait for her to bring it up. It was awkward, unsettling, and a bit unnerving at the same time.

"Why don't we start by introducing ourselves to Joan," Dr. O'Brien suggested, motioning toward the others.

Doug spoke first. He'd lost his wife a couple years ago and had come a long way in the healing process. Phil had noticed Doug's keen interest in Mary Lou of late, although the woman seemed oblivious. It could be she had read the signs and decided to ignore Doug's attention.

Sally was next. "I'm Sally, and Mary Lou's right, we need another woman around here to balance everything out. I'm so glad you're here."

Sally was in her mid-seventies and widowed within the last year. Like Joan, she struggled with the loss of her husband and had trouble traversing the unfamiliarity of living life alone. She spoke of how uncomfortable it was for her to assume the tasks her husband had always done. Her children were a big help, but she realized she couldn't rely on them too heavily.

The rest of the group shared their names. Warren. James. Glenn. Sherry.

When it came to his turn, Phil simply said his name and didn't add any other pertinent information, as a couple of the others had. Each had offered a welcome, and he did the same, almost by rote.

"Joan," Dr. O'Brien said, "would you like to tell us something about yourself?"

Her gaze flew to Phil. Her look resembled that of a deer trapped in the light of an oncoming vehicle.

"Ah . . ." she started and hesitated. "As I said earlier, I'm a widow."

"Me, too," Mary Lou inserted. "And so is Sally."

Joan offered her newfound friends a weak smile. "Jared died four years ago, and I've mostly kept to myself since then." She added a few details about how her husband's sudden death upturned her life.

"I know exactly how you felt," Sally said when Joan finished. "My husband had a heart attack and was gone before the ambulance arrived. We had booked two cruises and had all these plans for when George retired, and then, poof, he was gone in the flash of an eye. We loved cruising, letting someone else pamper us."

"But, Sally, tell Joan," Mary Lou inserted. "You went on those cruises anyway and had the time of your life."

Sally grinned. "I did. My best friend from high school came with me. In the beginning, I didn't want to go, since they were planned for George and me. My kids were the ones who insisted I follow through, and I'm so pleased I did.

"In some ways, seeing Spain and Italy was exactly what I needed. I wished it could have been with George, but every site I visited, I felt he was with me in spirit. Those cruises and this group have helped me realize that, while George is gone, I have a whole lot of life left in me."

Mary Lou looked toward Joan. "There is life after a significant loss, Joan. Each one of us is here because we're working to forge a path to find meaning again. You will, too. I'm happy you've decided to join us."

Joan nodded. "I'm beginning to see that."

Dr. O'Brien looked well pleased.

Doug shared next and said he'd gone onto a dating website, even setting up a profile.

"Oh," Warren said, perking up, all ears. "You find anyone interesting?"

Warren was a younger member of the group, around fifty, Phil guessed. They weren't that far apart in age. His wife died of cancer several years back. His youngest daughter was in college, and he'd mentioned dating a time or two with little success. It was clear he was interested, although shy and unsure of himself.

"No one I'd seriously consider," Doug answered. "But I've got to say checking out what interested these women scared me plenty. We all know the importance of being careful these days. Women look at my picture and all they see is dollar signs."

Both Mary Lou and Sally burst out laughing, and Phil noticed that Joan had a hard time holding back a smile.

"What age span are you considering?" Dr. O'Brien asked, clearly amused herself.

"I was thinking someone in her forties."

"Forties," James scoffed. "You old coot. What would a woman in her forties see in you?"

"I'm not that old," Doug insisted. "I'm thinking a twenty-year difference isn't that much. Not in this day and age."

"In other words, you're looking to date a woman young enough to be your daughter?" Sally asked.

"Or granddaughter," Mary Lou added.

Doug's face flushed pink. "Go ahead and tease me all you like. It's still worth a try."

Phil didn't envy his friend entering back into the dating world. At this stage of life, finding the right woman was bound to be difficult. While he knew Doug was partly joking, he was serious, too. He suspected the older man's sudden interest in dating was an attempt to spur a reaction from Mary Lou. If the smile she struggled to suppress was any indication, Doug's plan had failed.

After an hour, the meeting came to a close. As was their tradition, several members met up afterward at a local restaurant for coffee and chitchat. Phil often attended, although this evening he needed to get home.

As he folded his chair and set it against the wall, he heard Mary Lou invite Joan to join the others for coffee. He didn't hear her response.

Exiting the room, he slapped Doug on the back and wished him well. "Don't give up hope finding the right woman," he said, sending his friend a subtle message regarding Mary Lou.

"I don't intend to," Doug responded with a grunt.

When he passed Joan, Dr. O'Brien was talking to her. He wanted to welcome her and tell her he hoped she'd return. He wanted to reassure her if she harbored any doubts about the two of them attending the same group. Standing around, waiting until Joan finished with Dr. O'Brien, would be awkward for them both, and so he left, determined to clear the air the next time he saw her.

He'd need to look at his schedule to confirm the next time he was due at her property. That was likely to be the best time for them to chat. With that in mind, he walked across the parking lot to where he'd parked his car and headed home.

Chapter 16

Maggie was eager to hear about Joan's experience with the grief therapy group, and she wasn't disappointed. From the moment she returned, Joan couldn't stop talking about the group and how it was unlike anything she'd expected. Apparently one of the widows had been a big encouragement. Joan mentioned Mary Lou several times and the fact that she had lost her husband as well. Everyone had been open and had welcomed her. She'd said her biggest fear was that the grief others had suffered would be a weight too heavy for her to bear, but that hadn't been the case at all.

That night Joan spoke to Maggie for the first time about what had happened to her husband. Until then, Joan hadn't mentioned Jared's name. All at once she seemed to have a lot to say about him and the aftermath of his sudden death.

"After I lost Jared, I was crazy with fear," Joan admitted. "I mean really afraid. There was the dental practice and all these people who relied on Jared for their health-care who I needed to inform. I spent days canceling appointments and dealing with the aftermath of the unexpected shock of it all."

"What happened to the practice? Did you close it down?" Maggie couldn't help being curious.

"No, I sold it, but not without a lot of angst. Everything hit at once. Not only was I grieving; I believe I was in some kind of emotional shock. I had a difficult time making even the simplest decisions, like what flowers I wanted at Jared's services."

"How awful." Maggie couldn't help being sympathetic. It was hard to think of this strong woman crazed with grief and confusion. It'd been much different when her mother passed. Elaine Herbert had lingered for days between life and death, so when the news came, it wasn't a complete shock. At the time Maggie thought she had mentally prepared herself for the worst. The loss hit her hard, and her father, too, although he showed his pain in different ways, comforting himself with beer and sleepless nights. The last week of her mother's life, Roy Herbert had stayed at his wife's side, never leaving her alone. When she'd passed, he'd completely broken down, sobbing as she'd never seen her father do before.

As Joan spoke about losing her husband, it brought up a lot of memories of when her mother had passed. Maggie was a good listener, and the two spoke late into the night as Joan poured out her heart.

"Do you think you'll go back to the group sessions?" she asked, although it was clear that Joan had enjoyed it.

"I will . . . only . . ."

"Only what?"

"You'll never guess who else was there," Joan said.

"You're right, I probably won't, so tell me."

"Phil Harrison."

"The landscaper?" That was a surprise.

"I assumed he was married, and now I'm unsure. He didn't mention why he was in the group, and I didn't ask."

Maggie noticed the way Joan twisted her hands. "Does it bother you that he's part of the group?"

"Not necessarily, although I'll admit he didn't say much. If anything, I believe he was as surprised to find me there as I was to see him."

"Did you talk to him after the meeting?"

"I wanted to," Joan admitted, "but I got distracted by Dr. O'Brien, who wanted feedback on how I thought the meeting went. By the time we finished, Phil had already left."

Friday afternoon, Maggie was in a good mood. She'd taken the last of her finals and felt confident she'd done well. The morning had started out gray and cloudy as she headed to work and then to the college campus. By the time she finished the exam, the sky was a dazzling shade of blue and the sun was out.

Maggie spent the early afternoon at the school with the two children she tutored. Both Caleb and Victoria had made progress since she'd started working with them on their reading problems.

"We only have three more weeks of school," Caleb reminded her, as if he was carefully counting down the days. It had been difficult for him to be still, and he repeatedly bounced against the back of his chair. "Mrs.

Patrick said if I can read at grade level, I won't need to attend summer school."

"That's amazing! You're almost there, Caleb." Maggie knew that would give him the incentive he needed to do his assigned reading homework. Grinning, Caleb nodded, as if it was a done deal.

"This doesn't mean you can slack off, you know."

One bounce, then two. "I won't, I promise."

"Good," she said with a wink.

Her next student was Victoria, who was a shy, sweet girl. Maggie suspected she didn't have a great home life and had little support from her single mother when it came to completing her schoolwork. With encouragement and praise, Victoria had made great strides in her reading.

"Look at you," Maggie said, praising the youngster, who had sounded out the word *magazine* without any help. "Pretty soon you're going to be reading at a college level."

Victoria blushed and offered Maggie a timid smile.

Maggie had grown close to both her students and was proud of the hard work they had put in and the progress they'd made. Feeling invigorated, she headed back to the house, her mind churning over ways to reward her star pupils at the end of the school year.

When Maggie arrived at the house it was after four. She found Phil busy at work, mowing the lawn.

"The yard is looking amazing," Maggie said, as she headed up the few steps toward the front door. His efforts had made a dramatic difference already.

Phil acknowledged her words with a gentle smile.

"When you see Joan, would you mind telling her that I

have a few things I need to go over with her when it's convenient?"

"Sure thing."

The instant Maggie entered the house, Edison galloped toward her, jumping up on his hind legs, begging for attention.

"How's my puppy doing today?" she asked, picking him up and nuzzling him against her chest. He really was a joy, and so energetic.

Joan peeked her head around the kitchen door. "How'd your test go?"

"Great. I have a good feeling about it." Like Maggie was with the two children she tutored, Joan had become her champion, supporting her with her own schoolwork. She didn't mention that a second scholarship had fallen through. Maggie refused to give up hope. There remained a chance still, and she was determined to remain positive.

"I never doubted you for a moment," Joan said, boosting Maggie's spirits. "Not with all the hours you put in studying."

"And now I have the next few weeks free. My supervisor at Starbucks was happy to give me more hours."

"I don't doubt it. She had nothing but praise for you when I talked to her."

It was a relief to know Maggie would be able to save for school in the fall. "Did Edison have any accidents today?"

Joan sighed and wrinkled her nose. "A couple, but he's learning. *Patience* is the word for the day."

"For sure." Maggie headed upstairs to change her clothes. With the sun out, she pulled on a pair of shorts and a summer top printed with strawberries. It was one of her favorites. She had her playlist going and bounded down the stairs when she remembered she hadn't told Joan that Phil had something to ask her.

Halfway down, she stopped abruptly when the front door opened, and Nick Sample walked inside. When he saw her, his smile froze. Their eyes locked like clashing swords before a frown settled on his face, twisting his features.

"Why are you here?" he demanded, ignoring Edison, who begged for his attention.

Maggie straightened her shoulders, her heart pounding with such ferocity it felt like it was about to fly out of her chest. "I live here."

"What the hell?" His eyes rounded with shock.

"Nick?" Joan came into the foyer.

"Mother," he returned, looking none too pleased. "You didn't tell me you'd taken in a boarder."

"No, I guess I forgot to mention it when we last talked. Oh yes, I didn't have a chance. The last time we talked was when you dropped off this puppy. And as I recall, you couldn't get away fast enough."

While playfully spoken, Maggie didn't miss the sarcasm.

"I had to get back to work." Nick had the good grace to look chagrined.

Joan shrugged, as if this was really none of his concern. "We discussed me taking in a boarder, remember?"

"And I said I didn't think it was a good idea."

"And I took your words into account and made my own decision," Joan returned without the slightest hesitation.

"Why rent it to *her*," he said, as if Maggie wasn't standing right there listening in on the conversation.

"What's wrong with Maggie?" Joan wanted to know, sounding perplexed. She looked from one to the other.

"Maggie and I have a difference of opinion," Nick said, as if that explained everything.

"What he means is that he asked me out and I told him no," Maggie clarified, infuriated that he didn't appreciate the position she'd been in when he'd asked her for a dinner date.

"It seems a lowly construction worker isn't good enough for Miss High and Mighty."

"That's not true." Maggie couldn't believe he'd say anything so asinine. Was that what he thought? "I . . . I figured out you were Joan's son, and I didn't know what to do. Surely even you could understand how awkward that would be."

"You should have said something," Nick flared back.

"I . . . couldn't . . . not with a line of people behind you ready to place their orders." He was smart enough to recognize her confession then and there would have been impossible.

"You made me look like a fool," Nick returned, apparently unwilling to accept her excuse.

"If anyone needs to apologize," Maggie flared back, "it's you. I heard what Kurt had to say about you ditching your mother on her birthday and then pawning the puppy off on her."

"That's enough," Joan said, coming to stand between the two. "I'm sorry to hear you two got off on the wrong foot."

Maggie folded her arms over her chest.

Nick narrowed his eyes at Maggie as though to say what he thought of her and crossed his own arms.

Joan exhaled and seemed to collect her thoughts. "Now, it seems both of you have jumped to conclusions about each other. This can all be easily settled. Maggie," she said, turning her attention to her, "Nick is a good son, and while he wasn't able to be with me on my birthday, he later treated me to dinner at a restaurant that meant a great deal to his father and me."

Nick smirked and nodded at Maggie as if to say he'd redeemed himself and she should appreciate his thoughtfulness.

"What about the puppy?" Maggie asked, and held back from reminding Joan of the sleepless nights they'd suffered when the puppy had cried and cried.

Joan glanced at her son with a pinched look. "Yes, well, that gift was a bit much and certainly unexpected."

"I gave you the dog because you were lonely," Nick insisted.

"But, Maggie," Joan addressed her again, "you have to admit that Edison has been a joy. Yes, those first few nights were a trial, but we survived. We've both come to love this puppy."

This was a truth Maggie couldn't deny.

"Like I said," Joan continued. "You two got off on the wrong foot. I would advise you both to reconsider your feelings toward each other. Knowing you're living with me is a shock for Nick."

"You can say that again," Nick muttered.

"I know my son and he's a great guy."

Maggie lowered her gaze and rubbed her palms together. Joan was right. She'd handled it badly when Nick had asked her out and she regretted not accepting and telling him the truth earlier.

"And about the puppy," Nick said. "My intentions were good. Edison had been abandoned at the construction site. When I found him, he was dehydrated and nearly starved to death. I brought him home with me and did what I could to nurse him back to health. But I work all day and I had to leave him in the crate. I was racing back to my apartment at noon and didn't even have time to eat."

Maggie remembered overhearing Kurt mentioning that.

"After a few days he was doing better," Nick added, "but I hated leaving him in the crate all day. My mother hasn't been herself since my dad passed, and I hoped this sweet little dog would help her. If you want to condemn me for that, then I'm grateful you turned down my offer for a date."

Maggie looked away, unable to respond.

"Nick, you should know," Joan said, "having Maggie live with me has been a blessing. I should have mentioned her earlier, but I hadn't heard from you and decided you'd find out on your own sooner or later."

"I wish you had said something." Nick sighed. "What I want to know is which bedroom did Maggie take?"

Joan shared a reassuring look with Maggie. "I gave her the option of either room, and she chose yours."

"No way . . ." Turning toward the stairs, Nick raced up, taking them two at a time. Maggie followed behind him and Edison attempted to follow, but his short, stubby legs wouldn't let him. Maggie reached down and pulled him into her arms, tucking him under her chin as she followed Nick.

She arrived just as he opened the door to her room and went stock-still. "What happened to my Coldplay poster?" he demanded.

"It's rolled up and stored in Steve's bedroom. I believe your mother put it in the closet." The puppy wiggled in her arms, wanting down. She set him on the carpet, and he happily bounced his way into Maggie's room.

Nick's gaze remained focused on the room. "And my Russell Wilson autographed football?"

"It's there, too, along with your soccer trophies."

He continued to stand just outside her bedroom, his shoulders slumped in defeat. He was acting as if she'd personally deprived him of everything important from his childhood.

Maggie sucked in a deep breath, deciding it was up to her to make things right with Nick. "Your mother is right. Perhaps we could start again?" she asked hopefully.

Nick hesitated, shrugged, and then agreed. "Is it true what you said about the company frowning on dating customers?"

"No . . . I made that up as an excuse."

"That's what I thought."

Rather than hash over her babbling response to his invitation, she said, "I want you to know how much I admire your mother. She's been a godsend to me."

"I haven't been around as much as I should have been. I knew she was lonely without my dad, but I didn't know how to make that better for her. I considered moving back home and would have if she'd asked, but I was afraid I'd become a crutch. Mom needs to find her own path."

"And she is."

He agreed with a half-smile.

"I'm hoping we can be friends, Nick. I'm sorry I turned you down. I figured out you were Joan's son when you mentioned the puppy and I didn't know what to do because you didn't know I was living here."

"I'd like for us to be friends, too," he admitted. "When I saw you here, I didn't know what to think."

"Your mom is wonderful. I owe her a great deal, and I promise you I'll do my best to be a good tenant."

"I'd appreciate that." He gave her a genuine smile.

Maggie felt a wave of relief. At least they were both of the same mind when it came to Joan. "Let's go assure your mother we won't be at each other's throats," she suggested.

"Let's. Can I hold Edison?"

"Of course."

Nick tucked the puppy into the crook of his arm. "Where did he ever get that name?"

"Your mother and I came up with it." True, Maggie had been the one to suggest it, but the idea had come from Joan.

"I like it. It suits him."

"Your mother said he brought light into her life."

"Which was exactly what I hoped would happen." Nick sounded pleased with himself.

Joan was busy in the kitchen. She turned when Maggie and Nick joined her. "Did you two settle your differences?"

Maggie glanced toward Nick to discover he was watching her.

"Yeah, all good," he answered. He set Edison down on the floor, and the puppy raced over to a chew toy.

"Excellent. Will you stay for dinner?" Joan looked to her son.

"What are you making?"

"Nick!" Maggie chastised.

"What?"

"You should be happy with whatever your mother has planned."

Nick snorted softly. "Okay, fine. I'll be happy, even if it's liver and onions."

"It isn't." Joan seemed amused at the banter between the two. "You stopped by for a reason?" She directed the question to her son.

"Can't I come see my mother anytime I want?" he challenged, grinning.

"Of course, but it's rare enough to pique my interest."

Maggie sent Nick a knowing glare, which he ignored.

"I came to see how you were faring with the puppy," he said, and added, "and if you needed anything."

"That's thoughtful of you," Joan said, as she opened the refrigerator door. "And seeing how worried you are about what's for dinner, I'll tell you. We're having crispy chicken salad with fresh tomatoes, olives, and shredded cheddar cheese."

"Sounds good. By the way, the yard is really taking shape."

"I hired a maintenance company, Harrison Lawn and Landscaping."

"It's a bit early to get started on dinner, isn't it?" Maggie asked.

As if unaware of the time, Joan glanced toward the

kitchen clock. They didn't normally eat until after six, and it wouldn't take long to assemble a salad.

Joan thought about that for a moment. "It is earlier than normal. I was hungry. I hadn't felt that way in a long while," she said, and cocked her head to one side as if the realization had surprised her.

"That's good, Mom. You've lost a lot of weight since Dad died."

"I have?" She didn't seem to have noticed. "Listen," Joan said, "why don't the two of you take Edison out for a walk? By the time you return, I'll have dinner going."

Nick looked to Maggie for the answer.

"Sure," she said, although Edison was a bit small for much of an excursion. She had put him on the leash before, without much success. He'd twisted his head around and tried to chew on the cord.

While Nick collected the leash, Maggie got the puppy. They were about to head out the door when Maggie remembered Phil had asked her to give Joan a message.

Glancing out the front door, she saw that his truck remained parked outside, so he was still at the house.

"Joan, I almost forgot. Phil asked to talk to you."

"Did he say why?"

"He didn't."

"Okay, thanks."

"You ready?" Nick asked, tugging Edison along behind him. Maggie could see it was going to take some effort to train the puppy to the leash. As she stepped onto the porch, Phil was coming up the steps.

"Tell Phil I'll be out in a minute," Joan called.

"Did you hear that?" Maggie asked the landscaper.

"I did. I'll just wait here."

"She won't be long," Nick added, and the two started down the street with Edison.

Edison resisted, and they ended up nearly dragging him along, to the point that they were both soon laughing.

Just maybe they could be friends after all, Maggie mused. Good friends.

Chapter 17

Joan walked over to the sink to wash her hands before venturing outside to talk to Phil. As the warm water poured from the faucet, she realized she was nervous. He'd said so little during the group session, and she feared it was because of her.

They'd both been flustered at the unexpectedness of finding each other there. While in the group, Joan had been completely surprised by the way everyone had welcomed her. Already she'd heard from Mary Lou, and the two had planned a lunch out. It'd been such a long time since Joan had enjoyed female companionship—that is, until Maggie had come to live with her. Mary Lou, however, was her contemporary. She felt an immediate kinship with the other woman.

Drying her hands with unnecessary zeal, Joan suspected Phil wanted to talk to her about the group, and secretly she would be glad to clear the air. It was best to talk this over so there wasn't any discomfort on either side.

"You asked to speak to me . . . ?" she said as she met him on the porch.

Phil nodded and motioned toward the flower bed. "I had a few ideas, and seeing how important loving flowers is to you, I felt obliged to offer a couple suggestions." His eyes twinkled as he spoke.

"You're going to enjoy teasing me about that 'must love flowers' comment, aren't you?"

"Yup."

She was pleased to see that any discomfort he had felt with her in the group didn't show.

"I was thinking blue star juniper would go nicely. It's easy to maintain and attractive to the eye."

Joan was familiar with the plant. Juniper was an excellent suggestion, and one Joan wished she'd thought of herself. The shrub was resistant to insects and diseases and a perfect complement to the lavender rhododendron she'd planted several years earlier. Rhododendrons were the Washington state flower. "I like that idea."

"If you're looking for a bit more color, how about a dwarf burning bush? It is a brilliant red and a hardy shrub." As he went on about why he thought it would flourish in her yard, Joan realized he was uneasy mentioning the elephant in the room.

Joan folded her hands in front of her. "That's another good idea. But I prefer the blue star juniper."

"Great, I'll get one ordered."

"Perfect."

Again, he hesitated, and Joan knew she would need to take the initiative. "Was there something more than the plants you wanted to discuss, Phil?" she asked, amused at the way he delayed what was really on both of their minds.

He exhaled and shrugged, aware she had found him out. "Suggesting the flowers was a good excuse, although I really do love flowers. They're a must," he added, grinning.

"They are," she agreed. "But I have the distinct feeling what we really need to talk about is the grief therapy group."

His shoulders relaxed. "Yeah, you're right. I wanted to apologize."

"Apologize?" She couldn't imagine why.

"The thing is, I'd wanted to tell you about the group soon after we met, thinking it might help you. I've found the support meaningful, which is why I'm still attending after five years. I regret that I didn't, and then when you arrived, I was kicking myself for delaying. Plus, I wasn't sure if I should mention that I already knew you or not."

"I was thinking the same thing. We were both being ridiculous, you realize. When you didn't say anything about knowing me, I thought it best to remain silent."

"That was my thought, too," he said, grinning now. "I'm sorry, Joan."

"Don't be silly, there's nothing to apologize for."

"Thanks." His relief was obvious. "I hope you'll return."

"I plan on it. I think if I was a no-show, Mary Lou would come get me."

Phil chuckled at that. "Then we're square?" she asked.

"We're square," he concurred, and gave her a dazzling smile.

Just then Todd came racing up to the front of the yard.

"Can I play with Edison?" he asked. "Mom said I could if it was all right with you."

"I'm sorry, Todd, but Edison is on a walk with my son and Maggie." Todd had already met Maggie when he and his sister had stopped off earlier in the week.

Todd hung his head in disappointment but recovered quickly. "Mom said if you offered me a cookie, I could have it."

Joan had baked a couple days earlier, seeing how often Todd and Ellie came by to play with Edison. "Let me check the cookie jar."

She entered the house, and when she returned, she saw Phil talking to the youngster. He was showing him a snapdragon plant that was in the bed of his truck, along with several flats of flowers. Todd's eyes were huge as he hung on every word Phil said.

"Joan, Joan, did you know snapdragons can talk? Phil showed me. It's really cool."

Joan handed him a chocolate-chip cookie and Todd's smile covered his whole face. "Thank you," the boy said, ever-so-politely.

"You're most welcome." Todd had chocolate smeared on both sides of his mouth as he quickly downed the treat.

"Guess what? Dad's getting the backyard fenced soon and then I can have a dog of my own," he said with his mouth full, too excited to swallow before he shared the good news.

"That's great," Joan said, exchanging a smile with Phil as he loaded his equipment into the bed of his truck.

"Hey, what about me?" Phil called out. "Don't I get a cookie, too?"

Joan chuckled and shook her head. "I'll see what I can

do." Returning to the house, she brought out a couple more cookies for Phil.

"You're a woman after my own heart," Phil teased. He climbed into his truck and, with a jaunty wave, drove off.

Joan watched as he turned the corner and was out of sight. She was disappointed that Phil hadn't mentioned what had brought him to the group. She wanted to ask, and would have if Todd hadn't shown up when he did.

Todd left soon after he finished his cookie, as a friend of his passed by on his bicycle.

Nick and Maggie hadn't come back from their walk yet, which boded well. She felt certain the two would hit it off once they got over their troubling start.

Feeling good, Joan decided she wanted to update her sister on the latest developments taking place in her life.

Reaching for her phone, she punched in Emmie's name.

"Hey," her sister greeted, her usual cheerful self.

"Emmie, you won't believe what's happened. I joined a grief therapy group."

"Oh Joan." Her sister breathed her name as if sighing in relief. "I have waited four long years for you to get the help you need. Tell me everything."

Joan, who normally avoided long phone conversations, talked nonstop for a good while, updating her sister on each member of the group. Best of all, Joan told her she hadn't broken into tears even once and how she'd found a friend in Mary Lou.

"Sounds like this group was made especially for you."

"Funny thing, the landscaper I hired is also in the group."

"Well, that's a surprise."

"It certainly was, and for him, too. He's a good person."

"I think he must be. I remember what you told me, about him helping Maggie collect her things from her father's house. Not everyone would have been willing to step in like that."

Joan agreed.

"So he's a widower?"

"No, I think he's married. He didn't mention who he'd lost. I have to assume it was a close family member. A child, or possibly a sibling."

"I'm just so happy that you're finally dealing with your grief."

Joan was pleased with the changes she'd made, too.

"Were there any eligible men attending the group?" Emmie asked.

Joan gently groaned. "Emmie, I'm nowhere near ready for any kind of a relationship."

"But you will be in time, right?"

"*In time*," Joan agreed, emphasizing the words.

They talked a few minutes longer, and then Nick and Maggie returned with Edison. Joan watched the two of them and smiled. If there was any romance brewing in this house, it was the one happening right before her eyes.

"Mom," Nick said, coming into the kitchen. "You've got a visitor."

"Oh."

"She said her name is Ellie."

Joan met Ellie at the front door.

Hands on her hips, Ellie asked, "Did you give Todd a cookie? Because Mom said he wasn't supposed to ask for one."

Joan tried hard to hide a smile. "I did. Would you like one, too?"

"I would," she said with a hard nod, satisfied now that she hadn't been cheated out of a treat.

"Do you want to come inside?" Joan asked.

"Okay," Ellie said, eager now.

Joan opened the door and realized that, in the span of such a short while, she'd opened the door of her heart as well.

Chapter 18

Humming to herself, Joan carted the bags of groceries from her car into the house. When she opened the front door, she gasped. Edison was barking like crazy, and when she saw why, she dropped the bag. The grapefruit spilled out and scattered haphazardly, rolling onto the kitchen floor. Edison stood on his hind legs in his crate, leaning against the wire to look at the stranger who'd invaded the house.

"Steve," she cried. "You scared the living daylights out of me."

"Sorry, Mom," he said, looking guilty. He must have let himself into the house, but she wasn't sure how.

As if reading her thoughts, he answered the unasked question. "The key hidden in the rock was still there."

"Of course." It surprised her that he remembered, seeing that she'd completely forgotten about it.

"I told you I was coming into town for a conference, remember?" Steve said, grinning. "By the way, I like what you've done with the yard. It looks great."

Joan couldn't take credit for the lawn, but the flower beds were quickly taking shape. She'd planted annuals, and the burst of color they added uplifted her spirits every time she stepped out the door.

"I was able to catch an early flight, after all. The conference doesn't start"—he paused and glanced at the time—"for another couple hours."

"That's great." Still reeling with the shock of finding him at the house, she had yet to collect her thoughts. "It's really good to see you."

"You, too."

They hugged, and then Steve went after the fallen grapefruit and set them on top of the kitchen counter.

Joan had ventured out to the grocery store run by Amazon for the first time. Maggie had casually mentioned it over dinner the night before. Curious, Joan had wanted to check it out. Since the pandemic, she'd almost always ordered whatever she needed online and had it delivered. With the possibility of exposure to the virus, it didn't seem necessary or prudent to risk shopping in person when she didn't need to.

"Is that all?" Steve asked.

"All?"

"Groceries?"

"Oh, sorry, no, there's a couple other bags in the car."

"I'll get 'em." He bounded out the front door, eager to help.

While Steve was collecting her bags, Joan freed Edison from his crate. She took him into the backyard to do his business, which he did in quick order. She brought him back into the house and rewarded him with a doggie treat.

Steve returned with the two additional bags, setting them on the kitchen counter alongside the grapefruit. Joan promptly unloaded the goods, setting aside the items to go into the refrigerator.

"Did you know," she said, full of wonder and enthusiasm, "at some stores you don't even need to go to a checkout stand? What is happening to our world? This is crazy. You put the item in the cart, and the cost is automatically calculated. Unbelievable!"

Edison chased a toy beneath the table.

"Mom, that's been around for a while now," Steve told her.

"It was a first for me," she said, still a little in awe of the entire process. Grocery shopping had been an eye-opening experience.

Her son grinned as if he found her enthusiasm amusing.

"That's not all. I was in the mall the other day, and I bought myself a new pair of shoes. The salesclerk said I didn't need to insert the credit card into the machine. All I had to do was tap it." That was another electronic marvel that had taken Joan by surprise.

Steve helped her load items into the refrigerator. "Mom, you've been living under a rock ever since the pandemic hit. These things aren't new, they've been around for ages." He said it in a teasing tone that took the sting out of his words.

"You're right," she admitted. "I can't help but wonder what other changes have taken place that I know nothing about."

"You'll find out soon enough."

No doubt she would. Now that all the groceries were put in place, Steve sat down at the kitchen table.

"Coffee?" she asked, remembering how much her older son enjoyed his java.

"Sure." He relaxed on the kitchen chair. Knowing how involved Steve was in his work, she was pleased he'd taken the time to stop by.

Joan brewed him a cup and then one for herself before taking a chair next to her son. She took a moment to study him. Steve was in his late twenties and handsome. He looked good. He'd always taken pride in his appearance. He was dressed in a suit and tie, which told her the conference he'd mentioned was important and likely one that would advance his career. He was the taller of the two boys, standing at six feet, with wide shoulders and a narrow waist. From the little he'd mentioned about his job, she knew he worked long hours.

"I will say the puppy is cute," he said, reaching down and setting Edison in his lap. The dog looked up at him suspiciously and then started chewing on Steve's fingers. "I wasn't pleased when Nick told me what he'd done. Ouch, his teeth are sharp." Jerking his hand away, he waved it several times.

Joan laughed. "It's your fault for giving him your fingers."

Steve grinned. "I'm glad it's worked out."

"Best gift I've had in years," Joan said, and reached over to pet Edison's head.

Steve set the dog back down on the kitchen floor. "You're being overly kind. He should have at least asked first."

"I'm glad he didn't, because I would have refused. Instead, he didn't give me much choice. It's worked out for the best, as Edison quickly wormed his way into my heart." She picked up the dog and set him in her lap. Content, Edison immediately licked her hand before settling down to nap.

"My goodness, it's good to see you." The last time had been the Christmas after they'd buried Jared, and then right after that the country had closed down. Steve had kept in touch, but not nearly as often as Joan would have liked. She accepted that Steve carried a lot of responsibility with his job. He'd always been ambitious. Reading between the lines of things he'd mentioned, her son was looking to be promoted to distribution warehouse manager within the year.

"It's good to see you, too." He crossed his legs and sipped his coffee, looking mature beyond his years.

Her sons appeared to be regularly communicating, and while that pleased Joan, she would have enjoyed a few more of those conversations herself.

"How's the boarder working out for you?"

"Does my having a boarder concern you?" she asked, her voice tightening with the question.

"Concern me?" Steve repeated. "Not at all. In fact, I think it's a good idea."

That was a relief. "Maggie's helped me adjust." She didn't feel the need to explain further.

"That's great, Mom."

"I'm becoming a regular social butterfly," she told him.

"A what?" He frowned with the question.

"A butterfly. You know, breaking out of my cocoon. It

was something Emmie said recently. Maggie's been a great support. She even encouraged me to attend a grief therapy group, though I had my doubts."

"Have you?"

"I did, and am seeing a therapist one-on-one as well. Dr. O'Brien runs the grief therapy group."

"You'll continue going, right?"

"I will. The group meets on Wednesdays." She'd agreed to one session and that was all, but she would be happy to return. Mary Lou had phoned earlier, and they'd met for coffee before Joan went to the store. "The group was different from what I expected; everyone was encouraging and kind. I . . . didn't say much," she added, but didn't give the reason. "Next time I won't hesitate, and I'll join the others for coffee afterward, which I understand is something the group does on a regular basis."

Edison studied Steve, cocking his head to one side as if to say her son had passed muster.

"No worries, little one, Steve is family."

The puppy appeared to amuse him. "From the way he reacted when I came into the house, it looks like he's going to be a good guard dog."

Time would tell. "I see that Nick's been updating you on what's been happening."

"We talk often. For a long time, our conversations revolved mostly around you."

"Me?"

"Mom, we were worried, both of us. You never seemed to adjust to losing Dad. I know it was a blow, but, Mom, it's been four years. You've been in this emotional black hole and neither one of us knew how best to help you."

"I'm moving forward."

"I can see that. I have to tell you it's a relief. Nick and I were unsure what to do. We were about to have an intervention."

She'd heard of these before, of course. Concerned family and friends confronted a loved one with their considerable worries. What bothered Joan was what they might have said and how she would have reacted.

The night of her birthday dinner, Nick had basically said that they'd both been at a loss on how to help her. She remembered how he'd mentioned not being able to talk to her or get her advice when he was considering buying a house. Her grief and inability to move on had deeply affected them. Caught up in her own loss, she hadn't given enough thought to the fact that her sons needed her now even more than before. They'd lost their father and were hurting, too. Being unable to look past her own pain, Joan had basically ignored her sons.

"It doesn't matter, because it's no longer necessary," Steve said, "and I for one am grateful. Neither of us was eager to confront you; thankfully, the matter took care of itself."

From Steve's apologetic look, he seemed to regret having said anything.

"You've clearly made some positive changes in the last few weeks," Steve continued. "It was what Nick and I had hoped would happen for a long time. Living in Arizona, I wish I'd been around more to help you. I should have phoned more often, and I'm sorry I didn't, mainly because I felt at a loss as to what to say or what I could do to help you."

"It's fine, sweetheart. No worries, I understand." Seeing him so rarely, she didn't want their conversation to dissolve into regrets from the last four years. Recovering as best she could, she set her gaze on Edison, hoping Steve wouldn't see the hurt in her eyes. She needed time to analyze how her sadness had affected her sons. That they'd been worried enough to discuss an intervention shook her to the core. Joan hoped she could make up for the years she'd been remote and emotionally unavailable to them. "Update me on what's going on in your life."

Steve shrugged. "Nothing much."

"Are you still seeing Zoe?" she asked, venturing into uncertain territory, hoping Steve would share what had happened to that relationship.

He shrugged as if it wasn't a big deal. "Off and on."

From earlier conversations it had seemed the two were in a committed relationship. Something had changed. The look he gave her seemed to suggest his girlfriend was a closed subject.

"What about work?"

Another halfhearted lift of his shoulders. "It's good. I put in a lot of hours."

"Are you saving your money?" Jared had been a stickler when it came to teaching his sons the benefits of saving a certain amount of every dime they earned. He made sure they understood the value of a dollar. While Joan and her husband could afford to buy each of their sons a car, Jared had insisted Steve and Nick contribute at least half of the total cost.

"You don't need to worry about me, Mom."

"I'm not worried," she rushed to tell him. "It's just that I'd like to know how you're doing, what's important to you and how I can be there for you."

"Thanks, Mom, that means a lot. For a long time, it wasn't easy to talk to you, you know?"

Guilt weighed her down, and then anger. This was Jared's fault. He was the one who'd left them. He was the one who had delayed his physical, too concerned about taking time off, claiming it was too hard to clear his schedule, even when Joan had assured him she could free up his time and that it was important. The doctor couldn't have predicted an aneurysm, but Jared was at fault, too, for not taking his health seriously.

"I'm sorry, Steve."

"Mom—"

"No, let me finish. I love you, son, more than words can adequately express. It's time I went back to being the mother you remember, an even better version of myself. To be the mother you can trust with your doubts, your pain, and your secrets. The one who was there to give you advice when you asked. The one person you could always count on to be in your corner."

"We're each to blame," he countered. "I should have been more available to you. Nick, too. We just didn't know how best to help you. As it's turned out, you seem to have found your own way. That's all Nick and I ever wanted for you."

"Thank you," Joan said, grateful they'd had this conversation. She'd avoided anything unpleasant or possibly unpleasant for so long, it felt good to speak freely. For her, and it seemed for Steve, too.

For a long time, her son didn't say anything. Then he nodded, and when he spoke his voice was full of emotion. "Could we start with a hug?"

"I think that's an excellent idea."

They stood and embraced. Joan felt this was a real turning point in her relationship with her children. It was different without Jared, now that he was gone, and it seemed the three of them were only now learning to adjust.

Chapter 19

Sunday morning of Memorial Day weekend, Maggie invited Joan to attend church with her. Joan hesitated and appeared to consider the invitation before declining. Her landlord looked like she needed a bit of cheering up, and Maggie was disappointed that Joan had turned down the invite. While the weekend was dedicated to remembering those who had died in service to their country, it was a time to honor all of those who had passed, military or not. It made sense that Joan was thinking about her husband. She'd mentioned that her older son had stopped by for a visit. Joan seemed introspective afterward, which left Maggie wondering what had transpired during his visit.

Maggie didn't visit her mother's grave often, only a couple times a year. As far as she knew, her father had never been there, not even once, since the funeral. The gravesite was a symbol of all that he'd lost, and he'd avoided facing the emptiness of his life since Elaine's passing. Since her mother's death, Maggie rarely celebrated holidays. Her father resented any effort she made, especially when it came to Thanksgiving or Christmas, which was understandable. Her mother had always gone overboard, cooking and baking. She'd made every effort to brighten their lives over the holidays.

"I'll attend with you another time," Joan said, as if sensing Maggie's disappointment.

By the time Maggie returned from the church service, it'd started to rain. Feeling carefree after a week of finals, she decided to splurge and take in a movie. Something she hadn't done in months. Unfortunately, all her friends from Starbucks and school already had plans for the holiday weekend.

While Maggie was keen to see the latest Tom Cruise movie, she didn't want to go alone, so she asked Joan to join her.

"No thanks," Joan said out of hand.

So much for that idea. The rain started to come down in earnest, the day a dark gray. It seemed every Memorial Day weekend it rained in Seattle, as if the heavens wept for those who had passed. Her second-best choice was a novel she'd been longing to read. Reading fiction was a rare treat. Any spare time allotted in her busy schedule was devoted to her studies.

Book in hand, she plopped herself down in a comfy chair in the family room. Edison was asleep, cuddled up at Maggie's side, and the gas fireplace was lit, with shadows dancing against the opposite wall.

Although Joan had made strides, Maggie could see something heavy was on her mind. Maggie had debated whether she should ask or pretend she didn't notice. Only she did, and it concerned her. She couldn't help wondering if this change in mood had to do with Joan attending the grief therapy group. Maggie knew Joan had connected with another widow in the group, as the two had gone to lunch. It'd only been since her son's visit that she'd grown quiet and introspective.

Dr. O'Brien had given Joan a workbook, and Maggie had seen her poring over the questions, writing down her thoughts. At one point, Joan had gotten upset over something she'd read and slammed the pencil down, causing Maggie to jerk with surprise. Joan had immediately apologized, although she didn't offer an explanation.

"Weren't you heading to the movies?" Joan asked, looking up from the puzzle. She'd set it up on a card table and had been diligently working on the border and hadn't seemed to notice Maggie was in the same room.

Maggie's hand gently petted Edison as she explained. "Everyone is busy, and I didn't want to go alone."

"I bet Nick would jump at the chance to go with you."

"Maybe," Maggie agreed, although she doubted Joan's son would be interested. True, they'd made peace with each other, but their friendship was new, and she didn't want to make assumptions.

"You won't know unless you ask," Joan encouraged.

"I don't have his contact information." This was true, and a way of telling Joan, who obviously would have his number, that she was reluctant to reach out to Nick with an invitation. He might get the wrong idea. Joan's son might believe she was interested in a relationship, and she wasn't. Well, maybe she was, but if that relationship didn't work out it might impact the one between her and Joan.

"I'll invite him to dinner," Joan suggested, "and you can ask him then."

"Please don't on my behalf," Maggie said. She feared putting Nick on the spot like that would do more harm than good. "You can invite him to dinner, of course, but please don't mention the movie."

"Why not? I thought you two had resolved your differences."

"We have," she said, and went back to reading her book, not wanting to belabor the subject.

No more than thirty minutes later, Nick popped in unannounced.

Joan looked pleased to see her son. "This is a welcome surprise," she said as Nick confidently walked into the family room.

"I like surprising my mom," he said, kissing Joan on the cheek. His attention swerved to Maggie. "It's a lazy Sunday afternoon, I thought I'd check in to see what the two of you were up to."

Joan didn't hesitate. "Maggie wanted to go to the movies, but all her friends are busy."

Nick perked up like this was the best news he'd heard in weeks. "I could see a movie. Let's go."

Maggie's spirits immediately lifted, although she didn't want to look overly eager. "You don't need—"

He interrupted her. "I want to. What time is the next showing?"

"Don't you want to know which movie I'd wanted to see?" she asked, tickled by his enthusiasm and a bit wary of it at the same time. "It might not be one that interests you."

"I'm okay with whatever it is, as long as it isn't a chick flick."

"Is there something wrong with chick flicks?" she wanted to know, staring him down.

"Well, yes, they're . . . you know . . ."

"I don't know, so kindly enlighten me." Maggie was amused, watching him squirm, knowing he was about to dig himself into a hole. She'd enjoy seeing him attempt to dig himself out.

Nick looked to his mother for help. Joan blatantly ignored him.

"Nick?" Maggie asked again. "What's wrong with a chick flick?"

Seeing that his mother wasn't coming to his aid, he buried his hands in his jeans pockets and said, "They're . . . girly."

"Girly," she repeated, letting him know by her tone she considered that ridiculous.

Nick sighed and shrugged. "Okay, fine. If you want to see a chick flick I'll go, but you're buying the popcorn."

Maggie laughed. "Deal." She reached for her phone and checked the movie times and purchased the tickets online.

"What are we seeing?" Nick asked.

"It'll be a surprise. I bought the tickets, so you're buying the popcorn." She didn't want Nick to think of this as a date as much as two friends spending a Sunday afternoon together.

"That sounds fair."

Good, he understood her intention. "We don't have a lot of time if we're going to make the show," she said, setting aside the book and bouncing up from the chair. Edison yawned and stretched his stubby legs while arching his back.

"That's my cue to take him outside," Joan said, rescuing the puppy from the chair and heading out the front door.

Maggie grabbed her raincoat and purse while Nick waited at the front door.

Joan stood on the porch steps out of the rain, while Edison quickly did his business.

"Good boy," Joan praised the puppy, and gave Maggie a thumbs-up. "Success," she said, scooping up Edison and taking him back into the house.

"I'll drive," Nick said.

"Okay." With the price of gas, Maggie wasn't going to complain.

By the time they bought the popcorn and drinks, the previews were running. This Tom Cruise movie had gotten a lot of rave reviews and Maggie wasn't disappointed. She could see Nick's relief that it wasn't a chick flick. She couldn't remember the last time she'd eaten buttered popcorn. This was a decadent treat, and she intended to savor every minute.

The movie was great. As they left the theater, Nick asked, "Do you have any plans for the rest of the day?"

Unwilling for Nick to assume she needed or wanted to spend time with him, she made up an excuse. "I should probably visit my dad."

He arched his brows as though confused. "You have family in the area?"

"My dad," she said, stating the obvious.

"Then what are you doing living with my mother?" He frowned disapprovingly, as though this news was a surprise, and not a pleasant one.

"That's my business," she said, "and none of yours." She took exception to his reaction. How dare he insinuate she had something other than the best of intentions living with Joan.

"Seeing that it's my mother, it is my business," he challenged, studying her with a look that suggested suspicion.

Maggie stiffened and crossed her arms. No way was she going to spend time arguing with him. Everything had gone well to this point, and now Nick had ruined a perfectly good afternoon.

"Please take me home."

"With pleasure," he snapped back. "I'm just wondering which one. Your dad's or my mother's."

She refused to answer.

The atmosphere in the truck as Nick drove to his family home was thick and tense.

Nick had barely turned off the engine when Maggie unbuckled her seatbelt and headed into the house.

"You're back early," Joan greeted, stepping out of the kitchen when Maggie returned. Her landlord seemed pleased with herself, matching the two of them up for the afternoon.

Nick barged in the door, following Maggie.

Joan looked from one to the other and seemed to instinctively recognize the tension between them.

"Mom," Nick said, glaring at Maggie and then focusing his attention on his mother. "Did you know Maggie has family living in the area?"

"Yes." She dried her hands on a terry-cloth towel. "What of it?"

"I want to know why she's living with you and not her own father?"

"Did you ask her?"

He glowered at Maggie. "She said it wasn't my business."

"Well, that's true. This doesn't have anything to do with you, son. Her reasons are my concern and not yours."

"It does concern me! You're my mother, and without Dad here to look after you, I'm worried. I've heard of cases where someone helps another out of the goodness of their heart, and it comes back to bite them."

"Oh Nick, you don't need to worry about Maggie."

"I would never . . ." Maggie immediately regretted opening her mouth, wanting to prove herself and realizing it was a lost cause. Her best response was silence. If nothing else, time would speak for itself.

Joan shook her head, revealing her disappointment and frustration with her son. "I hope you would trust my judgment, Nick. Having Maggie live with me has been a blessing. You're off base here."

"Then reassure me," Nick said. "Why would she choose to live with you over her own family? Something's up and I want to know what it is. If Dad was alive, would he approve of you taking a stranger into our home?"

Maggie had heard enough. Despite her determination to remain silent, she couldn't anymore. "You're impossible, do you know that? Frustrating and impossible. It was a bad idea to go out with you today, and I already regret it. There won't be a second time." With that, she headed up the stairs to the bedroom that had once been his, then turned around and added, "For someone who is supposedly smart, you can be incredibly stupid."

Continuing up the staircase, Maggie wished with all her heart she would have taken Steve's room instead. Angry as she was, she decided to switch bedrooms. Joan wouldn't care. Even sleeping in a room that had once been Nick's was more irritation than she needed.

With her door closed, Maggie didn't hear the discussion between Nick and Joan, and she was grateful to be left out of it. She paced for several minutes until her temper cooled.

At around six, Joan called Maggie to dinner. The buttered, salty popcorn that had been a rare treat hadn't settled well in her stomach, no thanks to Nick and his accusations. She came downstairs, grateful to find he'd left.

Joan was busy getting out bowls from the cupboard.

Maggie stopped her. "I'm not hungry, but thank you."

Joan frowned and studied Maggie. She'd set two places at the table, while a kettle of stew simmered on the stove.

Any other time, Maggie would have enjoyed the meal. It was perfect for such a dreary Sunday afternoon.

"I know Nick upset you," Joan said. "I apologize for the things he said. I've rarely seen him jump to conclusions like this." Joan seemed to be mulling it over, and after a moment shook her head as if she couldn't make sense of it even now. "Frankly, I don't understand my son."

Maggie dismissed Joan's apology. "It's fine." The problem was with Nick and not his mother.

Worry clouded Joan's face. "You aren't considering moving, are you?"

"No way!" She refused to give Nick the satisfaction.

Nodding approvingly, Joan murmured, "Good girl. Give Nick time and he'll come around."

It didn't matter to Maggie if he did or didn't; she wanted nothing more to do with him.

Being Monday was a holiday and she got paid time and a half, Maggie chose to work an eight-hour shift. She didn't have any specific plans and the money was good. Any extra income automatically went into her fund for school.

Starbucks was busy with a steady line of customers from the moment she clocked in. After the rain on Sunday, the weather report had forecasted afternoon sunshine and it seemed everyone in the Seattle area had decided to take advantage of it.

Maggie was assigned to take orders from the drive-through, which was one of the areas she enjoyed working. She made sure she greeted everyone with a welcoming smile and wished them a good day after delivering their order. Starbucks made it a policy that all employees could work any station, which was a good business practice. Every position could be filled in a pinch, and no one was irreplaceable.

At around ten, Maggie leaned out the window to collect the money before she handed over the iced chai latte to a woman in a blue Tesla when she noticed Nick's truck. He was waiting for his order directly behind the woman with the latte.

The coward.

He hadn't come into the building as he normally did. Instead, he'd placed his order through the drive-through, as if to avoid her. Fat chance of that. Nick Sample was in for a big surprise.

When he rolled up to collect his Americano, he couldn't hide his reaction. His eyes rounded when he saw Maggie, and he immediately avoided meeting her gaze.

"That will be four-twenty-five," she said in a business-like tone, without a smidgen of friendly overtures.

He handed her a ten. "Keep the change."

In the past he'd been generous, but never quite this generous. She resisted the urge to tell him he couldn't buy an apology, if indeed that was what he intended.

"Thank you," she returned flatly, and then because she was feeling generous herself, she said what she did with every customer. "Have a good day."

Nick Sample had a long way to go if he intended to get back in her good graces.

Chapter 20

Joan had done her best to ignore the holiday weekend, with minimal success. She phoned Steve in Arizona, but the conversation was brief. He was on his way into work. On a holiday, no less. Memorial Day. On *Jeopardy!* the night before, the question—or rather the answer—had been the original name for the holiday.

Decoration Day.

Joan had missed the question. She seemed to be missing a lot these days. The workbook Dr. O'Brien had given her had brought to the surface a lot of memories she'd struggled hard to forget. She'd dreaded holidays, choosing to ignore them rather than face them alone. All of what had been happy times became painful reminders that she was by herself. The workbook's pointed questions had forced her to face the distracting measures she'd taken rather than dealing with her grief and anger. Several times while going through the exercises, she found herself growing irritated to the point she could barely hold in the rush of negative emotion.

Mary Lou had mentioned how much journaling had helped her. Joan had taken her newfound friend's words to heart. After their talk and following the prompts, Joan wrote down her thoughts. She realized that, for at least the first six months after Jared's passing, she'd been numb, forgetful, and confused. She'd bottled up and ignored any emotion she felt as best she could rather than face reality, because when she did, the pain was so sharp she found it difficult to breathe. In the process, she'd unintentionally lost sight of the most important relationships in her life, those with her sons. And somewhat with Emmie, too, although her sister hadn't made herself easy to ignore.

Her concentration skills had faltered, which was one reason she'd taken up putting together jigsaw puzzles and working through books and books of Sudoku. They'd been a wonderful distraction. Lately she'd lost interest in both, and she knew why. For the first time in four years she was looking grief in the face and not backing down.

The flood of emotions was overwhelming, but she refused to go back. From now on, with determination, she was looking ahead instead of falling into the trap of memories.

Once again, she felt the sting of anger, felt it grow to monstrous proportions. Joan was furious with Jared for his lackadaisical attitude toward his own health. For a time, she'd blamed herself, thinking she should have insisted he get his annual checkup. She'd reminded him, wanted to make the appointment, but he'd continually made excuses. Twice that she remembered he'd mentioned having headaches, a sign that he'd chosen to ignore, claiming he was too busy to take time away from his practice.

The anger brewed inside her until it felt like a volcano about to explode. For four long years Joan had left everything that had belonged to her husband exactly where it was. His clothes remained in the closet. His personal items, golf clubs, tools . . . Everything was exactly where he'd left it. In retrospect, she accepted this was her way of holding on to him, as if her need for him was strong enough to bring him back to life. How sad, how ridiculous. How wrong. She'd cheated herself out of four years. Four years in which she could have broken ground to a new life for herself.

Joan wasn't holding on to Jared any longer. Joan wanted every bit of him gone.

Tossing her pen down on the table beside the journal, she raced into their room with a vengeance. Sensing her urgency, Edison followed behind, barking loudly. Stepping into their shared walk-in closet, she wrapped her arms around Jared's dress shirts, lifting ten at a time and then tossing them down on the floor. Unable to satisfy her anger, she stomped on them. She continued until every piece of his clothing that had hung in the closet was discarded in a giant pile.

Her shoulders heaved with the exertion. Exhausted, she moved to the king-size bed they'd once shared and sank onto the side of the mattress until her breathing slowed and her heart rate returned to normal. Tears filled her eyes, and she furiously swept them away, angry that she was so weak as to give in to the emotion. Edison sat at her feet, and she lifted him up, holding him beneath her chin, needing his warmth and his comfort. The puppy licked the moisture from her face as if he understood what she needed.

"I have shed my last tear for you, Jared Sample." There, she'd said it aloud, and she meant it.

Once her anger cooled, Joan's shoulders sagged, and she felt the need to weep all over again. She'd created a huge mess, one she'd need to deal with sooner or later.

She decided on later.

With Maggie at work, the house felt empty. It had rained for two days straight without a break, and now the sun was out. She'd basically ignored the holiday. Because she was dealing with the raw emotions with the grief group, journaling, and reading through the workbook, she'd done nothing to decorate Jared's gravesite. With the fury of her anger spent after clearing out his belongings, she felt she needed to visit her husband and get her frustration out. Vent if she needed to, release him once and for all.

Filled with purpose now, she cut a few purple rhododendrons from the bush in the backyard. While there, she tenderly looked over the two azalea bushes she'd recently planted. She'd loved working in her yard again, planting and weeding. Such simple tasks that had brought her back to herself, nurturing her soul.

Once inside the house, she arranged the rhododendrons in a vase and headed to the cemetery.

It'd been a while since her last visit, more than a year. Needless to say, she hadn't forgotten him. It was hard to equate that the man buried in the ground had been her husband, and visiting the cemetery only confirmed a reality she hadn't been ready to face.

It took a few minutes for her to locate his gravesite. She noticed a ragged-looking bouquet had been placed at his headstone. Steve. He hadn't forgotten his father when he'd been in Seattle for the conference.

"Jared," she whispered. It always felt awkward to be talking to a stone marker. Not that she was expecting a reply. "I am so upset with you. I want to blame you even though I know dying wasn't your fault. I'm alone now, and I don't like it. I'd hoped to grow old with you, to travel, spoil our grandchildren, all the things we'd once talked about. We had such wonderful dreams for the future. Now all those plans are as dead as you. I thought we would always be together, but then you had to go and ruin it."

The sprinklers had run their course, and the sun shone down and glistened off the freshly watered lawn. Joan would rather have had it rain. The bright sunlight was ruining her sour mood.

"You've upset everything. Did you even once consider how your death would affect our family? The boys need their father, and where are you?"

Joan lifted her face to the heavens and closed her eyes. She thought about Steve, living in Arizona. Something had happened with Zoe, and he refused to talk about it. And Nick, he was so skeptical and distrusting. That, too, could easily be attributed to her reaction to losing Jared.

She set the vase down at the top of the headstone next to the one Steve had left and stepped back. "This is it, Jared. I've come to my senses and I'm letting you go. I can't hang on to you any longer because it's killing me.

Killing me," she shouted, her anger echoing through the cemetery.

She wiped the moisture from her cheeks. Shocked at her outburst, she hung her head, stepped back, and whispered, "Good-bye." And then, because she felt guilty at the rage that had spewed from her lips, she added, "Rest in peace." That said, with a heavy sigh, she returned to the parking lot.

Twenty-four hours later, Joan was in Dr. O'Brien's office. The counselor sat in her chair with her legs crossed in front of the sofa where Joan was seated with her hands pressed between her knees. The counselor wore high heels and one shoe had slipped from her heel and was balanced on her toes. Funny how such a little thing as a shoe could be so distracting.

"I'm anxious to hear what you thought of the group now that you've attended a couple times," Lannie O'Brien asked.

Joan would be forever grateful that Dr. O'Brien had suggested she attend at least one meeting before she made her decision. "It's really helped."

"I understand you and Mary Lou have become fast friends."

Joan nodded. "She's great. Sally, too."

"Every person in the group has been where you are, Joan. They know exactly what you're feeling because at one time or another, they've been in the same place themselves."

"I've been going through the workbook."

"Wonderful. Is it helping?"

Joan told the counselor about visiting the cemetery and yelling at Jared and then feeling both guilty and foolish.

"That is understandable and necessary. Not to mention a giant step in the right direction."

Joan agreed. When she'd returned home, it seemed like a giant weight had been lifted from her heart. The anger had been cleansing. Joan realized this was only the first step and there were many more issues around Jared's death that she had yet to address. She would, though, in time, and that encouraged her.

"Now that you are coming to terms with the loss, Joan, you can start to look forward to the life ahead of you. There are two ways to consider this."

"How do you mean?" Joan leaned forward, anxious to understand.

"You can continue to cope as you have been," Dr. O'Brien said, "but I can see that you've already done that to the best of your ability, and it appears it's no longer working."

Joan realized Dr. O'Brien was right. Her coping skills, sequestering herself in the house, working jigsaw puzzles, and ignoring anything outside her front door, no longer offered solace.

"The other way may prove to be one of the most difficult aspects of grieving for you to reconcile."

Joan wasn't sure she understood.

"From what you've said, it feels like you're ready to move forward and make the best of what you have."

"Yes. Definitely."

"And yet there's the desire to remain connected to Jared."

That was also true. She couldn't simply erase the years or forget all that they'd once shared.

"The two go hand in hand, Joan. Back and forth, side by side. Moving forward yet staying connected. Does that make sense?"

Joan still wasn't entirely sure it did. "Can you give me an example?"

"Of course. Moving forward is attending the group and staying connected is visiting the gravesite. You removed Jared's clothes from the closet; that was moving forward. Looking through the photo albums was remaining connected. It's a delicate balance."

"It is," Joan agreed. She hadn't removed Jared's golf clubs or any of his woodworking equipment, thinking it would be a waste to give it up when one of her sons might want those items later.

"Tell me how you're feeling right now?" Dr. O'Brien asked.

Joan took a moment to assess her feelings. "Better, I think." It felt good to tell someone what she'd done and how angry she'd been. "Taking in a boarder was also a step in the right direction."

"It's difficult to face being alone," the counselor said, "especially when you and Jared were together twenty-four/seven."

That was the crux. If they hadn't worked together, it might have been just a little easier to accept his passing. The fact that they were always together, nearly attached at the hip, made the adjustment to being single even more difficult.

"There's a difference between loneliness and aloneness, Joan. As your healing process takes root, you'll find ways of belonging again, only it won't be as it once was. I'm grateful you're continuing with the group. Finding sources that help you grow out of your shell will offer new opportunities."

Joan could see this was already happening.

"While you and Jared were together, there were times when you were apart, right?"

"Of course."

"Even when you were alone you weren't actually lonely because you had a partner. Someone to eat with, share ideas with; someone to help you make decisions. You had a social life together, friends, outings, vacations. You were a couple. Much of the loneliness after the death of a mate is the loss of identity. When it happens abruptly, as it did in your case, it's only natural to feel disoriented and lost."

Joan had never thought of this aspect of loneliness, but now that she had, it resonated deeply. Her identity had been shaken. She no longer knew who she was. After being a wife and coworker for all those years, abruptly she was neither.

"I read ahead in the workbook," she admitted, fearing Dr. O'Brien might frown on her eagerness to move forward. "Is that all right?"

"Of course. Did you have a question?"

Joan nodded. "I noticed it mentioned helping others as beneficial."

"It amazingly is. The more effort we put into others, the stronger we begin to feel ourselves."

Joan let her mind soak in those words. Helping Maggie had been huge for her. It was as if her subconscious recognized this was beneficial for her as much as for Maggie.

Dr. O'Brien glanced at her watch and frowned. "Unfortunately, our time is up, but Joan, you're doing exceptionally well. I'm proud of you."

"Thank you."

"I'll look forward to seeing you at the next group therapy session."

"I'll be there."

"Good. Before you go, I'd like to recommend a book I feel you'll find helpful."

"Of course."

"It's C. S. Lewis's *A Grief Observed*."

Joan was willing to do anything that would free her mind and her heart. "I'll order it right away."

Dr. O'Brien led her to the door and Joan left. When she was in the parking lot, she slowly exhaled—so grateful she had taken these steps toward recovery. It was painful and traumatic, but then she remembered all that the butterfly had to endure to break free.

Chapter 21

Maggie finished an eight-hour shift at Starbucks, and while she hated to admit it even to herself, she was disappointed Nick Sample hadn't stopped by. His loss. She hoped he went hungry. In the days since the movie and the confrontation afterward, her attitude toward him had shifted slightly. He was right to worry about his mother, but at the same time, he should trust Joan's judgment.

She'd enjoyed his company when they'd attended the movie. They'd shared a large bucket of buttered popcorn and laughed together. Then as soon as he learned her father lived in the area, Nick had become wary of her and openly suspicious. Maggie had a lot to be grateful for, and she was deeply relieved that Joan had countered her son's doubts with her faith in Maggie.

In the brief time since she'd moved in with Joan, Maggie felt a sense of home that had been missing ever since she'd lost her mother. She knew her presence had helped Joan, too. They'd needed each other.

Maggie intended to do everything she could to show

Joan how much she appreciated becoming her boarder. She would rather be on the street than take advantage of Joan. That Nick would even suspect Maggie would use his mother for her own selfish purposes was an insult.

As she headed toward where she'd parked her car, Maggie reached for her phone and skimmed through emails. When she saw the one from Hurst Review, she went stock-still and held her breath.

For a long moment all she could do was stare at the heading. She'd applied for their nursing scholarship, along with several other scholarships and financial aid. Her best hope, she believed, was with Hurst. Their scholarship would be life-changing for her.

When she couldn't stand not knowing any longer, she opened the email and quickly scanned the contents. She had to read it twice before she believed what was right in front of her.

She'd been awarded the scholarship.

For the next two years her school expenses would be paid as long as she maintained the conditions listed in the email. Overwhelming relief and happiness flooded her heart. Right where she stood, there in the middle of the parking lot, Maggie started laughing, jumping up and down, while pumping her fist into the air in a wild display of triumph.

This news was too good to keep to herself. The first person she thought to tell was Joan, who had encouraged her when the other scholarships had fallen through one by one. But Maggie remembered that Joan had an appointment with Dr. O'Brien that afternoon.

Almost against her better judgment, Maggie felt the need to tell her father. It was unlikely he'd be happy for her, but that didn't matter. She felt it was important that he know all her hard work had reaped dividends.

It went without saying at this time of day her father wouldn't be home. Most afternoons were spent at the local watering hole with his drinking buddy, Al.

Sure enough, that was where she found him, sitting at the bar at the Half Pint with his cronies, a beer mug in his hand. The interior of the room was dark, and the scent of beer and cooking grease wafted about the room.

"Maggie?" Roy Herbert spoke first, his greeting full of surprise.

"Hi, Dad."

He frowned and looked worried. "You okay?" The question was full of concern, although his voice was gruff.

"I'm good," she assured him. "More than good, actually."

He turned around on his stool to get a better look at her. His brow had nearly folded in half, as if he couldn't fathom what had caused her to seek him out.

"This your daughter?" the man on the stool next to her father asked.

This must be his friend, Al, that her father had so often mentioned.

"That's Maggie," her father said, as a means of introduction.

"She's pretty."

"She takes after her mother."

"You should be thankful she didn't take after your sorry puss." Al laughed, as if he found himself hilarious.

"Shut up, Al." Her father slid off the stool and led Maggie over to one of the empty tables, of which there were plenty. Business this time of day at the Half Pint was apparently slim.

Maggie took a seat and offered him a weak smile.

"What's going on?" her father asked a second time. His look told her he was conflicted, still angry that she'd left him and at the same time concerned, but unwilling to show it.

She shrugged. "Nothing much."

"You doing okay with that widow lady?" His eyes darkened, as if convinced she'd made a terrible mistake by leaving him.

"It's working out."

He accepted her words with a tight nod, but his look said he wasn't sure he believed her.

"How about you?" she asked.

He glanced down at the floor. "Gotta say, it's a bit lonely without you traipsing in and out of the house at all hours of the day and night."

Wow. That he'd be willing to admit he missed her was huge, especially after the way he'd acted when she'd moved out. It sounded like a concession on his part, his way of saying how badly he regretted his actions. This was big. Double wow.

"Are you taking care of yourself?" Maggie asked.

He snorted. "Gloat if you want, but the house seems empty without you there bugging me about my drinking and insisting I eat something." It seemed her time away had mellowed him out a little.

"Glad to hear that," she assured him, quickly quelling her amusement.

"You gonna offer your daughter a beer?" Al shouted from the bar.

"No," Roy answered. "She doesn't drink." Then, turning to Maggie, he asked, "Right?"

"Right." She didn't feel the need to mention the occasional glass of wine. His asking gave her an idea, though. She'd buy a bottle of champagne to share with Joan later. Cheap champagne, as that was all she could afford.

Her father continued to stare at her, as if waiting for her to divulge the reason she'd sought him out.

Holding her breath, she decided to tell him, unsure of his reaction. "I got an email earlier. I've been awarded a two-year nursing scholarship." His response was far and away beyond anything she could have anticipated.

Tears filled his eyes.

He blinked furiously, as if to keep them at bay, swallowing tightly. "Your mother would be proud." His words were little more than a whisper. At first Maggie didn't make them out. When she did, she placed her hand on his arm. "What about you, Dad?"

He ignored the question. "Last time I saw you, what did I say?" he blurted out instead, his voice harsh.

Say? She didn't remember much about their last meeting. She'd stopped by shortly after collecting her things and he'd assumed she'd returned home with her tail between her legs. "Sorry?"

He huffed, as though that was exactly what he'd expected. "I said if you come around you needed to bring me a Whopper."

Maggie smiled. "Looks like I failed you once again."

"It's what I expected."

"I'll make sure I don't disappoint you the next time," she promised.

A hint of a smile touched his eyes. "You do that."

Maggie scooted out of the chair and stood. Looking toward her dad's drinking buddy, she said, "Nice to finally meet you, Al."

The Black man saluted her. "Glad to meet you, too, after all your dad has told me about you. He might not say it, but he's right proud of you."

"Shut up, Al," her father barked.

His words cut her up short. Her father was proud of her. That was a surprise. He made it sound as if Roy had bragged on her. Would wonders never cease? She glanced toward her father and noticed his face reddening. Yup, that was what she thought. While he might do his best to tear her down and discourage her studies, in his heart of hearts he was pleased she'd done all she could to continue her education. Although, heaven forbid he let her know.

Maggie left the tavern with a bounce to her step. On the way back to Joan's she stopped off at Safeway for a bottle of champagne. She found one that had reasonably good reviews for twenty bucks. It was twenty bucks she couldn't really afford, but if there was ever a reason to spend money frivolously, this was it.

Maggie parked in her usual spot and raced up the porch steps, letting herself into the house.

"Joan," she cried, too excited to not yell. She held up the champagne bottle as she hurried toward the kitchen.

Joan stepped out of the room. She wasn't alone.

Nick was with her, holding Edison in his arms. It seemed she'd been too excited to notice his truck parked outside.

The joy left her like water bursting from a fire hydrant. Her gaze clashed with Nick's until she could almost see the sparks.

Maggie slowly lowered the bottle. "Sorry, I . . . didn't realize you had company."

"What are we celebrating?" Joan asked, eyeing the champagne bottle.

Shrugging as if it was of little importance, Maggie said, "I got a two-year scholarship."

Joan's face broke into a huge smile. "That's wonderful news."

"Congratulations," Nick added. His eyes held hers for a long moment.

Maggie did her best to pretend to ignore him, finding him hard to read. He sounded sincere, but she wasn't convinced she should trust him. "I'll put this in the refrigerator to chill and we can open it later." With Nick at the house, she needed to disappear. It went without saying that her presence made them both uncomfortable. "I'll go to my room."

"No need," Joan said, in an effort to stop her.

Maggie didn't stick around long enough to argue. Instead, she headed up the stairs. She was almost to her room before she realized Nick had followed her.

"What?" she asked, turning to face him.

He raised both arms as if she'd pointed a pistol at him. "If you give me a minute, I'd like to apologize."

"Apology accepted. Think nothing of it."

He placed his hands in his jeans pockets. "I wish it was that easy."

"What do you mean?"

"It matters to me. I was an ass."

She crossed her arms and cocked her head to one side. "I'd say that's an accurate statement."

"Listen up, okay?"

She was a captive audience. "All right."

"You remember Kurt? He's the other guy who comes into Starbucks with me."

"I do, but what does he have to do with anything?"

"His mother had hip replacement surgery a while back. She had the daughter of a friend come in to help her after she got home from the hospital. Her bedroom was upstairs . . . Well, that doesn't matter. The point is, she brought this young woman into her home."

Maggie wasn't sure why this was important information, but she decided to hear him out. "What's that got to do with me?"

"Nothing, but it might help explain my reaction. Only after Kurt's mom was able to climb her stairs again did she realize several valuable items were missing from her jewelry case. Kurt was furious that someone had taken advantage of his mother. He confronted the girl, who adamantly denied stealing anything. She was outraged at the suggestion. It ruined the relationship between his mother and her best friend. Kurt started checking around pawn shops and eventually found several of the missing pieces. The sad part is that his mother trusted someone unworthy of that trust. I . . . I didn't want the same thing to happen to my mother."

"And you're telling me this because you were afraid I might steal from your mother?" Nick wasn't helping himself any.

He shifted uncomfortably. "Yes, and I was wrong. I'm sorry, Maggie, and I hope you'll be willing to give me another chance." He lifted his head to meet her look. "I jumped to conclusions when I learned you had family in the area, thinking there wasn't a good reason for you to be living with my mom when you had other alternatives."

She considered his explanation. Admittedly, she might have had her own suspicions had their situations been reversed. Especially after hearing what had happened to his friend's mother.

"Mom mentioned that your situation at home wasn't ideal."

Maggie didn't confirm or deny it.

"Well?" he asked. "Do you think we can put this behind us and be friends?"

She let him sweat it out for a few seconds before she smiled and gave him her hand. The thing was, she liked Nick. She'd had a great time at the movie with him. He was fun, and while she'd been hurt by his distrust, she understood he was looking after his mother's best interests.

Nick's smile took up half his face as he eagerly took her hand and shook it. Then, surprising her, he pulled her forward into a tight hug. "Congratulations on the scholarship."

"Thanks," she said, hugging him back. Her spirits were too high after the positive news to hold on to her anger for long. His arms felt good, and she breathed in his warmth and genuine delight at her award. She was happy he'd been at the house so she could share the good news with both him and Joan.

"My guess is that champagne is cold by now. Let's celebrate."

"Let's," she agreed.

Side by side, they bounded back down the stairs.

As if anticipating their arrival, Joan had brought out three flutes and set them on the kitchen counter.

Nick opened the refrigerator and removed the chilled bottle.

With an expert hand, Nick twisted off the foil and wire before taking hold of the bottle and twisting it instead of the cork.

"It looks like you have experience opening champagne," Maggie commented at the knowledgeable way he handled the bottle.

"I worked for a caterer while I was a senior in high school," he mentioned. "My supervisor said there was no need for the cork to pop if the bottle is opened properly. As I recall, he said that if I did it right, the sound would be the sigh of a contented woman."

Joan burst out laughing. Maggie smiled, too, before turning her attention to the widow. Something had changed for Joan, as well, if her smile was any indication. Maggie suspected it had to do with the widow friend Joan had found in Mary Lou and the counseling group.

Nick expertly poured into each glass before distributing them to his mother and then Maggie.

"To the future Florence Nightingale."

Maggie made a short bow.

Edison barked and all three laughed before clicking their glasses together and sipping the champagne.

This day had been full of wonderful surprises. The scholarship, the visit with her father, and Nick's apology. Happiness flooded Maggie's heart.

Briefly, she closed her eyes and was certain she could hear her mother's voice reminding Maggie how very proud of her she was.

Chapter 22

Late Wednesday afternoon, Joan carefully chose her outfit before settling on tan pants and a flowered teal shirt with a light white sweater. It'd been far too long since she'd given a second thought to her appearance. She studied her reflection and could see the difference. Her haircut had certainly helped. It was more than a hairstyle, it was her attitude. She felt almost free; it went without saying she had a long way to go. Progress had been made, though, and she was eager to continue along that path, eager to face the future, no matter what it held. She was finished with burying her head in the sand, hiding from the world because it'd felt impossible to face the future without Jared.

She was about to leave when Maggie came bouncing down the stairs. The young woman seemed full of life and light. She looked amazing in a sleeveless yellow summer dress printed with white daisies. The strapless sandals were a perfect complement. In the few weeks that Maggie had lived with her, she hadn't dated. Not as far as Joan could tell. The girl was always working, studying, or tutoring, although from what she'd said, that job would end shortly when the children's classes were dismissed for the summer.

"Looks like you have a hot date," Joan said, pleased by how happy Maggie looked.

Maggie's cheeks flushed. "Nick asked me out . . . You don't mind, do you? I mean, he said they were a member short on their trivia team and asked if I could fill in this week. I—"

"Heavens no, why should I mind?" If anything, having her son take an interest in Maggie thrilled Joan. If she were to have a daughter, Joan would want her to be someone exactly like her boarder.

Maggie visibly relaxed. "It looks like you're heading out yourself."

"It's Wednesday. I'm meeting Mary Lou for the grief therapy group."

"That's great."

It definitely was. Although they talked nearly every day now, Joan had resisted asking Mary Lou about Phil's wife. He'd been by the house, per the contract for lawn maintenance, several times. They'd exchanged pleasantries, but his wife had never attended the group. Joan would be interested in meeting her. Joan had grown fond of Phil, not in a romantic way, though. He was a good man, conscientious and caring, with a subtle sense of humor. His wife must be a special woman, and Joan hoped that one day they could all be friends.

Phil was something of a mystery, though. He drove an expensive Tesla, and she remembered him mentioning that he'd left his former job to take over Harrison Lawn and Landscaping when his father retired. Joan couldn't keep from wondering what he'd done before. She'd wanted to ask but hadn't because it never seemed to be the right time and she didn't want to pry, either.

Nick came to collect Maggie, and Joan noticed that he'd cleaned up. He'd shaved and wore a pair of Dockers and a button-down shirt. Joan couldn't remember the last time her son had cared that much about his appearance. Even when he'd taken her to dinner, he'd worn jeans. This told Joan her boy had strong feelings for Maggie. The two had had their troubles, but somehow they'd managed to come to a meeting of the minds.

With barely an acknowledgment, they were out the door. Joan noticed them holding hands, which to her way of thinking was a good sign that their relationship was progressing along nicely. That made her heart glad.

Edison cried pitifully as she placed him inside his crate, and, gathering her purse, Joan prepared to leave herself. She felt guilty leaving Edison, especially when he looked up at her with his dark brown eyes. The one bonus was how happy he would be when she returned. He'd all but leap for joy. The puppy, along with Maggie, had helped her with the healing process, she realized, grateful for them both.

Nick opened the truck's passenger door for Maggie. Because it was a stretch for her five-foot-three frame to climb inside, he helped by giving her a boost. "Thanks," she said, scooting as gracefully as she could manage into the seat. Men and their trucks!

Nick joined her and started the engine. He appeared

to be in a happy mood, and for that matter, so was she. She'd been excited and pleased when Nick had asked her to join him and his friends for what was sure to be a fun evening.

"Tell me about your trivia team," she said, wanting to be prepared.

"You already know Kurt."

"Right." He was the one who came in each weekday morning with Nick.

"He has a lot of general knowledge about movies, actors, and that sort of thing."

She nodded.

"Then there's Bruce. He's an engineer, so the technical stuff is his thing."

"What's your strength?" she asked.

He shrugged. "I'm hopeless with pop culture, but I read a lot, mostly history and science, which is why Kurt calls me Einstein."

Maggie smiled.

He glanced away from the road. "Does Kurt's nickname for me amuse you because it annoys me?"

"It isn't your nickname I find laughable, it's your humility," she said. "I suspect you invited me for my medical knowledge."

"Yeah," he agreed, and then grinned as if hiding a secret. "The truth is it was a good excuse to spend the evening with you."

Maggie had her suspicions. "Are you really down a team member?"

He hesitated before answering. "Okay, confession time. Each team is allowed four members. The three of us are pretty competitive and show up every week. Not so much with Tyler. He's more of a floater and comes when he feels like it. He hasn't shown up for the last two weeks. We can't depend on him, so I called him earlier and said we had a fourth person this week."

"You did not!"

"I did," he confessed. "Besides, when it comes to anything having to do with medicine, Kurt, Bruce, and I are at a loss."

"Now I understand. You invited me for my brain?"

"Rest assured there are other parts of your body that interest me as well."

Maggie blushed and let the comment pass. She wouldn't say it aloud, but there were parts of him that interested her, too, and more than his apparent intelligence.

"Obviously your input on medical questions will certainly help the team," he said, briefly looking away from the road and at her. "On the other hand, I wanted a chance to get to know you better and this felt like the perfect opportunity. Are you upset?"

"I'm actually flattered."

"Good." He reached for her hand and gave it a gentle squeeze.

Within a few minutes, Nick pulled into the parking lot of a restaurant and angled into an empty space. "The trivia game is played in the bar. We order a few appetizers and beer, but if you want anything else, let me know."

"Appetizers and beer sound perfect."

"Kurt insists beer sharpens his intellectual skills."

"I'll have to give that a try, then," she said, her good mood rising with each minute. Maggie hadn't gone out for a fun evening like this in ages. She couldn't recall the last time she felt this carefree without the burden of her father weighing her down. She'd struggled for so long, and it felt heavenly to relax and be with friends.

Helping her down from the truck, Nick claimed her hand and led her through the restaurant to the bar in back. Several high-tops were situated around the room in front of what looked to be a small dance floor. A table was set up there with a microphone resting on the top. People of various ages milled around, waiting for the competition to start.

Kurt saw them from across the room and raised his arm, indicating that he already had a table. When Nick led them over, he introduced her to Bruce.

"Do you work with Nick and Kurt?" she asked, sliding onto the raised chair at the high-top.

"Yes, but I'm in the engineering division of Harbor View Construction." He reached for the pitcher of beer in the middle of the table and poured himself a mug.

Nick claimed it next and filled both his and Maggie's mugs.

"Nachos and chicken wings are on their way," Kurt mentioned, sipping his beer.

A server stopped by and delivered pencils and papers. One sheet was for the answers, and there were several smaller ones, which Maggie guessed were provided for them to share their responses without any other team overhearing.

"Are there prizes?" Maggie asked, surprised she hadn't thought to ask earlier.

"First place is light-up shot glasses."

Maggie had no idea such a thing existed.

"Second place is Washington state lottery tickets."

"You mean to say the shot glasses are more valuable than lottery tickets?"

"A bird in the hand," Bruce said, setting down his beer.

"And third place is a five-dollar Starbucks card."

"Yahoo." Maggie raised her fist in the air.

"She works at Starbucks," Nick explained.

"And your team routinely wins?"

"I wish," Kurt grumbled. "See the table over there?" He pointed to a team three tables over. "The Wizards are in the money every week. We don't even know their first names and we hate them."

Maggie laughed, knowing that was an exaggeration.

A middle-aged man with a balding head and a stomach that hung over his belt buckle spoke into the microphone. "Welcome, trivia buffs. I'm Darrin, your friendly and fair trivia master. Is everyone ready for tonight's competition?"

A cheer of hopeful responses filled the room.

"Now, everyone raise your right hand and say along with me: *It's only a game.*" A chorus of unified voices followed.

Darrin nodded approvingly. "I've counted ten teams. We welcome back the regulars," he said, calling out the team names. "And give a nod to our newest team The Quizzie Rascals."

A few people called out, "Welcome."

"Just more competition," Kurt grumbled.

Having said his piece, Darrin continued. "All right, let's get down to business."

"Which team are we?" Maggie asked in a whisper, leaning close to Nick.

"Beer Today, Gone Tomorrow," Nick whispered back.

Maggie rolled her eyes.

Darrin glanced at the screen on his iPad. "First question: What was the title of Bruce Springsteen's memoir?"

Maggie's mind was completely blank. She didn't realize one of her favorite performers had written a memoir. Most of her reading material related to her schooling.

"I got this," Kurt said, and quickly scribbled down his answer on one of the small pieces of paper. He turned it around so the others could read it: *Born to Run*.

Nick, Bruce, and Maggie didn't have an answer so Nick, the team leader, wrote that response down on the answer sheet.

After a few minutes and mumbling around the room, Darrin continued. "Next question. Where was Catherine the Great born?"

Maggie thought she knew. With her own German heritage on her mother's side, she recalled that Catherine had invited immigrants from Germany to settle in Ukraine. She quickly scribbled down "Germany" and saw that both Bruce and Kurt agreed.

Nick shook his head and twisted his paper around to reveal his answer. Poland.

"No way," Kurt insisted, and pointed to his answer.

Nick remained adamant. "I read her biography years ago. Trust me."

While her teammates continued to look skeptical, Maggie sided with Nick. "I think we should trust Nick. He's the smart one, remember?"

Bruce scoffed a laugh. "Is that what he's been telling you?"

There were ten questions, and while they couldn't be

entirely confident they were all correct, Maggie felt they had a good chance of placing.

Darrin gave the teams a few minutes to review the ten answers. Maggie noticed that a number of the teams had their heads together, silently discussing and debating the questions.

Breaking into the waves of whispers, Darrin continued in a raised voice, "For tonight's bonus question, there are double points."

"I never do well with these bonus questions," Kurt complained. "I'd have better luck with the answers in Final Jeopardy."

Maggie glanced his way. Kurt didn't look like the type to watch *Jeopardy!*, but then it was probably a good source for learning trivia answers. He obviously took the game seriously.

Darrin paused and then spoke. "This is a four-part question, and there are double points for each correct answer. What are the four main types of tissues in the body?"

Nick looked to Maggie, as did Kurt and Bruce. She instantly felt the pressure. Reaching for her pencil, she bit into her lower lip and wrote: muscle, connective tissue, nerve tissues, and . . . the fourth one remained a blank in her mind.

"That's only three," Bruce whispered. "Think, Maggie, think. This answer could get us over the top."

She closed her eyes and remembered this very question had been on a recent test. She should know the answer.

"Leave her alone," Nick said. "She can't think with you harping on her."

All at once it came to Maggie, and she quickly wrote down: epithelial tissue.

Nick penned her answers on the sheet and was one of the last of the team captains to hand it in to Darrin.

Chatter erupted while Darrin scored the sheets. It didn't take long for him to announce the winners. "Third place goes to our newcomers, The Quizzie Rascals. Congratulations."

The new team gave a shout of surprise and clapped excitedly.

Maggie heard someone close by mumble, "Beginners' luck."

Darrin handed them four five-dollar Starbucks cards.

"Second place goes to The Wizards."

A gasp followed.

Maggie looked to her team, not understanding.

"They routinely place first," Nick explained.

Bruce seemed elated. "Over the last few months, they've collected enough lighted shot glasses to light up the Space Needle. A little humility will do them good."

"I really thought we'd place this week," Kurt murmured, looking discouraged.

"Maybe I got the bonus question wrong." If so, Maggie would feel dreadful.

"First place," Darrin said, "is Beer Today, Gone Tomorrow."

From the way her fellow team members reacted, one would think they'd won the lottery. Bruce and Kurt high-fived each other, and before she realized what he was doing, Nick wrapped his arms around her waist and lifted her several feet off the ground. "You did it for us, Maggie."

If she was surprised to have her feet dangling above the floor, she was even more so when he kissed her. Maggie cupped his face and kissed him, then threw back her head and laughed.

"I'm calling Tyler," Bruce declared, "and I'll tell him he's been replaced. Maggie, welcome to the team."

"Thank you."

With Nick's arm around her waist, they returned to where the truck was parked, proudly touting lighted shot glasses. Even if Maggie had no idea what she would do with them, it was something she would always treasure.

Chapter 23

Joan arrived at the counseling office the same time as Mary Lou. She noticed Phil's blue Tesla was in the parking lot.

Mary Lou walked toward her as Joan exited her car. The widow was a petite blonde with a fondness for hats. Her smile was contagious, and Joan suspected she had never met a stranger. If so, they didn't remain one for long. She'd taken Joan under her wing, and for that Joan would always be grateful. "I hope you'll come to Shari's with us after the meeting this week," Mary Lou said, as they met up close to the building's front door.

Most of the group gathered for coffee and pie following the meeting. Up to this point, Joan had refused. "I wish I could."

Disappointment showed in Mary Lou's eyes. "Is it because of the puppy again?"

Joan tucked her purse strap over her shoulder and nodded. "Maggie is out, and I really can't leave the poor fellow alone for hours on end."

"Edison is in his crate, right?"

"Yes . . . but."

"No more excuses," Mary Lou said. "Tonight you're going. I get as much from that time as I do the meetings. You need to come."

Joan's impulse was to refuse. The words were on her lips, and she intended to use Edison as a convenient excuse as she had in the past. She abruptly changed her mind. "You're right. Edison should be fine for a couple hours. I'll join you."

"It's the best way to get to know the others," Mary Lou reminded her. "The meetings are helpful, don't get me wrong. Half the time, though, it's the coffee afterward where we get down to the nitty-gritty of adjusting to our new lives."

Joan remembered what Dr. O'Brien had mentioned in their session, about the loss of identity after a spouse dies. The group would help her find a new one, Joan realized. New friends, new experiences, and a shared understanding of who she was as a single adult.

When they entered the room, four others had arrived and taken their seats in the circle. Dr. O'Brien acknowledged Joan and Mary Lou with a smile. Joan took a seat next to her friend. Phil sat across from her, next to Dr. O'Brien. It wasn't long before every chair was filled.

The conversation was friendly as they discussed their week. When there was a short lull, Joan had a question.

"Recently I had an unpleasant discussion with my son. He made a comment that brought me up short."

Dr. O'Brien leaned toward her. "What was it, Joan?"

"Something I hadn't thought of until recently." As difficult as it was to admit, she'd been caught up in her own grief and had ignored her own sons' feelings. "Nick, my younger son, was concerned that Maggie, the young woman living with me, might be taking advantage of me. Out of the blue he said if his father was alive, he would disapprove."

"That brings up an excellent point," Dr. O'Brien said. "Studies show us that sixty-five percent of sons after losing their fathers say it affected them more than any previous loss in their lives."

"It isn't only Nick," Joan added. "I'm afraid my older son, Steve, has withdrawn from me. I feel like I've failed him."

"My son had a hard time when his father passed," Mary Lou mentioned. Her hands were tightly clasped in her lap, and Joan could see how painful it was for her friend to admit this to the group. "I wanted to help him, but I was so deep into my own grief, I wasn't much help. He started drinking heavily and ended up with a DUI." She hung her head as though ashamed, as if her lack of awareness had caused her son to falter.

"You can't accept blame for your son's behavior," Phil said.

"Phil's right," Dr. O'Brien added. "Let me ask you a question. What was Mike's relationship with his father before his death?"

"Not so good. Dennis was a great father, but when Mike was in his teen years, the two repeatedly clashed. For the last part they tended to avoid each other."

"It's understandable that a son who had a negative relationship with his father would be left with regrets, guilt, and anger, feelings that can linger for years unless addressed."

"What can I do for Mike?" Mary Lou asked, her tone pleading.

"Talk to him, ask him to consider getting counseling."

"I will," Mary Lou said, and then, looking to Joan, she added, "I appreciate you bringing up your son, Joan. I've been hesitant to mention Mike, but you addressing how your relationship has suffered gave me the courage to speak up."

"I don't mean to change the subject here, but I've got a problem," Glenn said. "Something is wrong with me." Glenn appeared to be in his mid-sixties, possibly early seventies. "Lucy always did the shopping, so getting groceries is a whole new experience for me. I made the mistake of going to Costco and came out with a case of sardines and an inflatable unicorn."

"You must have a fondness for sardines," Sally said.

Glenn shook his head. "Hate 'em, Lucy was the one who liked sardines. She used to put them on a peanut-butter sandwich. I thought it was disgusting, and here I was purchasing an entire case."

"Why do you suppose you did that?" Dr. O'Brien asked.

Glenn lowered his head and didn't answer for a couple painful moments. "I suppose that was my twisted way of admitting how much I miss my wife. I've always been my own man. I put on a good front after Lucy died, and I expect the only one I fooled was me."

Joan could identify. After Jared died, she made his favorite dinner—turkey meatloaf—when she much preferred beef over turkey. At the time, she knew what she was doing and that it would likely end up in the garbage can. It was wasteful, and she'd done it because it made her feel a connection with her dead husband. Silly. Ridiculous. Yet at the time completely necessary for her mental health.

Phil leaned forward and with a smile said, "I don't think I want to know what prompted you to purchase a blow-up unicorn."

The entire group laughed.

"That was for the grandkids," Glenn insisted, laughing himself.

As the session was about to end, Sally addressed Joan. "How long have you been a widow?" she asked.

"Four years." It felt a whole lot longer, though—a lifetime.

"How come it took you so long to seek help?" she asked, as if she found it difficult to understand Joan's hesitation.

Joan knew Sally was only curious and didn't take it personally. "I believe we each come to recognize when it's time, and I suppose for me it took longer than most. Nevertheless, I'm here now."

Sally nodded and smiled in understanding.

After the meeting drew to a close, the group gathered together in the parking lot.

"Shari's?" Glenn asked.

"I like meeting there better than McDonald's," Sally said. She looked around the small group for confirmation.

"I'm in," Phil said.

"Me, too," Joan added.

Before she climbed into her car, Mary Lou gave her the

address to the restaurant. She sent Maggie a text to tell her she'd be later than expected, and if she got home first, to be sure and let Edison out.

By the time she arrived at Shari's, the others were already in place. They'd pushed two tables together and left a chair empty for Joan, which warmed her. It was a way of saying she was one of them now.

The server came forward with a coffeepot and menus. Joan and Sally ordered tea and the rest of the group had coffee. Several ordered a slice of pie to go with their drinks. The list of pies was impressive, and Joan was tempted.

"You going to order pie?" Mary Lou asked Joan.

"I'm considering it."

"If you do, I will, too."

That was all the encouragement Joan needed. Before she had second thoughts, she added a slice of sour cream raisin pie to her order.

The discussion around the table was lively and friendly. An outsider would never guess they were part of a grief therapy group. They laughed and shared jokes, and when Sally started to cry, there were words of encouragement. Both Mary Lou and Joan had mentioned their sons, and after finishing off a slice of apple pie, Glenn mentioned his daughter, who hadn't dealt well with her mother's death. That led to a whole other discussion.

Before Joan realized it an hour had passed. It felt like fifteen minutes. She was happy Mary Lou had encouraged her to join the others. If she'd declined, she would have missed this bonding time and the laughter. No one seemed willing to let Glenn forget that blow-up unicorn.

Mary Lou walked with her into the parking lot. "I'm

so happy you're part of this group. You know Sally didn't mean anything by questioning why it took you so long."

"I know. I didn't take offense."

"Good. Is the group what you expected?"

"Not at all," Joan told her.

"How so?"

"Well, for one thing, I didn't expect to laugh so much. I completely understand what led Glenn to buying sardines, but that inflatable unicorn got to me."

"There've been sessions when we laugh more than we cry. This group is the one place where we can share our feelings without judgment or regret. We've all survived a body blow that has left us weak and lost. Together we're finding a way back."

"I am, too."

What Mary Lou said was true. Joan had been foolish to wait as long as she did. In retrospect, Joan wasn't sure what had kept her away, other than her own stubbornness. In reality, the group session hadn't been all that different from the private counseling. Dr. O'Brien's main role was to listen and ask an occasional question. Only rarely did she add a comment. The counselor was there to monitor the group, but she let those attending do the talking. The goal was for each one to find their own path to healing, helping one another.

Confession time. "I didn't want to attend the group session because I was afraid," Joan admitted. "I feared I wouldn't be able to bear hearing about who others had lost. I had trouble dealing with my own grief, let alone anyone else's."

"It isn't like that," Mary Lou commented.

It wasn't until she'd attended the group session that Joan realized it.

A minute later, she waved her friend off and headed to where she'd parked her car. She noticed Phil's Tesla remained in the lot, which was mostly empty now.

"Hey, Joan," he said, coming toward her. "Good to have you join us."

"Thanks. I enjoyed the banter, not to mention the sour cream raisin pie." She pressed her hands against her stomach. She could only imagine how many calories were in that one slice. However many, it was worth every single one.

"Don't tell anyone, I'm addicted to their cherry pie myself," Phil said.

"Mary Lou and I were talking about Sally wanting to know why I took so long to come to therapy."

"Sally didn't mean anything by it," Phil assured her.

"I don't know that I would ever have found the courage if not for Dr. O'Brien."

"Over the years," Phil said, "I've come to believe that God's timing is perfect. You arrived at precisely the time that was right for you. When you made the appointment to see Dr. O'Brien, you were ready."

"You're right. The timing was perfect. I've struggled not to cry, but seeing others feel free to display their emotions has helped." When Sherry mentioned the loss of her son in a recent session, Joan hadn't been able to hold back tears. He'd been in the military and was killed in a training exercise.

"None of us worry about displaying our pain," Phil said. "We all do at one time or another. Tears, I've learned, can be cleansing, a release. For myself, they were the roadway that led to healing."

Joan briefly lowered her head, as if confessing to a fault. "I didn't cry for a long time after Jared died. Don't get me wrong, I wept a river of tears in the months that followed, but not in the beginning."

Phil held her gaze, his eyes warm and sympathetic. "I believe it, especially when the one we love is gone without warning, in a split second of time, it takes our hearts a while to absorb the shock of it."

Joan agreed. "For the longest time, I couldn't accept that he wasn't at my side the way he had been all the years we were married."

"That's understandable, Joan. I think what you experienced is fairly common. I know it was with me, and we aren't alone. Time and again I've heard others in the group say the same thing."

Joan found his words reassuring.

"Sadly, some of us never find the courage to move forward."

Joan felt the wisdom of his words. "Can I ask you something?"

"Of course."

"You so often mention needing to get home because dinner's on the table, but you haven't said anything about your wife. Is there a reason she doesn't attend the group with you? I'd really enjoy meeting her."

The shocked look that came over him stunned Joan. "I'm sorry, did I say something wrong?"

"My wife?" he repeated. "I'm not married."

"You're not . . . I'm sorry, I didn't realize . . ." Joan didn't know what to say. "Did your wife die?" He'd never mentioned whom he'd lost, and Joan had been left to speculate.

"It isn't my wife I'm heading home to see," Phil explained. "It's my dad. He lives with me and does all the cooking. Amanda's mother and I divorced years ago."

"Amanda?"

"My daughter. She died five years ago in a car crash."

Chapter 24

"You lost your daughter?"

Phil looked off into the distance as if to say how difficult it was to speak of his daughter's death even now.

"Oh Phil, I'm so sorry." Joan couldn't imagine how difficult it would be to lose a child. The very thought of burying Steve or Nick made her stomach hurt.

"I no longer have any contact with Katelyn, Amanda's mother," he admitted, and then as if he wanted to change the subject, he explained, "It makes sense that you assumed I was married. After Mom died, Dad was never the same. It wasn't long after her passing that he retired. He lived alone, and I did as well, so it made sense for us to combine our households. Dad likes to cook, and it gives him purpose besides advising me on the business and handling the bookkeeping. Amanda's mother and I haven't spoken in years."

"Oh." Joan felt incredibly foolish. "I'm sorry."

"Don't be. Given the circumstances, it's understandable. Dad was the one who suggested I get help after I buried Amanda. Losing her broke me, Joan. I was lost in a sea of grief and drowning with every breath I drew."

Hearing the agony in his voice, Joan reached for his hand, curling her fingers around his. Silently she let him know she understood. She had the strongest desire to hug him and hesitated, thinking how inappropriate it would be to touch someone in such a familiar way, and yet she couldn't stop herself. She knew this pain, had walked this rut-filled path herself. Following the impulse, she wrapped her arms around his middle and gave him a gentle squeeze.

"Thank you." He briefly hugged her, and it seemed he had something more he wanted to say but held back.

"Forgive me . . . I . . ."

"No, please don't apologize. I welcomed that hug." Joan hardly knew what to say, and so she remained silent.

"Like Jared was to you, Amanda was my whole world," Phil said. "Katelyn and I divorced when Amanda was three. She'd gotten pregnant while we were in college, and we married. It was never a good marriage. Katelyn felt trapped and quickly grew disillusioned with being a wife and mother. She left to find herself and instead found the man she told me was her soulmate. Apparently not, because they divorced sometime later. She granted me full custody of Amanda and moved on, rarely connecting with our daughter, so it was always just the two of us.

"I was her soccer coach, her Sunday school teacher, and her calculus tutor. I stayed up all night with her after she broke her arm on the school grounds."

Knowing how difficult it was for him to speak of his daughter, Joan briefly closed her eyes, as his pain was clearly visible. "You don't . . ."

"No, I want you to know what happened." Phil appeared to gather some inner strength before he continued. "Amanda was brilliant and graduated from high school as the class valedictorian. I was so proud of her on graduation day. I sat in the audience, and it felt as if the buttons would burst off my shirt. She gave a speech that stirred me and several others to tears." His voice cracked, and he hesitated before continuing.

"Oh Phil, this is too painful. I'm so sorry."

"I know."

This was a phrase Joan had often repeated when friends spoke of their own feelings at Jared's loss. She didn't want Phil to explain anything more, seeing how difficult this was for him.

"No, it sometimes helps to talk about it. It reminds me my daughter lived and isn't forgotten."

She admired his determination to bare his soul over a loss that had clearly devastated him.

"Amanda, as you can imagine, had the opportunity to attend any university she wanted. After giving it a lot of consideration, she chose the University of Washington, the main campus right here in Seattle. We'd toured Pepperdine, and it was my first choice for her, but the decision was hers. When it came down to it, she wanted to be independent and at the same time close enough to run home with a load of wash if she wanted. It was where her mother and I attended, and while she never said as much, I think that's the real reason she chose there."

Joan smiled. So typical of a teenager, wanting to be on their own but close enough to home for when the need arose. And to follow in her father's footsteps.

"Amanda quickly became friends with her college roommate. The two did everything together. Julie, her roommate, and Amanda were excited to attend a concert at the Gorge."

Joan knew the Gorge, in eastern Washington, was a huge venue for bands and major artists, plus several rising ones.

"Julie drove and the two decided to head back that night following the concert. As best we can figure, Julie fell asleep at the wheel. Amanda was instantly killed, while Julie walked away with barely a scratch." He paused long enough to take in a deep breath, as if it took all his strength to finish explaining what happened.

Joan gasped at the horror of it. "Oh Phil, what a terrible shock her death must have been."

He shook his head as though to dismiss her words. "No more surprising than you losing Jared. At first it felt unreal, like there'd been some terrible mistake . . . like a nightmare I would wake up from sooner or later. Even after I was notified, I refused to believe it until I saw her body."

Joan had felt all that herself when the kind doctor in the ER had told her there was nothing more the medical team could do for Jared. He was gone. She remembered standing there, her knees growing weak as she shook her head back and forth, wanting to dismiss his words, wanting to say that he was wrong, that Jared would be fine once he got the care he needed.

"I'll admit I didn't deal well with losing my only child," Phil continued as he wiped his hand down his face. "I went through several stages of grief: The first, of course, was denial. That didn't last long, seeing that I had to make the arrangements for her funeral. All the details leading up to the services sort of hit me in the face with the fact that I was burying her."

Joan remembered how painful that time period had been for her as well. She'd relied heavily on her two sons and her sister, who'd immediately flown to Seattle to help her through that first couple weeks while she dealt with the funeral arrangements and the dental practice.

"I was so angry," Phil said, and Joan heard the regret in his voice. "I lashed out at Julie, wanting her to assume some responsibility." He exhaled, as if he found it difficult to continue.

She understood his determination to reveal his path to healing.

"In the end, I realized how unfair that was. Julie was devastated, overwhelmed with grief herself. It took her a full year before she was able to get behind the wheel of a car again. In the years since, I've found I could understand they were both at fault and should never have decided to drive back to Seattle that night. In my heart I knew Amanda wouldn't have wanted me to lay the blame on Julie."

Joan admired Phil for his compassion and understanding for Amanda's friend.

"I don't know if I could have done that," she told him, letting Phil know how deeply his willingness to release her friend from this awful guilt inspired her.

Phil held her gaze for a moment before he continued. "For months afterward I wallowed in sorrow and depression. My partners were sympathetic for a time, but as the months progressed, they lost patience with me."

Partners? She held back her questions.

"About a year after I buried Amanda, I snapped out of

the depression and was able to continue with a full work-load. Dad was instrumental in helping me. He encouraged me to join the grief counseling group. The group made all the difference. I was a basket case the first few times. I didn't share, didn't speak. It was all I could manage to make a showing.

"As the weeks progressed, I realized I wasn't alone. Others had suffered the same as me and, with time and patience, had learned to move forward and live again. The group became my lifeline, and between the other members and Dr. O'Brien, I learned coping skills and eventually was able to look toward the future instead of dwelling in that black hole of isolation and grief."

"I relate to this so much," Joan whispered. The lump in her throat was huge as she listened. "I used distractions to help me cope for a long time." She wallowed in her own pain for far too long.

"You aren't alone; several of those who have come and gone from the group have done the same. They were willing to do anything to take their mind off what they'd lost. I remember one woman who'd been widowed used baking as a distraction. Every week she'd arrive with an array of homemade goodies, bread, cookies, pies, you name it." He smiled for the first time since they'd started talking. "We had to ask her to stop because we were all gaining weight."

"I so understand her need for a distraction. It helps for a time, but then there's still the reality that can only be ignored for so long."

"So true."

"Did you use a distraction?" she asked, thinking their paths in loss seemed to have flowed in the same direction.

"Work, for a time, but then I lost interest and decided to make a change."

"You mentioned you had partners?"

"Before I took over Harrison Lawn and Landscaping, I was a partner in a prominent Seattle law firm. We did family law, which means I saw firsthand how difficult it could be to blend families. It was important for me to always put Amanda first and for her to know she was my top priority."

"You mean to say you didn't have a serious relationship the entire time she was growing up?"

He shrugged. "I dated now and again, but I never let any relationship develop beyond friendship."

That told Joan how serious he was about keeping his daughter his main priority.

"My partners assumed I'd lost my mind to give up a thriving practice, and frankly I can't say that I blame them."

From the outside it must have seemed ridiculous for Phil to leave everything behind to ride a lawn mower.

"I suppose in some ways becoming a landscaper was a distraction. Dad needed me, and I needed to be needed. It wasn't long before I realized how beneficial taking over the business was to my mental health."

"Dad was miserable living by himself and was going through the motions with the business, tending only to his longtime customers. When he saw me working in my own yard, digging and planting, he asked if I'd be interested in taking over for him. He listed the advantages and offered to guide me and handle the bookkeeping. Planting flowers, growing my own vegetables, helped bring me back. Letting that seed die in order to produce new life. I found comfort in the warm earth, feeling it with my hands and sifting the dirt through my fingers. It was a reconnection with life. It fed my spirit and led me back to a time and place where I could find acceptance after losing my daughter. The promise of spring and the seeds growing and bearing fruit showed me I could learn to live life without Amanda. It didn't take long for me to realize stepping in for Dad would be good for both of us."

"I'm searching myself," Joan admitted. "I worked as Jared's assistant, bookkeeper, and janitor for all those years, and now I do little but twiddle my thumbs all day."

"Do you need to work?"

"Financially, no. At the same time, I don't want to waste what remains of my life. I'd like to find something to do that's meaningful and needed."

"There are any number of worthy charities that would welcome you, Joan."

Dr. O'Brien had said as much and had encouraged her to reach out to aid others in need.

How crazy it was to share such a meaningful conversation in a Shari's parking lot. "Thank you, Phil. Would you mind if I gave you another hug?"

He grinned. "I wouldn't mind at all."

Phil hugged her back. She'd been impressed with him before, especially after he'd helped Maggie. Her admiration grew even deeper after learning about his daughter.

Chapter 25

Maggie arrived at work, excited for the upcoming day. As always Starbucks was hopping with early morning traffic.

Leanne noticed her friend's chipper mood right away and pulled her aside.

"You got a hot date with Einstein again?" Leanne asked, arching her well-shaped brows with the question.

"As a matter of fact, I do have a date, but not with him. It's the last day of school."

Leanne frowned, drawing those same brows together in a sharp inverted V. "I thought your classes let out a couple weeks ago."

"Mine did," she confirmed. "It's the last day for Caleb and Victoria, the second-graders I tutor. I promised them a reward if they could raise their reading level to third grade, which they'll start in September. I'm taking them to Wild Waves."

Leanne looked at her as if she'd lost her mind. "Are you nuts? Do you have any idea of what a crazy place it is, especially at this time of year?"

"Not really. I've never been." Not that it mattered. Maggie had gotten permission from both parents, then collected Caleb and Victoria's swimsuits and beach towels and stored them in her car's trunk. Neither student had any idea of what she'd planned. All they knew was that Maggie had a surprise especially for them. They'd both worked hard to improve their reading skills. Best of all, they were now eager readers, going through books by the dozens, as if they couldn't get enough. There was a world of difference from when she'd first started working with them.

Leanne pulled her aside. "Girl, take it from someone who knows. Wild Waves is a madhouse, with a bazillion kids, running around like banshees. You won't have a moment's peace. Don't even think about lounging on the beach for fear of stampeding eight-year-olds."

All Maggie knew was what she'd heard from the kids at the elementary school. The park had more than a wave pool; there were carnival rides and booths that sold all the typical fair food. Maggie was quite certain neither Caleb nor Victoria had ever been, as both came from single-parent families and lived in a low-income area.

"Did you take a loan from the bank?" Leanne asked next. "Because you're likely to need one."

"Ah . . . the entrance fee didn't seem overly outrageous." It'd been a stretch in Maggie's already tight budget, but she didn't hesitate before ordering their tickets. Both children were small, and she was able to get a discount because of their age. The website said that the one-day pass included all the rides plus the water park.

Maggie had packed a lunch and had hoped to avoid buying overpriced snacks. She hadn't seen anything on their website that prohibited bringing in food. That wasn't the case in many places.

Leanne chuckled and shook her head. "You're a better woman than me."

Maggie promised to update her come morning.

"If you survive, that is." Leanne patted Maggie's back and wished her well as Maggie left the building.

Now that her shift was over, Maggie drove to the school. She'd already told the children to wait for her there. As she parked outside the building her phone buzzed. Caller ID told her it was Nick.

He rarely phoned, almost always communicating via text. They'd been to dinner and Maggie had participated in the trivia night with him twice now. She'd had a lot of fun, and not just because she was able to answer the majority of the medical questions when no one else could. It'd been almost a week since she'd last had contact with him. The construction project was on a deadline, with huge fines to be leveled against the contractor if the work wasn't completed within a certain time period. This meant Nick was working a lot of overtime hours, which resulted in them being out of communication.

"Hey, what's up?" she asked, surprised to hear from him.

"I've got the afternoon off, and a friend loaned me his sailboat. How about we head out to Lake Washington? It's a perfect day and the wind is good. You game?"

Instant regret filled her. "Oh Nick, I can't."

A shocked silence followed. "How come?"

She didn't need to explain herself, but for the sake of peace did. "I already have other plans."

"Plans? Can you change them? I mean, this is the first

afternoon I've had off in weeks, and I'd hoped we could get together. I realize it's last-minute and all. One of the contractors didn't pass inspection and we can't continue work until he makes it right, which shouldn't take long."

"I'm sorry, but I can't. Any other time I'd like nothing more, but I can't disappoint Caleb and—"

"Who's Caleb?" The question came at her like a bullet.

He was jealous and he didn't bother to hide it. They weren't exclusive, and he seemed to be reading more into their relationship than was warranted.

"Nick," she said, keeping her voice even. "I'm sorry to disappoint you. I've already made plans for the day, and I won't change them. To ask me out of the blue like this and be annoyed when I say no is unfair. I hope you have a good time."

Caleb and Victoria came out of the school and looked around for Maggie.

"I have to go."

"Maggie, wait—"

"I'm sorry, Nick, my date is here." She probably should explain who Caleb was, but decided against it. It would do him good to think he had competition, even if it was selfish of her.

Maggie climbed out of the car and met the two children. They looked up at her, both wide-eyed with excitement. They'd been eagerly waiting for the reward she'd promised.

"Are you going to tell us what our treat is now?" Victoria asked. "Caleb said you were taking us for ice cream. Is that it?"

"Nope," Maggie said, and shook her head. "It's better than that."

"What can be better than ice cream?" Caleb asked, grinning and showing off his missing two front teeth.

"I think I know what it is," Victoria claimed. "We're going to the zoo."

Maggie had a hard time keeping the secret. "Good guess, but that's not it." She gathered them in the car, buckled them into the backseat, and headed south on the freeway toward the Enchanted Parkway and Wild Waves.

"Where are we going?" Caleb asked, looking out the car window.

"You'll see."

"Is it far?" Victoria asked, stretching her neck to view the scenery around her.

Maggie took the exit for the park. It wasn't long before both children saw the sign for Wild Waves.

"Is it the water park?" Caleb shouted, unable to hide his enthusiasm.

"I told you it would be better than ice cream," Victoria touted.

By the time Maggie pulled into the parking lot, both children were bouncing up and down with excitement. She gathered their swim gear and her own from the trunk of her car, along with the picnic basket. They walked what felt like a mile through the huge parking lot to the entrance.

After changing into their swimsuits, Maggie and the two children charged into the water, not stopping until they were nearly fully immersed. Both Maggie and Victoria gasped at the first rush of water, shocked by the temperature. It was cooler than what Maggie had imagined, although her body quickly adjusted.

The day was perfect, with temperatures close to eighty along with a warm wind. She hated to refuse Nick and would have enjoyed her first sailboat ride. But this time with these children was by far more important. Maggie was convinced both Caleb and Victoria would remember this day for a very long time.

The two kids giggled and repeatedly raced back and forth, jumping into the waves. Their laughter caught on the wind, their joy spilling over. They couldn't get enough of leaping into the waves, it seemed.

It wasn't long before Caleb wanted to go down the water slide. Victoria held back, unsure until she saw Caleb glide down and make a big splash in the water. He came up sputtering and tossed his arms triumphantly into the air.

"Come with me," Victoria pleaded, pulling on Maggie's arm.

"Me?"

"Please? Go down the slide with me."

Maggie couldn't refuse the little girl, who'd worked so hard. When they reached the top of the slide, Victoria demanded that Maggie go first. She felt a bit ridiculous, as this was the smallest slide and she was the only adult. Refusing to be self-conscious, she slipped down the water-slick slide, laughing all the way. She reached the bottom with a plop and went completely underwater, surfacing with a mouthful, choking and laughing at the same time.

Victoria followed and landed in Maggie's arms, hugging her close as she cried. "I did it! I did it!"

"You sure did," Maggie told her.

The three of them returned to where they'd parked their towel and lunch. "Are you two hungry yet?"

Both adamantly nodded. Maggie opened the basket and brought out the sandwiches. She saw the disappointment in their eyes as they viewed the peanut butter and jelly. The hamburger stand must be close by, because the scent of cheeseburgers lingered in the air.

"I have . . ." She didn't get to complete the sentence. A familiar face caught her attention, and she saw Nick walking toward her, as if this had been the plan all along. He was dressed in his swimsuit and had a beach towel draped around his neck.

"Nick?" Her mouth had gone completely dry. She wanted to ask him what he was doing at Wild Waves, but she couldn't seem to form the question.

"Hey," he said, as if she'd been expecting him all along. Both Caleb and Victoria stared up at him as if he was an action figure from their favorite television series. Maggie had to admit, with his bronze muscles and washboard abs, he caught the eye of more than these two children.

Maggie's mouth sagged open until she finally found her wits. "Caleb and Victoria, this is my friend, Nick."

"Hi, Nick," Victoria said.

Caleb continued to stare at him as if viewing a Greek god.

"How did you know I was here?" Maggie asked the obvious. It was shocking that he'd found her in the huge park with literally hundreds of guests.

"Mom," he said, as if that explained everything. Then, noticing that she'd opened the lunch basket, he asked, "What's on the menu?"

"Looks like peanut butter and jelly," Caleb answered, and didn't bother to hide his disappointment.

Nick shook his head. "You can't eat peanut butter at Wild Waves, it's against the rules. I guess Ms. Herbert didn't know that. When you're here it's hot dogs and cheeseburgers and cotton candy and ice cream."

Maggie gently elbowed him in his side. "I can't afford that," she said out of the corner of her mouth.

Nick ignored her. "Come on, kids, let's get lunch. I'm going to need help carrying it all."

He didn't need to ask twice, as he quickly acquired two eager volunteers.

"Nick?" Maggie whispered again.

"You better put in your order, Ms. Herbert," Nick said.

Maggie blinked against the sun a couple times, unable to answer. It would take time to absorb the fact that Nick had given up his chance to sail on Lake Washington to spend his free afternoon with her and two children.

"Cheeseburger it is," Nick decided for her. Taking Victoria's hand, and with Caleb walking at his side, Nick headed in the direction of the food vendors.

While he was away, Maggie got out the drinks, spread the beach towels out along the bench of the picnic table, and prepared for their return. It seemed to take a long time before Caleb came racing back, his face a huge smile.

"Nick got us ice cream *and* cotton candy."

"We had to eat the ice cream first because it was melting," Victoria added, as she joined Caleb. She carried the drink container, being careful to keep a good hold on the carton.

Nick had the burgers, hot dogs, fries, chips, huge pickles, cookies, and cotton candy. From what Maggie could see, he'd bought out the store.

Caleb and Victoria climbed onto the picnic table bench, and Maggie opened up their hamburgers and sliced them in half, wondering if their small stomachs would be able to hold all this food.

Caleb's mouth was full as he scarfed down a hot dog. "This is the best day of my life," he said, before he swallowed.

Maggie didn't want to ruin it by reminding him of his manners.

"My life, too," Victoria agreed. "I've never been on a water slide before, and had both cotton candy and ice cream in the same day."

After lunch the children wanted to take a few rides. Maggie was afraid with full stomachs it might be too much, but they insisted they were fine.

"I'll keep a close eye on them," Nick promised.

After the Ferris wheel and several other rides geared toward their size and age, they wanted to go back into the water. By five o'clock, both children were dragging, their energy spent.

When Maggie suggested it was time to leave, they both protested. "Not yet."

"Please, can we stay a bit longer?"

"I want to go down the water slide again," Victoria pleaded, her eyes huge as she stared hopefully up at Maggie.

She couldn't refuse them. "Then rest for a few minutes first."

As she suspected, they were both asleep within seconds. Maggie sat at their side, her arms wrapped around her bent knees.

Nick stretched out next to her, leaning back on his elbows and crossing his ankles.

"You checked up on me with Joan, didn't you?" she asked, knowing full well he must have. While she shouldn't be pleased, he'd been wonderful with the two children. One afternoon and they viewed Nick as their hero. She had to admit the purchased food was a lot more appetizing than the lunch she'd packed. Besides his generosity in buying all the treats, Nick had been patient with the kids, laughing and teasing with them. He carried Victoria around on his shoulders and took her into the deeper part of the water, swimming with her on his back and then doing the same with Caleb. He even went down the big water slide, holding on to Caleb as the two flew into the water, landing several feet away from the end of the slide.

"Are you upset with me?" Nick asked Maggie.

She threw a question back at him. "Should I be?"

He hesitated before answering. "Probably. All I heard when we spoke was that you had plans with someone named Caleb. It knocked me off-balance. I wasn't expecting Caleb to be a second-grader."

"So you checked with your mother to see if I was dating some guy named Caleb."

Nick chuckled softly. "I did, and Mom laughed at me and told me I was jealous of a seven-year-old."

"You were jealous then?"

He exhaled and shrugged. "I didn't do a good job of hiding my feelings, did I?"

"Not really."

"I know we got started off on the wrong foot, Maggie,

and then I took another misstep. I like you, and every time I take one step forward, I take two back."

Maggie couldn't deny the truth of that and wasn't about to disagree with him.

"When Mom told me you'd taken Caleb and Victoria to Wild Waves I knew I had to come. I was here a full hour before I found you."

"That long?"

"Don't suppose you've noticed there are about five hundred people here today, did you?"

It was a packed park.

"I needed you to know spending the afternoon with you and the kids was far more appealing than sailing by myself."

Maggie couldn't hide how pleased she was. "You should know you're Caleb and Victoria's hero."

"More important, am I yours?" His gaze held hers.

Maggie couldn't keep a smile hidden had she tried. "That remains to be seen, Nick Sample."

Chapter 26

All the talk about sons from the last grief therapy session had stayed in Joan's mind for a long while, bringing with it doubts, to the point that she felt she had to confront her apprehensions. Her relationships with both Steve and Nick were important, and she wanted to make sure they knew that. She was grateful for the talk she'd had with her older son, as it had helped her understand how her grief had negatively affected them both.

In her conversations with Steve, she'd noticed how he avoided talking about Zoe. Whenever she asked, he quickly changed the subject, letting her know anything having to do with her was off-limits. It used to be that her son could talk to her about most anything. That had changed and worried her.

She feared Steve assumed her hearing bad news would somehow cause her to relapse. Or it could be that he hadn't resolved his feelings about the loss of his father. She could be way off base, but she needed to know and was determined to find out. With these thoughts weighing on her mind, she was uncertain how best to approach the subject.

The house was quiet. Maggie was out and Edison was napping in his crate. That seemed to be the place her puppy loved best. Joan had gotten him a comfortable, fluffy bed that he liked to circle around several times before nestling down for sleepy time.

Gathering her courage, she reached for her phone, hoping Steve was home on a Saturday afternoon.

Steve answered on the second ring. "Hey, Mom, what's up?"

As usual, he sounded busy. He never had been one for lengthy phone conversations.

"Am I catching you at a bad time?" She needed his full attention.

"Now's fine. Is everything okay?"

"It's great."

"Glad to hear it. What's up?"

"I . . . I'm clearing out some of your father's things."

"Good," he said, sounding encouraged. "That's a step in the right direction."

"I gave his clothes to the Salvation Army; they were happy to get them. Your dad had a couple high-end suits." Both boys were taller and more muscular than Jared. "You didn't want anything out of his closet, did you?"

"No thanks." His answer was quick and to the point.

"That's what I thought."

"Are you still playing golf?" she asked, thinking Steve might be interested in Jared's irons.

"On occasion. I work a lot of hours, Mom."

"You need time to relax." Everyone needed to get away from the job now and again.

"If I want to get ahead in this company, that means putting in the sweat equity."

Joan let his words sink in. "There's more to life than work, son."

Her words were met with stilted silence. "I know you mean well, but this is beginning to sound like a lecture, Mom."

"Okay, I won't mention it again." Sooner or later her son would recognize what was most important in life, and it wasn't his job title or how high he rose within the company.

"Good. So . . . what else is going on?" he pressed.

"Like I said, I'm cleaning out your dad's things and wanted to know if there was anything you wanted."

He hesitated and then admitted, "I can't think of a single thing."

"I thought for sure you'd want your dad's golf clubs. You two spent so much time on the golf course. Heaven knows there's a golf course every few blocks in Arizona."

"We did," Steve agreed with a sigh. "I appreciate the offer, Mom, but I don't have time for golf any longer. I work most weekends now. Give the clubs to Nick."

"He doesn't play golf." It was on the tip of her tongue to comment again on the long hours her son put in at the warehouse. She would if she didn't want to continue their current conversation.

"Nick's athletic; he might take it up in the future."

"What about your father's tools?"

"Nick will want those." He sounded impatient now, as if he was eager to get off the phone.

"Isn't there anything of your father's that you'd like to

have?" It hurt how easily Steve dismissed every effort she made to give him something of his father's.

Steve paused as if mulling it over. "Not really."

"Nothing? What about a tie clip or cuff links?"

"Mom," he said and groaned, as if she was far behind the times. "No one wears that stuff any longer."

His refusal to hold on to anything from Jared pained her. "I'd hoped you would have some desire to hold on to his memory."

He must have heard her disappointment because, once again, he hesitated. "I'm sorry, Mom. You're right. I should keep at least one memento of Dad."

She hoped her voice didn't betray the lump in her throat. "I assumed you had a good relationship with him."

"I did," he was quick to tell her. "The thing is, I left home a long time ago. And Dad and I were different. He was a good father and I'm grateful to have had him in my life. I have all those memories, and really that's what's most important."

Steve was right. She, too, had her memories, and like her son, she would treasure those. Then, gathering her courage, she asked, "Can I ask you something, and please, I need your honesty?"

"Of course."

"Have I failed you as a mother?" She closed her eyes, fearing his response, the guilt eating at her.

He seemed to weigh his words as if he was afraid of hurting her feelings. "No way. I always knew I could depend on you. You've been a good mom," he added, as though it was important that she know that. "And Dad was a good father."

"You mean I was a good mother in the past," she added, her words more breath than sound, afraid that in her grief she had abandoned her children.

"You were always there when it mattered most. Nick and I aren't kids any longer. We're adults, and not once did I ever feel you'd failed us. I can't speak for Nick, but I think he'd agree. If anyone failed, it was the two of us. You were so deeply depressed, and we were at a loss on how best to help you. Forgive me for that, Mom. I should have made a bigger effort to come see you, to be there for you."

"It's all worked out for the best," she whispered. "A friend recently reminded me that everything happens in its own time, and I shouldn't question having waited as long as I did to get the help I needed. You don't owe me an apology, Steve."

Steve released a sigh. "I guess it's just the mood I'm in lately."

This was the opening Joan had been waiting for. "What's going on, Steve, and please credit me with some intelligence? For the longest time I've felt there's something troubling you, and my guess is it has to do with Zoe."

"Mom, please. It's nothing. I'm busy. I carry a lot of responsibility and it wears on me. You wouldn't believe how many meetings I attend in a week or problems that arise at the warehouse that I need to fix. The demands on my time are constant."

Joan wasn't willing to listen to excuses. "Why do you change the subject every time I bring up Zoe's name?"

The question fell like a nuclear bomb blast between them.

Complete silence.

"My relationship with Zoe is off-limits," he snapped, after an awkward moment.

Joan had never met his girlfriend. It was rare for Steve to mention his relationships, so when he told her about Zoe, Joan knew she meant a great deal to him.

"I assumed the two of you were serious," she said, ignoring his warning.

"Mom," he said, as if upset that she was venturing into unwelcome territory.

"Why it is that every time I bring up her name, you change the subject?"

"One would think you'd take the hint!"

"Recently you said you two were on and off. What does that mean?"

"Mom," he said and groaned. "Leave it alone."

"I can't, because I want to know what's happening with you. I don't want our relationship to be surface level. I want you to share your thoughts and concerns with me, be open and honest."

"Fine, you want me to be open. You first! What's with you and this landscaper?"

The question came at her out of the blue. "Phil? Nothing. He's in the same grief counseling group I am. I barely know him."

"Are you dating anyone?"

"No." She laughed at the absurdity of even thinking along those lines. "Why would you even ask?" She knew the answer as soon as the words left her mouth. Nick must have mentioned him. "Rest assured, Phil is a friend, nothing more."

Steve scoffed. "Nick said the two of you were out late one night."

Joan found this highly amusing. "Some of us go out for coffee after each session. Phil was there, and so was I. Trust me, there's nothing happening. I only recently learned he's divorced."

"So you're saying he's just a friend."

"Steve," she said slowly to make her point, "I know what you're doing quizzing me about my landscaper. You're diverting the subject away from you and Zoe."

Her son's response was weighed down with a heavy sigh. "If you insist on knowing, Zoe and I have parted ways."

"I'm sorry." This was what Joan had long suspected.

Another sigh, this one clearly pain-filled. "Yeah, me, too."

"I don't suppose you want to tell me what it's about, but I hope you will." Joan didn't want to pry too deep. Her wish was that her son would want to explain what'd happened to a promising relationship.

He didn't hesitate as she assumed he would. "Zoe wants to get married."

Joan didn't understand why that would be a problem if they were in love.

"We've been dating two years exclusively," Steve continued, "and all of a sudden she put pressure on me to make a commitment."

"Do you love her?" Joan asked, although she felt she knew the answer.

"Yeah . . . I do."

As she suspected. "Would you be comfortable spending the rest of your life with her?"

"I would," he said, a bit more convincingly this time.

"Then what's the problem?" It had to be something more than Steve's unwillingness to make a commitment.

His voice mellowed as if he had lowered his guard. "Zoe wants a family."

"And you don't?"

"I do, just not anytime soon. Maybe in the next seven to ten years. I mean, the time has to be right. You don't bring a baby into the world unless you have a home with a fenced yard, and a substantial income, and a secure future. It's the same with getting married."

"You want a house before you marry?" Joan had a hard time computing the list of what Steve felt was necessary.

"Yes."

"My goodness, Steve, if your father and I had all those stipulations in place, you and Nick might never have been born."

"Times were different back then," he flared.

"Really?"

"Yes, Mom, really," he insisted.

"And you feel Zoe is being unreasonable to not want to wait until the solar system is aligned with your list of what's necessary." She didn't mean to sound sarcastic, but if anyone was being unreasonable, Joan felt it was her son.

"Yes," he snapped. "I didn't want to lose her, so I asked her to marry me. I even got her a ring, which was what she wanted. But when I refused to set a date for the wedding, she had a coronary."

"You mean she got upset?"

"She said she wasn't willing to wait for five years,

which is when I feel I'll have everything in place to be the husband I want to be. Condemn me for that if you want. It's the way I think. I'm goal-driven, and having a wife now, or anytime in the near future, doesn't fit into my plans. I'll have the right income by then, perhaps sooner, but even that's no guarantee. I might be named the warehouse manager next year, but that's only the first step in my five-year career plan."

Joan didn't fault Zoe for not wanting to wait that long. If Steve was truly committed, he would marry her.

"She said she didn't believe I'd be ready in five years," he mumbled. "She made it seem like I was leading her on, and that my list of reasons to wait was only an excuse to keep her hanging."

"So it sounds like she gave you an ultimatum?"

"She said if I couldn't agree to a wedding within a year, we were finished."

"You didn't believe her?"

"I . . . didn't appreciate the pressure, and I felt she was being unfair about my goals."

Joan could appreciate how stubborn her son could be when given an ultimatum. "What happened?"

"When I told her I wouldn't be ready in a year, she gave me back the ring." It seemed, even now, he had a hard time believing she would walk away.

The shock of it rang in his voice. Shock, disappointment, pain.

"I'm sorry, Steve."

"Yeah, well, she's apparently moved on. I saw a post on Facebook with her and some other guy."

"I bet that stung."

He snickered. "It sure didn't take her long to find someone else."

"Sounds to me like she made her point," Joan murmured.

"The thing is, if she came back to me today and said she'd changed her mind, I'd laugh and tell her she's too late."

"Oh Steve, that's both stubborn and foolish. We both know that's your pride talking."

"Yeah," he reluctantly agreed. "I miss her. She made everything better. Zoe was the best friend I've ever had. I . . . feel empty without her. There wasn't anything I couldn't tell her. She's smart, and savvy, beautiful, and wise. Nothing feels right without her."

That sounded like love to Joan. "Then tell her how you feel."

"I can't; she won't listen."

"Don't be so sure. You two were together a long time, son. She's got to be missing you, too. You need to think about what your life will be like without her. Why does marriage terrify you?"

"I . . . don't know," he confessed, sadness leaking into his voice.

"Could it have anything to do with losing your dad?" Joan asked, hoping it wasn't so.

"I don't see how it could."

"Give it some thought."

"Thanks for pressing me about the issue with Zoe, Mom. I feel better having talked to you. I'll think about what you said and let you know what I decide."

"Good. I'm here for you anytime you want to talk, Steve."

"I know."

"Let's connect again soon. Okay?"

"Sure thing." They were about to end the conversation when the door opened and Maggie came inside, following her shift at Starbucks.

Joan and Steve said their good-byes, and Joan turned her attention to her boarder. "Hope you had a good day."

"It was long. Our oven broke down and it's going to be a week before we can get it repaired. Customers weren't happy."

Joan had to smile. The horror of having to do without egg bites was too much to bear.

Maggie's phone chirped and she groaned as she answered. Her eyes immediately grew large as all color drained from her face.

"What is it?" Joan asked as soon as Maggie disconnected.

"That was the hospital. Dad collapsed at the Half Pint and was taken in by ambulance."

Chapter 27

Maggie rushed into Swedish Hospital, where the ambulance had taken her father, and went straight to the counter. "I'm Maggie Herbert. My father was brought into the ER. Can I see him, please?"

The receptionist told Maggie she'd need to step over to the window marked SECURITY. When asked by the guard, she provided her identification, and was given a name tag and buzzed into the ER. A nurse directed her to the room where her father lay on a gurney.

"Dad," she cried, as she hurried to his side.

"Maggie." He half-raised himself up on his elbow, extending his arm to reach for her. When he grabbed hold of her hand, his punishing grip was so hard she nearly yelped in pain.

"I'm here," she said, stating the obvious. "What happened?"

Her father shook his head. "Don't know. I wasn't feeling well, haven't been for some time now. I was at the Half Pint, and Al was chattering away how he does. The man never shuts up. The next thing I knew some guy was leaning over me, and I was lying flat on the floor with Al looking to the heavens and praying out loud asking God to spare me. Guess he thought I was dying. The paramedic from the fire station said I'd passed out."

"Oh Dad, you've got to take better care of yourself." This was exactly what Maggie had feared. His drinking had finally caught up with him. None of her pleading had helped, nor had her moving away.

"Maggie," he whispered. His eyes were full of desperation. "You've got to get me out of here."

She gave his hand a reassuring squeeze. "Not yet, we need to find out what's wrong first."

He adamantly shook his head, his eyes pleading with her. "Get me out of this place. People die in here."

Despite herself, Maggie grinned. "Let's talk to the doctor first."

"They're going to kill me. Mark my words, Maggie, they keep me, and I'll be dead in a week." His fear was palpable. He sincerely believed all hope would be lost if the hospital decided he needed additional care and didn't release him right away.

The doctor stepped into the room, a chart in his hand. His gaze was on the paperwork. Her father's hold on Maggie's hand tightened even more. She stayed close to the side of the gurney, letting him know she wasn't leaving him alone.

The physician's name tag identified him as Dr. Lael. When he looked up, his gaze went from Roy to Maggie and then returned to her father.

"Mr. Herbert, I'm Dr. Lael."

Maggie's father glared at the physician. "I can read,

you know. That badge has your name on it. Lael. Funny name. Who are your people, anyway? Undertakers?"

"Dad," Maggie protested. She looked apologetically at the doctor and added, "You'll have to forgive my father; he's suspicious of hospitals. I'm Maggie Herbert, his daughter."

Dr. Lael grinned, clearly amused. "Sorry to disappoint you, Mr. Herbert, but there isn't a single undertaker in the family."

Roy Herbert made a scoffing sound, as if he didn't believe him for a moment.

The physician glanced down at the chart and addressed Maggie. "The blood tests we took show that your father is suffering from liver disease."

Maggie had suspected that was likely the problem. Her father's diet consisted mostly of beer, and it'd been that way for years. Dr. Lael went on to give her the medical information that pointed to his conclusion. One look at her father's jaundiced eyes had already raised her suspicions. Even his complexion looked yellow, and she'd noticed several bruises on his arms as well.

"Mr. Herbert," Dr. Lael addressed her father, his expression serious, "you're going to need to lay off the alcohol."

Her father reacted with a snort. "Barely touch the stuff."

"Dad," Maggie protested. "You drink every day. You were at a tavern when you passed out."

"I drink beer. Hardly ever sample the hard stuff."

"Dad," she said, as gently as she could. "Beer, in excess, can be just as damaging as hard alcohol."

What color remained on Roy's face quickly disappeared. "I have to give up beer?"

"Yes, Dad, if you want to live, you're going to need to abstain from all alcohol."

Roy looked deep in thought and then shook his head. When he spoke, his voice was emphatic. "I'd rather be dead."

"Dad!" Maggie's shoulders slumped with defeat.

"Got nothing else to live for," her father said. "Your mother's dead, and you've left me. The only friend I've got is Al and he's a jabbering fool. My one pleasure in life is beer and *Wheel of Fortune*."

"You enjoy *Jeopardy!*" Maggie knew those were the two television programs her father continually watched.

"Right!" he declared. "Except I don't come up with the answers as fast as I once did."

"I'm releasing your father," Dr. Lael said, as he wrote out the prescription and handed it to Maggie. "See to it that he takes this every day. It will help some. If he continues drinking, his disease will likely advance to cirrhosis of the liver."

Maggie felt a lump growing in her throat. "I'll do my best."

She waited with her father while the hospital prepared his release paperwork.

"This mean I can go home?"

"Yes, but you need to remember what Dr. Lael said. You've got to wean yourself off beer, but Dad, you're going to need help."

"I'll be fine, don't you worry none. Just fine."

"No, you won't," she insisted. "I'm going to search for clinics where you can get the help you need. You've got to stop drinking."

Roy crossed his arms as if he'd had his final say on the subject. Maggie fought down the frustration. She couldn't force him to stop drinking any more than she could get him the help he'd need to get and stay sober.

Roy Herbert was a stubborn cuss. Always had been and likely always would be, and there was little she could do to change him.

The nurse helped her father off the gurney and into a wheelchair. She handed Maggie the release papers and the prescription Dr. Lael had written out. He'd also included the names of several rehabilitation clinics in the Seattle area. It went without question that these places would be far and away from what Maggie or Roy could afford. But first she had to get her father to agree that he needed help.

As they moved into the waiting room outside the ER, Al stood with his ragged-edged baseball cap in his hand.

"Al," Maggie said, recognizing him.

"I got here as fast as I could. Was here when you arrived, but you didn't see me and then they let you in right away. I tried, but they said I couldn't go in unless I was family."

"You could've lied," her father grumbled. "If you'd been thinking, you'd have said you were my brother."

"I'm Black, Roy," Al reminded him.

"Oh yeah, right," Roy said.

The exchange amused Maggie when little else had since entering this hospital. "I'm taking Dad home. Would you like a ride, Al?"

"If it's not too much trouble, I'd appreciate it." He set the cap atop his head and followed them outside.

"It's no trouble. Would you mind staying with Dad while I get his prescription filled?"

"Be happy to."

"He'll talk my ear off," her father grumbled. "I could be dying, and I don't want the last thing I hear to be Al talking about his time working for the railroad."

"You're dying, Dad, but it won't be today, so you should be appreciative that you have a friend as good as Al."

"She's right," Al said with a hard nod. "Listen to your daughter."

Maggie had one more request of her father's only friend. "And while I'm gone, make sure he doesn't have any beer."

Her father huffed like there was no way Al would be able to stop him.

"Dad, I'm warning you . . ."

"Or you'll what?" he flared. "Move out and leave me to my own devices? You already have, and good riddance."

"He don't mean that," Al said under his breath. "He misses you something fierce. Tells me every day he's sorry you're gone."

"Don't tell me what I mean and don't mean," Roy snapped, glaring at Al.

Maggie left Al with her father while she collected her car. She brought it around to the area where she could pick him up. She climbed out and opened the passenger door while her father continued to grumble. Because he was light-headed, she wrapped her arm around his waist, supporting him as best she could. He didn't protest, which told her he was worse off than she'd realized. This diagnosis was serious. Either her father changed his drinking habits or he would soon fall victim to his disease. If he continued on this path, he would be signing his death warrant. It was true, Maggie and her father had their share of differences over the years, but he was her father, her only living relative.

"I'm not an invalid," he complained, "no matter what that doctor said. I can manage to get inside a car without the two of you fussing over me. A man can't breathe with the likes of you crowding around me."

Maggie left him to close his own door. He nearly slid off the seat and onto the pavement with the effort. Al made himself comfortable in the backseat. The Seattle traffic didn't make the commute any easier. Nearly thirty minutes later Maggie pulled up in front of the family home and breathed a relieved sigh. Her father complained the entire way, insisting she'd purposely taken the wrong route. Maggie didn't argue but rolled her eyes, aware that if she had followed his advice, it would have taken a full hour before they'd arrived home.

Knowing better than to help him out of the car, Maggie waited until he was out before she wrapped her arm around his elbow and led her father into the house. When Roy sank into his recliner, he exhaled loudly, as if this was his rightful place and everyone could leave now. He apparently wanted them to think he'd be perfectly fine without either of them.

Al claimed a seat on the sofa.

"I'll be back as soon as I can," she told her father's friend.

"Where you going?" Roy demanded.

"To pick up your prescription. I won't be long."

"Don't come back without a Whopper," he shouted after her, as Maggie headed toward her car.

When she arrived at the pharmacy, she had to wait to give the prescription to the woman behind the counter.

"Can you tell me how much this will cost?" she asked, almost afraid to find out.

"I'll need to ask the pharmacist."

"That's okay, I can wait."

The woman left and returned a few moments later and mentioned an amount that caused Maggie to blanch.

"Is there a generic option for this drug?" The generic pill was bound to be cheaper.

"This is the generic price."

"Oh," she said, and swallowed tightly.

"Do you still want it filled?"

Given no other option, Maggie nodded. "Please."

"It will take a few minutes. You're welcome to sit in the waiting area to the right."

With her heart heavy, Maggie slumped into a chair, closed her eyes, and prayed. As hard as it was to admit, her father needed her. He would never be able to give up drinking without her there to encourage him. As much as she hated the thought of moving back in with him, it seemed the only viable option. One thing her father needed to understand was that once he was fully sober, he had to stay away from alcohol. If he was determined to drink, there was nothing more she could do; she had no intention of sticking around and watching him die a slow, painful death because he was too stubborn to admit he had a problem.

With her mind set, she waited until her name was called. She paid for the prescription and headed home. As she parked in front of the house, she couldn't remember any aspect of the drive, as she was distracted by the consequences of her father's illness.

When she entered the house, the first thing she noticed was her father sitting in front of the television with a beer in his hand.

"Al," she cried. "You were supposed to make sure Dad didn't drink."

Al raised both arms in defeat. "I couldn't stop him."

Her father's look was stubborn. "Told you earlier, I'm not giving up beer."

"Yes, you are." Maggie said, so angry tears filled her eyes. "I just forked over nearly seven hundred dollars for this prescription. That was my entire paycheck and now I have nothing. I worked hard for that money, and I refuse to let you waste it."

"How much?" His eyes revealed his shock.

"You heard me the first time."

His face crumpled and tears filled his eyes. "Why would you do that?"

"Why?" she cried. "Because you're my father."

He blinked several times and seemed to close in on himself. "I . . . I don't know that I can give it up."

"You can; you have to. There are places and people who can help you. If you promise to do your best, I'll try to get you into a rehab center. You can't do this on your own, Dad; you're going to need help. I'll do everything I can to help you, too."

"I'm not an alcoholic," her father insisted.

Maggie shook her head. "Deny it all you want, but your liver says otherwise."

He lowered his gaze to the beer can he was holding. "I . . . I can't, Maggie, especially without your mother and now you . . ."

He didn't finish what he was going to say. He didn't need to; Maggie already knew. "I'll move back home," she said, knowing that was the only thing she could offer that would convince him to give up drinking.

His head shot up. "You will?"

More than anything, Maggie hated the thought of leaving Joan, but she couldn't see any other option.

A tear leaked down his cheek. "If you do that . . . move back, I mean, then . . . then I'll consider it."

"I'll help, too," Al claimed.

"How you going to help me?" Roy demanded.

Al stood up from the sofa, removed his tattered ball-cap, and spoke as if stating a solemn vow. "I promise I won't drink in front of you."

Her father snorted. "A lot of good that'll do."

"Dad," Maggie said, chastising him. "Al is your friend, and if I understood you right, you told me he's your only friend."

"I never said that," her father lied.

Maggie looked to Al and whispered, "Yeah, he did."

Roy shook his head. "And I haven't decided if giving up my one joy in life is worth you moving home. You're too much like your mother."

"I consider that a compliment."

"You should," he snapped back, mulling over the decision.

Al grinned, and Maggie noticed he had a gold tooth in

front. "Thank you for being a friend to my dad. He's going to need one if he keeps to his promise."

"Cry me a river," her father barked. "Both of you leave me be. I need to think this through." Al started out the front door, but Roy stopped Maggie. "You serious about moving back home?"

"If you agree to go into rehab. After your body has adjusted to going without, if I smell or see you with a beer or any other alcoholic beverage, I'm gone."

He heaved a sigh, signifying this was a weighty decision.

"And if I'm paying for your prescription, I won't be paying you rent."

He looked her in the eyes then and nodded, indicating that was understood. "Okay, it's a deal. When you plan on moving back?"

"Soon, Dad."

"Good, and when you return, bring me a Whopper. Now get, the both of you. I'm a sick man and I need my rest."

Chapter 28

Joan was too upset to think clearly.

Maggie had returned from the hospital, and even before Joan could ask what had happened, Maggie started up the stairs.

"My dad is sick and needs me. I hate this, but I can't desert him now. I need to move back home."

Joan followed her, attempting to make sense of what had just happened. "This is rather sudden. Have you thought this through?"

"It isn't what I want, Joan. I love living here with you, but I can't ignore my father when he needs me." Maggie tugged the suitcase from beneath her bed and started opening and closing drawers as she pulled her clothes out to place inside the one piece of luggage. "He has to stop drinking or it's going to kill him. I enabled him for far too long. I knew when I gave him money he would spend it on alcohol. I should have stood my ground. I've got to find somewhere for him to detox; he'll never be able to do it on his own."

"Oh Maggie, you can't blame yourself."

"I don't. Dad is the one who chose to drink, not me. I know him well enough to realize if he'll ever find the way to recovery, he'll need my support and encouragement." Rehab would help and AA, too, but she was his only child, and he would need her at his side as much as possible.

"Aren't you putting his problem on your shoulders?" Joan asked.

The tears ran unrestrained down Maggie's cheeks. "This isn't forever, Joan. I'll set boundaries with him so that he understands and make sure he accepts the consequences. I'll be there to watch his diet, too.

"Believe me when I say I hate to leave you, I really do. Living with you has been life-changing for me. I can't thank you enough for everything you've done."

Edison stood in the doorway and barked as if he, too, was distressed.

Maggie picked up the puppy and kissed the top of his head. "I'm going to miss you both so much."

Joan felt like weeping herself. Maggie had changed her entire world. She couldn't imagine the young woman returning to the ramshackle house and her alcoholic father. While Maggie felt she had to move, Joan feared it would all be for naught. Having her move back was exactly what Roy wanted, and he'd use every means available to make sure she stayed there. Her heart hurt just thinking about Roy's coercion tactics.

Maggie wiped the moisture from her face. "I . . . I told him I'd move back home to help him, but if he drinks again I'll leave."

"Maggie, don't you see he's manipulating you? Your

father would say anything to convince you to come back."
All Joan knew of Roy Herbert she'd learned from Maggie
and their one meeting.

Maggie paused in her packing. "Moving home wasn't
his suggestion, Joan, it was mine."

"Yours?"

"My relationship with Dad hasn't been the best since
Mom died. My leaving was a good thing, and now we
have the opportunity to make it something better."

Joan wanted to believe Roy Herbert had come to appreciate his daughter since her move and missed her. This
seemed far too convenient for him to have this epiphany
when he needed Maggie to care for him. It may have been
selfish thinking on her part, but Joan didn't trust the man.

"Dad's going to need an expensive medication, and I'll
need to be the one to make sure he takes it properly."

"Is it rent money you're worried about?" Joan asked.
She would happily let Maggie live with her for free.

"Not at all," Maggie assured her, as she continued collecting her things.

"What about Medicaid? You mentioned once that
your father's on disability. He should qualify."

"I'll apply, but knowing the government, it will take a
couple months for any financial help to kick in, perhaps
even longer." With her head down, Maggie stepped
toward her closet.

"You can't live in that house, Maggie. I saw the condition it was in."

"I know," she said with a sigh. "I admit, it's awful, but
what other choice do I have?"

"Surely there's some other way?"

"I wish there was."

She turned to face Joan, a handful of shirts and dresses draped over her forearm. "I called Nick on the way here and . . . he doesn't understand; he said I was being foolish."

"Are you?" Joan's thoughts mirrored her son's.

"He's my father," Maggie reiterated. "I'm the only person he's got."

"He doesn't deserve you." Joan probably shouldn't have said that. The words escaped before she could censor them.

"Maybe . . . a couple of months ago I would have agreed with you. But like I said before, things have started to change between Dad and me. I don't want to lose that. For the first time since my mother passed, I feel like I'm seeing a glimpse of his heart. For the first time I have hope for a real father-daughter relationship."

"Oh Maggie." The lump in Joan's throat was growing thicker by the moment. The young woman didn't seem to realize that Joan needed her, too.

The front door opened. "Maggie?"

It was Nick.

"Up here," Joan told him.

He climbed the stairs in record time. "You can't go through with this," he declared, barging into the bedroom.

"Nick, please," Maggie said with a groan, "leaving your mom is hard enough; don't make it even more difficult."

They stood facing each other, as if neither one knew what to say next. Fresh tears clouded Maggie's eyes before she tossed the clothes onto the bed. With abandon, the young woman flew into Nick's arms, hugging him close, her soft cries muffled as she buried her face in his chest.

Nick held her close, knotting his fists at the small of her back. "I can't let you do this."

"You think I want to leave?"

"Your dad doesn't care what this move will cost you. You belong here. Can't you see what he's doing? He brought this on himself; he should be the one paying the consequences, not you."

Joan knew the two of them had been seeing each other, and it had seemed they were getting along well. The emotion they shared now told her their relationship had grown much closer than she'd realized.

"You don't need to leave here to help your dad," Nick insisted. "You know the kind of man he is. He'll take advantage of you every chance he gets. You need to give yourself space. Don't make a rash decision you'll later regret."

"No." Maggie shook her head. "I know what I'm doing. My mind is already made up. I need to do this, Nick. Please try to understand."

Nick raised his head and put space between them. "You're not thinking straight. You're reacting emotionally. I'm not going to let your father use you like this."

"Use me like—"

Nick immediately cut her off. "You know he's using you, and I can't let this happen."

"You can't let this happen?" Maggie flared, her eyes widening. "You have no say in my life, Nick Sample. I don't know what makes you think—"

"I care about you," he shot back. Anger flashed in his eyes and then softened as he added, "A lot."

Maggie opened and closed her mouth as if she had more to say and then changed her mind. "I care for you, too. I'm sorry." She glanced toward Joan then. "I have to do this, to give Dad a chance to change his life. He needs me. I know my father, and he's going to require a lot of emotional help if he's going to kick this addiction."

"What about Alcoholics Anonymous?" Joan asked, disliking the fact that Maggie was tackling this task on her own.

"I've already looked up meetings in the area. He'll definitely need those once he's released from rehab."

"Has your father agreed to go into a rehab center?" Joan asked.

"Either he goes or I move back here. That is, if you'd take me." She paused, as if she hadn't considered that she might not be welcome.

"You're welcome to come back anytime," Joan assured her. Like Nick, the last thing Joan wanted was for Maggie to return to her father's house. The atmosphere and the building itself were toxic.

"The decision is up to my father. He understands the consequences if he starts up again. I made it clear, either he gets the help he needs and stops drinking or I'm gone."

"Manipulation doesn't work, Maggie," Joan gently reminded her.

"I don't believe I'm doing that. As far as I'm concerned, this is his one and only chance."

As if to emphasize her point, Edison barked.

"I still don't like it." Nick made sure his feelings were known.

"Luckily, it isn't up to you," Maggie reminded him.

Nick looked pleadingly toward Joan. "Mom, say something."

As hard as it was to let Maggie go, Joan felt she had no choice. With emotion tightening her throat, she offered her son a watery smile and addressed Maggie. "Let me help you carry what you've packed to your car."

"You don't need to do that," Maggie said.

"No, she doesn't," Nick said flatly. His fists were clenched at his sides. "You're making a huge mistake, Maggie, a huge mistake."

"Maybe so, but it's mine to make."

Nick remained dissatisfied. "We both know your father hasn't got it in him to stop drinking. He's weak."

Hands akimbo, Maggie glared at Nick. "You've never met my father."

"I . . ."

"How quick you are to judge him. He might be everything you claim, but you know what, he's my father, and I refuse to abandon him."

Nick stuffed his hands into his pockets, and took a step back, as if emotionally distancing himself from Maggie. "I can't stand by and watch you do this. I . . . I won't be able to see you give your life to someone who has done nothing to deserve it. Your father is an alcoholic. He'll drink because he won't be able to stop himself, despite all your efforts. I care too much about you to see that happen and remain silent."

For a long moment Maggie froze, as if she needed time to assimilate Nick's words. She swallowed hard, and with tears shining in her eyes, she slowly nodded. "I care for you, too, and I think we had something good happening between us, but I can't turn my back on my only family, no matter what you think or say."

"And I can't stand by and watch someone use you. I can't do it, Maggie. I just can't."

She frowned, as if she had trouble understanding what he was saying. "What does that mean?"

"It means if you decide to move back in with your father, we're through."

Joan wanted to groan, knowing Nick spoke impulsively and would soon regret those words.

Maggie blinked several times, squared her shoulders, and slowly nodded. "You have to do what you feel is best, Nick. I . . . understand. I guess this is good-bye, then."

"It is. Good-bye, Maggie," he muttered, and left the room as if escaping a burning building.

Joan followed her son down the stairs. "Nick, stop . . ."

"Not now, Mom," he called over his shoulder as he barreled out the front door.

Before Joan could stop him, her son was gone. She heard the truck's engine rev loudly as he drove away.

No more than ten minutes later, Maggie started loading up her car. When she finished, she returned to the house where Joan stood waiting.

"I don't have the words to thank you for all you've done for me," Maggie whispered, her voice cracking with emotion.

Joan hugged her close. "I wanted to say the same thing. You're welcome back anytime; just say the word and I'll come get you if needed."

Before she drove off, Maggie picked up Edison. "Gonna miss you, little one."

"Please say you'll stop by and visit often," Joan urged. It was important that Maggie understand how deeply Joan had come to care for her.

Tears brimmed in Maggie's eyes as she nodded and hugged Joan once more. "I will; I promise."

After Maggie left, the house felt empty and silent.

The pie she'd baked that afternoon sat forlornly on top of the stove. Joan had no desire to try a slice. Freezing it seemed the best option.

Her hands trembled as she struggled to wrap the pie in foil. Losing her temper, she tossed the box onto the countertop and covered her face with both hands.

She'd only started to compose herself when her phone rang. Caller ID told her it was Mary Lou.

"Hello," she said, doing her best to keep her voice even.

"Joan? You okay?"

"Mostly yes, why do you ask?" As frustrated, empty, and miserable as she felt, she didn't want to go into details. The sooner she got off the phone, the better it would be. She didn't want to drag Mary Lou into her troubles.

"You weren't at group this evening."

Looking toward the clock, Joan noticed the time and was shocked. With daylight savings time, it didn't get dark until nearly nine. "It . . . slipped my mind." She pressed her hand to her forehead. She'd been looking forward to this week's session. Every group discussion had helped her see some aspect of her life in a new light. She'd come to appreciate each member. That she had forgotten the meeting entirely was evidence that she was more upset than she realized.

"It is Wednesday, isn't it?"

Mary Lou chuckled. "Last time I looked."

"I'm sorry I missed . . . I'll be there next week for sure."

"Everyone asked about you."

Hearing that should have warmed her heart. Instead, it upset her even more. She could really have used this meeting and the friends she'd made there to help her deal with Maggie moving away.

"It's nice to be missed." Somehow she managed to get out the words.

A short silence followed, as if Mary Lou wasn't sure whether she should speak or not. "You said the meeting slipped your mind?"

"It did . . ." She wasn't able to say anything more for the lump in her throat.

Again, a short hesitation. "Okay, girlfriend, what's going on?"

When Joan talked to her sister, she'd been able to keep her feelings under control. With her friend, it was the exact opposite. She felt the emotion building up inside her until it was all she could do to keep from sobbing.

"I'm sorry," she blurted out, the words crowding into each other. "It's Maggie . . . She's moved back home to help her father. I'm sorry, Mary Lou, I really can't talk . . . about it right now." She disconnected. She hadn't meant to hang up on her. Continuing the conversation, however, was more than she could handle.

Slumping into the kitchen chair, Joan tried to tell herself she was being selfish, wanting Maggie all to herself. She reached for a tissue, reminding herself she was a strong woman. This was only a small blip in the course of her life. It wasn't like she wouldn't ever see Maggie again.

As for Maggie and Nick, eventually they'd work things out.

The doorbell rang, and inwardly Joan groaned. She wasn't up to having the neighborhood kids visit Edison.

If she'd been thinking clearly, Joan would have realized it was too late on a school night for any of the children to stop by.

Instead, when she opened the door, Phil stood on the other side. Joan's eyes widened with surprise.

"You weren't at group tonight. Is everything okay?"

Unable to speak, tears filled her eyes and she slowly shook her head.

Phil gave her a knowing look. "That's what I thought. Come on, I'll make you a cup of tea and you can tell me what's upset you."

Chapter 29

It took Maggie a full week to find space in a rehab center for her father. It was hellish as her father had stopped drinking, which was exactly what she wanted. However, he was terribly sick and suffered from withdrawal. She'd begged and pleaded, claiming how desperately her father needed help, but there was no space available for those first torturous days.

She missed Nick and Joan something terrible. She'd hoped once Nick got over his anger, he'd regret breaking up with her. Apparently not, as she hadn't heard a word from him. A dozen times a day she had to stop herself from texting him. She might have given in if her father hadn't required nearly constant attention.

Once Roy Herbert decided to get sober, he gave it his best, weaning himself off all alcohol. She spent countless hours on the phone searching for a rehab center. When she was able to locate one, she learned they charged astronomical fees, far more than what either Roy or Maggie could possibly pay.

"I don't know what to do." Completely overwhelmed, Maggie wept over the phone to Joan. She stood on the lawn, or what was left of it, in front of the house as she replayed the information she'd been given.

Joan had been the lifeline Maggie had desperately needed. They spoke every day, often more than once, and Joan had stopped by the house to relieve Maggie when she was scheduled to work.

"What did the bank say about getting a loan?" Joan asked.

With the cost of the rehab facility, the only way Maggie could make it happen was to mortgage the house. Joan had been the one to make the suggestion. With the value of homes in the Seattle area escalating, it was the only viable option. Maggie had sat with a loan officer earlier that day.

"As I'd hoped, the title to the house is free and clear. That's a blessing, but I'm afraid that once the bank sees the condition of the house, they won't even consider the possibility."

When she wasn't caring for her father, Maggie had spent every minute doing what she could to make the house livable again. She'd scrubbed and cleaned as best she could. After three trips to the garbage recycling center, the house's interior was in the best shape it'd been in since before her mother's passing. That, however, wasn't nearly enough. Not with a leaking roof and a badly needed paint job, front steps that were crumbling, and a multitude of other problems.

"Things have a way of righting themselves," Joan told her. "Don't lose faith just yet."

"I'll try not to." But it was hard. Her father was sober,

and that was a step in the right direction. Maggie would be risking everything if he lost his sobriety. She wasn't entirely sure he understood the full ramifications of what getting this loan would mean.

"Have you heard from Nick?" Joan asked.

Maggie swallowed down her disappointment. With everything in her, she desperately hoped he'd have a change of heart. Clearly, he'd meant what he said, and they were finished. Although she tried to put him out of her mind, it was impossible. She'd given up hope of hearing from him and wondered how the trivia team was doing without her. That he could so lightly dismiss her from his life told her everything. Her heart was broken, but she had more problems than an ill-fated romance to occupy her mind. Nick was avoiding her. No longer did he frequent Starbucks. It was as if he'd completely wiped her from his life. That he could walk away so easily proved he hadn't felt nearly as strongly for her as she did for him.

"Maggie?" Joan asked, breaking into her musings.

"No, nothing," she answered, trying hard to hide the hurt. "Have you?" Maggie had resisted asking Joan, not wanting to draw her friend into the middle of her and Nick's disagreement.

"Not a peep," Joan said, her words heavy with sadness. "I'd thought one of us would have heard before now. Don't lose faith. My son can be stubborn as a mule, if you'll excuse the cliché. I believe in time he'll come around. He cares about you."

Maggie wanted to believe that, too, but she had serious doubts.

"How's your dad today?" Joan asked, changing the subject away from Nick.

"Better, I think. He's miserable and cranky." Her father cursed until he lost his wind and could barely breathe to lambaste her, the world in general, and all creation.

To his credit, even with the cravings and physical discomfort, Roy had remained determined to stay sober. Maggie could only pray that same resolve would carry him through each day for the rest of his life. She could handle his mood swings knowing that was the release he needed from his discomfort. Twice in the last week, he'd taken her hand, looked at her with tears in his eyes, and whispered, "Thank you." Both times, Maggie had to battle back her own tears.

Keeping his word, Roy had attended an AA meeting every day, even when he insisted they were no help. He still wanted to drink. Nevertheless, he'd gotten a sponsor who had fifteen years' sobriety. Maggie had met Lyle and liked him. Like her father, Lyle had been addicted and had nearly lost his family. Lyle was an encourager and had done his best to help steer Maggie to the rehab center that had been life-changing for him. He'd even called the facility himself to help smooth the way.

"I need to go." Maggie was reluctant to end their conversation. Even with helping her father as best she could, she still needed her job. The Starbucks manager had given her every shift she'd asked for and had been understanding. Maggie was grateful.

"Do you need me to stay with your dad?" Joan asked. She'd come twice in the last week, giving Maggie a badly needed break, helping with Roy, cooking, and encouraging Maggie. Joan wasn't someone who would put up with Roy's attitude and had put him in his place, reminding him of the sacrifices Maggie had made on his behalf.

"Al's already here." Maggie told her. "He's been a trouper and he's kept his word. He doesn't drink in front of Dad, and although he hasn't told me, I have a suspicion he's attended a couple of AA meetings with him, too."

"Good for him. Your father needs his friends now more than ever. I might stop by anyway to check on things, if you don't mind."

"Of course not. You're welcome anytime."

After disconnecting the call, Maggie returned to the house, where Al sat with her father. As she came through the door, she overheard the two men talking and caught the last of their conversation.

"Maggie's getting a loan on the house to pay for that fancy place she feels I need. Every time I feel the urge to drink, I realize if I do, I take the chance of losing her and my home, too. I've lost too much already."

Sober a week and already Roy was more of a father than she could remember from her entire childhood. She wanted to believe he was sincere, and that with the help of AA he would find the wherewithal to turn his life around.

"What are you doing?" he demanded, along with a few snide comments about people who listened in on conversations.

Maggie ignored him and collected what she needed for work. Her father might be sober, but he was no Mr. Rogers.

"I'm getting ready for work," she answered. She kissed him on the cheek, smiled appreciation at Al, and headed out the door.

———

Phil's father glanced up from the book he was reading. He sat in his recliner, his feet crossed at the ankles, looking far more relaxed than Phil felt.

"Something on your mind, son?" he asked.

Phil ceased his pacing. "No, why?"

Setting the novel aside, his dad carefully studied him. "You've been fussing about the house ever since you returned from the dentist. Dr. Shaffer give you news of a root canal?"

Phil grinned. "No, all is well with my molars."

His father knew him and recognized the signs of Phil's restlessness. He might as well spew what was on his mind. "I was at Joan's property today."

"Joan? Oh, right, she's that must-love-flowers gal you mentioned a time or two."

"Right. She wants to help Maggie and her father and intends to drive over there on her own."

His dad nodded as if he knew exactly who Phil was referring to. Phil was certain he'd never mentioned the details of Maggie's ordeal with her father.

"I'm not sure what Joan has in mind, and frankly, I don't like the idea of her heading over to the Herberts' house by herself." Plus, he had an inkling this wasn't the first time Joan had gone out of her way to help Maggie with the girl's father.

His dad cocked his head to one side and frowned. "Seems like a simple solution to me. Go with her."

He'd stepped in between Maggie and her father once before. That was true, but things were different now, with Roy fighting for sobriety. Phil had no idea what the other man's mood was, and was worried Joan could be walking into a hornet's nest.

Phil had concerns. "What about—"

Before Phil could explain, his father cut him off. "Don't worry about dinner; it'll keep. Go help your friend and put your mind at rest. You jumping up and down every few minutes is starting to bug me."

It didn't take long for Phil to acknowledge his father was right. He grabbed his truck keys and headed toward the door. "I don't know what time I'll be back."

His father shook his head. "Just go."

"All right, all right." Smiling to himself, Phil left the house.

Less than ten minutes later he parked in front of Joan's house and was grateful to see her in the front yard, planting peonies. He relaxed, knowing he'd caught her before she'd left.

When she saw him, she paused, surprise lighting up her face. They'd been friends for a while now, and Phil enjoyed her company. Joan had added a great deal to the support group, and to his life, too. She had a gentle way about her, and was quick to laugh and quick to encourage others. She didn't take herself seriously, either. Phil had rarely been more comfortable with a woman than he was with Joan.

"Phil," she said, as a way of greeting. "Did you forget something?"

He'd been by the house earlier in the day for coffee. It'd been an impromptu visit, and they'd sat on the porch with Edison and talked for nearly an hour, following his dentist appointment. It was then that she'd told him her deep worries about Maggie and how the young woman had been stressed to the max, not knowing how best to help her father. The prohibitive cost of the rehab facility had left Maggie reeling after her talk with the bank.

Phil wasn't entirely sure how to explain his arrival. Nervously, he tucked his fingertips into the back pockets of his Levi's and met her halfway up the sidewalk.

She paused, waiting for him to explain himself.

"Are you heading to the Herberts' house?" he asked.

"I am, although I'm not entirely sure what I can do on my own. I'm not much good at carpentry work and wouldn't even consider attempting to repair the front steps. The one thing I can do is clear out the weeds from the flower beds and brighten up the yard."

Phil was relieved Joan hadn't decided to tackle anything inside the house, which would mean having to deal with Roy Herbert.

"Do you mind if I accompany you?" he asked.

Joan's eyes widened with surprise. "You want to come with me?" And then she asked, "Why?"

He shrugged and did his best to explain. "The flower beds are a good start, but you and I both know that lawn is a disaster. We can work together. I'll get the yard back into shape while you're clearing and planting."

"You'd do that?" Even after his explanation, Joan sounded amazed.

"Yup. I'd feel better if you weren't alone with Roy Herbert," he said, revealing his concern. "Plus, I want to help Maggie, too. That young woman could use all the support she can get."

"Oh Phil, this is so thoughtful of you." It looked for a

moment as if she wanted to hug him. She didn't, although Phil would have welcomed her embrace.

"Come on, then. You can ride with me, and we'll stop off at the nursery. I'll pick up what we need there." He led the way to the truck and held open the passenger door for her. Already he felt better and the anxiety that had nagged at him ever since Joan told him of her plans eased.

Once they were on the road, Joan said, "I don't think you need to worry about Roy. I've stopped by the house a couple times, and while Roy hasn't exactly tossed out the welcome mat, he's been decent."

"Maggie was there with you, though, right?"

She twisted her mouth to one side and then the other before confirming the truth. "Not always." She hesitated before placing her hand over his. "Thank you."

"No problem," he said, surprised by the warmth that went through him at her gentle touch.

After collecting what they needed at the local nursery where Phil routinely did business, they drove directly to Maggie's house. Phil would have helped Joan out of the truck, but she climbed down before he could get around.

Standing on the sidewalk outside the house, Phil was struck anew with all that would need to be repaired and fixed before any bank in town would agree to give Maggie a loan.

He collected the lawn mower from the truck, while Joan carried the tray of flowers to the porch.

The front door opened and Roy Herbert stepped out, letting the screen door bang behind him. He placed his hands on both his hips and looked none too welcoming, glaring at them both through narrowed eyes.

"What are you two doing here?" he barked.

"Hello again, Roy," Joan answered in a voice as cool and collected as if Roy had asked her if she wanted a cup of coffee. "You remember Phil Harrison, don't you?"

Roy turned his attention to Phil and answered with a gruff snort and a dismissive gesture. "Still don't know why you're standing on my property like you own the place."

"We're here to help," Joan explained.

"Don't need no help," Roy insisted.

"You do if Maggie is going to get that bank loan," Joan returned, without a hint of censure.

"Don't need no help and don't need no loan. Now scat, the two of you, before I call the police."

Phil found the threat humorous. "You'd make a nuisance call to the police because two volunteers are cleaning up the front of your yard?" he asked, in a joking kind of way. "I don't mean to sound sarcastic, but my guess is they'd laugh you off the block."

Roy continued to glare at the pair as if weighing his options. After a minute, he snorted loudly and shook his head as though admitting defeat. "Go ahead, then, wear yourselves out."

"Thank you, Roy," Joan said generously.

Roy returned to the house, slamming the screen door behind him. The wire mesh was torn and flapped with the force of it.

While Phil surveyed the yard to remove trash and empty beer bottles, Joan started in on clearing the flower bed, an ambitious project for sure. After years of neglect, it was difficult to tell where the lawn stopped and the beds started.

"You need any help?" he asked.

Before she could answer, the front door opened and an elderly Black man stepped outside. He stood on the porch and removed his hat, holding it politely in front of him.

"Roy won't say it, so I will. He appreciates what you're doing. He knows it's not for him but for Maggie, and that's why he's letting you stay." He nodded once, replaced his baseball cap, and returned to the house.

"That was nice," Joan said.

Phil agreed. He stood beside Joan and noticed a smudge of dirt on her cheek. She must have touched her face after she set the tray of flowers on the porch step. Not giving it much thought, he removed his glove and brushed the offending earth aside.

Joan blinked with surprise.

"You had some dirt on your face."

Embarrassed, Joan moved her hand to her cheek and brushed again in case any remained. When she noticed him staring at her she asked, "Did I miss some?"

"No," he said, and looked away as if self-conscious at being caught watching her.

Grinning, Joan elbowed him playfully in the ribs. "Quit your jabbering and get to work."

Chuckling to himself, Phil headed for the lawn mower.

When Maggie returned from work, she noticed Phil's truck in front of the house. She parked behind him and saw Phil and Joan diligently working in the front yard.

"Joan? Phil?" They looked up as she approached, both grinning.

Roy Herbert stood behind the torn screen door, cursing up a storm.

"Dad," Maggie shouted. "Keep your mouth shut."

Her father's eyes widened with shock before he glared at her as if to say she was a traitor to all that was right and good. Maggie ignored him, as she so often needed to if she intended on keeping her sanity.

"What are you two doing?" Maggie asked her friends, although it was obvious they'd been working in the yard for hours. Phil had mowed what lawn there was, while Joan tackled what had once been flower beds. The wheelbarrow was filled to capacity with clippings and weeds. The sun-parched lawn had been enhanced with what looked like a green spray.

"What do you think we're doing?" Joan asked, leaning on a rake. "If you're going to get that loan, we need to get this house into shape."

"I've got the lawn mowed," Phil said, "and spread seed, which is why the lawn has this green tinge. I was about to water it. If the seeds take root, your dad will need to water it every morning and night."

"I'm clearing the flower beds," Joan said, and motioned with her gloved hands toward the semicircle she'd shaped on both sides of the porch. From the way the sweat dampened her bangs, she had labored long and hard. Flowers had always been Joan's weakness. To her friend's way of thinking, no home was complete without flower beds. She'd once told Maggie that flowers said everything about a home and its occupants.

"Where did you get the hose?" Maggie asked, knowing full well her father didn't own one.

Phil answered her. "It was one I had lying around, taking up space."

Maggie was overwhelmed. Putting the yard in order

was a small fraction of the work that needed to be done, but it was a start. She was deeply touched and appreciative, even if her father wasn't.

"I don't know what I ever did to deserve such wonderful friends," she whispered, near tears.

Joan set aside the rake and hugged Maggie. "We love you," she whispered. "If I'd had a daughter, I would want her to be just like you."

That was all Maggie needed to let the tears flow. It'd been a hellish week with her dad. She missed Nick and lived in fear that everything she had sacrificed would be in vain if her father gave in to the lure of alcohol.

"Thank you," she whispered back, hardly able to get the words out.

Maggie had Saturday off. She woke to the sound of her father moaning, leaning over the toilet, emptying everything that remained in his stomach. The space at the rehab center would be available soon, thankfully. When she went to him, he cursed and told her to leave him be. As she had in the past, she ignored him, got a fresh washcloth, and gave it to him to wash his face.

An hour later he was sitting in front of the television, looking pale and out of sorts. Maggie had gotten him to eat a slice of toast and a banana. His appetite had been nonexistent since he was completely off alcohol. It was a triumph that he ate both.

"Time to water the lawn," she told him, as she turned off the television.

He looked at her as if she was insane. "Do what?"

She wasn't putting up with his attitude or arguing.

"My friends planted a lawn, and it needs to be watered. I'm doing everything I can to keep us afloat, Dad, and I refuse to do it alone. I need you to pitch in. You aren't helpless."

"I . . . I have a bad back."

"You have a bad attitude. Now get your butt outside and water that yard." It looked like he was about to argue. He managed a few less than choice words as he made a spectacle of himself getting out of the chair. To her amazement, he did as she asked.

When he finished, he glared at her. "You happy?"

Maggie checked his work, smiled, and said, "Good job, Dad."

He grumbled under his breath and fell into his recliner as if completely spent.

Maggie went back to her laptop, looking online for how to repair the stovetop burners. Only one was serviceable. The oven hadn't worked in years. Her hope was that it would be an easy fix.

"What in the hell!" her father shouted. "Maggie, Maggie, do something. Stop the noise."

Intent on reading the instructions listed on her computer, Maggie hadn't heard anything until her father started yelling. The sound was of someone hammering.

Leaving the kitchen, she went to the front of the house. To her shock she found Nick prying away the porch steps that were about to collapse.

"Nick." She whispered his name, hardly able to believe her eyes.

He must have heard her because he looked up and then, without a word, continued. Opening the screen door, Maggie stepped outside.

Nick seemed unaware that she was standing less than two feet away. That didn't stop her, though. "Nick Sample, look at me."

He looked up, and before he could say a word, she flew off the porch and into his arms. The force knocked him off-balance and he nearly toppled. He dropped his hammer and grabbed hold of Maggie around the waist, lifting her from the ground.

"What the—"

Maggie didn't give him a chance to speak. Wrapping her legs around his waist, she kissed him with everything that was in her heart. At first he resisted, but it didn't take long for him to return the fervor. Slanting her mouth one way and then another, she continued kissing him until they were both completely involved with each other.

"You came to help!" Maggie could barely believe her eyes. Seeing Nick meant everything. Still angry, she slapped his shoulder.

"Hey," he cried. "Okay, okay, I'm an idiot just the way Kurt said."

"Yes, you are. First you're furious I came to live with your mom and want me gone, and then when I do leave, you're furious again."

Nick blushed at the truth. "You're right. I can be a real bonehead, but in my favor, I am willing to admit my flaws. I've been miserable without you and hope you have a forgiving nature."

To show him she did, Maggie kissed him again, and they quickly became so caught up in each other that they didn't hear her father until he started shouting.

"Dad," Maggie said, sliding down Nick's body. "This is Nick."

Her father scowled at Nick; his eyes narrowed. "Are you taking advantage of my daughter?"

Nick stiffened and met her father's gaze head-on. "Are you?"

"I asked you first." The two men glared at each other like gunfighters at the O.K. Corral.

"I hope to take full advantage of your daughter when the time is right," Nick admitted.

Maggie burst out laughing. "If I don't take full advantage of you first."

Her father wasn't finished with him. "What the hell are you doing tearing up my house?"

"I'm repairing these steps, old man, and you should be grateful. Fact is, I could use a bit of help, so get out here."

"Like hell I will."

The standoff continued.

"Then I'm leaving, and you will only have half a porch."

"Good riddance."

"Dad," Maggie cried, staring her father down.

Cursing everything he could think to blaspheme under heaven and earth, Roy opened the screen door and stepped outside. Nick handed him a hammer and told him what he needed to do. While her father was busy taking apart the steps, Nick worked on repairing the screen door.

Maggie had a dozen questions she wanted to ask him. Standing on the other side of the door, the screen between them, she watched him work.

"Nick." She said his name as if it was a prayer. "I've missed you every minute of every day."

He shrugged as if to say he'd gotten along just fine without her.

Maggie smiled to herself, knowing from the way he'd returned her kiss that he felt as strongly about her as she did about him.

"You told my dad you intend to take advantage of me," she reminded him.

He shrugged. "That's what your dad's doing."

"If you believe that, then why are you here?"

He looked up and sighed. "Because I couldn't stay away. God knows I tried. Then Mom told me what you're doing and that you need a bank loan. She said it was unlikely with the house in its current condition." He met her gaze. "I figured you could probably use a carpenter, and so here I am."

"This old house needs more than a few new steps," she said, feeling more than a little overwhelmed.

"You can say that again," Nick said, looking around him.

He was right; it all felt so hopeless. "I called for a bid to see the cost of what it would be to paint the house and it was thousands of dollars."

"Can you afford the paint?"

"I . . . I don't know." She wasn't sure why he was asking.

"Seems to me between you, your dad, my mom, and me, we could work on getting it painted a bit at a time. Phil would probably help, too."

Maggie bit her lower lip and nodded. "We could do that."

"I couldn't let the woman I'm falling in love with

tackle this all on her own," he said, meeting her gaze through the filter of the screen.

Maggie placed her hand over her heart and then set it on the screen. Nick grinned and pantomimed her gesture, their hands pressing against each other with the screen between them.

In the background, Maggie heard her father continuing to cuss away. It was all she could do to keep from laughing.

Chapter 30

Joan was exhausted and at the same time exhilarated. She'd spent the day helping Maggie and Roy Herbert, with Nick and Phil working at their side. They'd been at it for two weeks and made vast improvements—enough for the bank to agree to a loan. Roy was in rehab and following the program, determined to maintain his sobriety.

Nick and a couple of his friends from the construction crew had repaired the leaky roof, the house had a fresh coat of paint, and they'd recently started work on the inside, painting and updating. Most all the updates in the furniture had come from the Salvation Army. The kitchen had been the first project Maggie had tackled, with freshly painted cupboards and an almost new table-and-chairs set. She'd been able to replace the stove's burners after trying to repair them and failing, and Nick had found a toaster oven on eBay for less than ten dollars.

The best news was that Roy was a resident at the Turning Point Treatment Center. Even better, Maggie had decided to move back in with Joan. Hearing the news had made Joan's day. She'd missed her.

The decision had come after the advice Lyle, Roy's AA sponsor, had given Maggie. Lyle had suggested Roy's daughter attend Al-Anon, a support group for those closely associated with alcoholics. After only a few meetings, Maggie decided she was fast becoming a crutch to her father's sobriety. She'd done everything she could to help start Roy on the right path. The rest was up to him. At this point, his mind was set, and he was just as stubborn as Joan had found him to be. She believed he was capable of remaining sober.

Maggie was committed to loving and supporting her father, but not if it meant sacrificing her future plans to finish her schooling. She had her own life, her own goals. Knowing her father, Maggie realized he would use every opportunity to keep her with him. Convinced she had done all she could for him, Maggie realized that sooner or later, Roy would need to stand on his own.

Sitting now in her kitchen, a glass of iced tea in her hand and Edison at her feet, Joan reflected on how much her life had changed since her birthday. She was happy, when not long ago she'd been convinced she never would be again. Her life was full. She'd forged new friendships.

The grief counseling group had been instrumental in helping her to look toward the future. She'd become good friends with Mary Lou. They had a lot in common and often met outside the group for lunch and the occasional movie. Her friendship with Phil had progressed, too, as both he and his father had lent a helping hand with Maggie's house.

When Joan's phone chirped, she barely had the energy

to pick it up and answer the call. Seeing that she'd left it on the kitchen counter, close enough to reach without major effort, she grabbed it.

"Hello."

"Hey, Mom, it's Steve."

She grinned at the sound of her son's voice. "Hey, yourself. What are you up to?" They communicated more often these days, and that pleased her. The deepening relationship with her children was another benefit that had come since May.

"What are you doing December fifteenth?"

She smiled at the question, thinking he was planning on sending her a Christmas surprise. Likely tickets to a show or something else he knew she'd enjoy.

"I don't have a single thing on my agenda."

"Good. How about flying into Phoenix for a wedding?"

Joan's heart stilled. "A wedding?" The question was filled with hopeful anticipation.

"Yes. I asked Zoe to marry me again, and she accepted. We decided to set the date right away."

"Oh Steve, that's fabulous news." The excitement in her son's voice told her how pleased and happy he was. She swallowed hard at the lump of joy that filled her throat. Her son had come to his senses. He loved Zoe and was willing to commit his life to her.

"Nick's agreed to be my best man, and Zoe already has her wedding dress picked out. Of course, she won't let me see it, not yet. She wants me to wait for the wedding, which is fine. We put money down for a venue and are talking to a catering company next week."

"Oh Steve, I'm so happy I feel like crying."

"Don't be silly. You should know I thought a lot about what you said earlier this summer. I knew I loved Zoe; I don't know why I was acting like such a fool. Pride, I guess. When I heard she was dating someone else, it made me sick to my stomach. I was miserable and lonely and realized what you said was true. You'll be happy to know I tore up that list."

"I'm so pleased." It was hard to hold back her excitement.

"It didn't take me long to realize it didn't matter how much money I had in the bank, or what my career goals were; if I didn't have someone to share life with, they meant nothing. Thank you, Mom. I don't know what made you reach out to me that day, but I'll be forever grateful that you did."

The call ended a few minutes later with Joan smiling so big her mouth hurt.

She barely had time to process the news when the front door opened and Nick and Maggie arrived.

Nick carted Maggie's suitcase up to the bedroom while she announced their arrival.

"It's good to have you back," Joan said, hugging her close. Because they'd been together practically every day since Maggie had moved out, it didn't seem that they'd been apart at all.

"It's good to be back."

Joan realized what a big day this was for Maggie and her father. "How'd it go?" she asked. The center had asked Maggie to attend a meeting with her father and she'd spent the morning with him.

Maggie looked pleased. "I got to see Dad for the first time since he checked in, and after the meeting, I prom-

ised him he could count on me to be there for any further
family counseling sessions. He's stayed sober this long."
This was said with both pride and a mixture of surprise.
"I can only hope he learns the skills he's going to need to
maintain his sobriety."

That was Joan's hope, too. Already she'd seen a
change in Roy in the three weeks since he'd taken his last
drink. He'd helped as best he could with the work on the
house. She didn't expect him to show his gratitude for all
those who'd stepped up on his behalf. To her surprise,
right before he entered rehab, Roy had thanked them with
tears in his eyes. Most of the time, he'd loudly complained and then made them iced tea. Maggie assured her
this was her father's way of showing his appreciation.

What Joan found the most gratifying was the change
in Roy's attitude toward Maggie. He actually showed his
daughter affection. Limited to a fleeting smile or a nod in
her direction, but still, it was there. Joan certainly noticed, and she was confident Maggie did as well.

"I didn't set anything out for dinner," Joan said, re-
gretting that she hadn't thought far enough ahead that
morning before she left to work at Roy's house.

"No worries, Nick and I are going out for pizza."

Her younger son entered the kitchen. "Want to join us,
Mom?"

"No thanks, I've got my group tonight." Tired as she
was, Joan wouldn't miss another meeting. Every week,
she came away with a fresh insight and deepening friendships. The coffee, and often pie, gathering after the meetings was its own therapy session. This was the time when
the deep friendships formed.

"I forgot it's Wednesday," Maggie said. Little wonder,

after all the hours the young woman had put in working on her father's house. Joan was there most days, and Nick stopped by after work and on weekends, often bringing along a few friends who owed him favors.

Nick had his arm around Maggie's waist. It went without comment that the two had fallen in love.

"By the way," Joan said, "I heard from Steve. It seems he told you about his wedding plans before me."

Nick grinned sheepishly. "Yeah, he was pretty pleased with himself. I haven't met Zoe, but I like her already."

"Me, too."

"They're coming to town Labor Day so we can all meet her."

This was news. Excited as he was, Steve had forgotten to mention that during their conversation.

Nick added, "Steve, Zoe, Maggie, and I are planning to attend Bumbershoot together."

Bumbershoot was an annual art and music festival celebrated over Labor Day Weekend. She'd attended the festival several times with Jared over the years. Bumbershoot. The word was a colloquial term for umbrella, which Joan found fitting for anyone living in the rainy Pacific Northwest. However, someone using an umbrella was immediately classified as a tourist. Those who lived in the region rarely bothered, as most of the rainfall came in the form of drizzle.

"Oh dear."

"What's wrong?"

"Nothing. It's just that I asked my support group to a barbecue that Saturday." She'd issued the invitation at their last session. Her small group of friends had sounded pleased and excited to see the beautiful yard Joan had so often mentioned, giving Phil credit.

Nick quickly dismissed her concern. "No problem, Mom. We'll be gone all day. You have your fun with your friends."

After unloading Maggie's vehicle, the two were off for pizza, their laughter echoing through the house as they left.

Joan showered and changed clothes before her meeting, eager to see her friends. When she arrived at the counseling center, Phil was in the parking lot, waiting for her.

He'd been wonderful with Maggie and Roy, helping out with far more than the work on the yard. Even his father had helped. Phil had given up his weekend to help paint the outside of the house. He worked next to Roy and the two had struck up what appeared to be an engaging conversation. Even better, during that time, Joan hadn't heard Maggie's father complain even once. That was a small miracle.

"Did everything go well with Maggie's meeting with Roy?" Phil asked.

"She seemed to think so. I have a feeling the session helped her as much as it did Roy."

Opening the door for her, Phil said, "That's good news, too. I hope you aren't wearing yourself out."

"I'm good." Joan's days had purpose now. "I talked to the school district about becoming a volunteer tutor." The inspiration had come from Maggie and also the neighborhood children, Ellie and Todd. They were frequent visitors these days. They used visiting Edison as an excuse, but Joan knew the cookies she offered them were an equal draw to their affection for her puppy.

"So you followed through with that?"

She smiled, because it sounded as if he'd doubted her. Last meeting was when she'd mentioned becoming a tutor. This evening she hoped to fill everyone in on her latest commitment. She'd stopped off as well at the local nursing home and set up a time each week to bring Edison in to lift the spirits of the seniors residing there.

When they came into the room, Joan noticed that Mary Lou had saved the chair next to her. Doug sat on her other side and Sally was there early, too. They didn't lack for conversation before three others joined, along with Dr. O'Brien.

The hour passed swiftly, as it did every week. It hardly seemed any time at all. Mary Lou and Joan walked to the parking lot together after assuring everyone they'd join them at Shari's for coffee and pie.

"Have you noticed how Doug makes a point of sitting next to you every week?" Joan asked her friend as they walked to their respective cars parked next to each other. "I think he might be interested in you."

"What?" Mary Lou adamantly shook her head. "You're imagining things."

"Maybe. Maybe not." She jiggled her eyebrows and enjoyed Mary Lou's flustered look.

Not to be outdone, Mary Lou returned, "Speaking of someone being interested, have you noticed the way Phil looks at you lately?"

"Phil? No. He doesn't look at me any different now than when I first joined the group."

Mary Lou slowly shook her head. "None are so blind

as those who cannot see. Isn't that how the saying goes? Why else do you think he'd give up his weekends to help at the house? It isn't for Maggie that he's put in all those hours painting. He did it for you."

"Do you think?" Joan needed to mull this over. Phil hadn't shown any outward signs of affection. Sure, he'd been the first one to volunteer, and had started with the lawn. When he'd returned later to pitch in as needed, she'd been pleasantly surprised. With so much work to be done, Maggie, and Joan, too, appreciated all the help they could get.

The parking at Shari's was often limited, so Mary Lou and Joan drove together. They didn't speak much. For her part, Joan was mulling over Mary Lou's insight into Phil. She had to wonder if Phil was interested, and, more important, if she was ready.

In another few weeks, it would be five years since Jared's passing. As Emmie was quick to remind her, Joan had a lot of life left in her. Of one thing she was certain: If she was ever thinking about a new relationship, she would like it to be with Phil.

From what he'd told her, Joan knew that Phil hadn't been in any romantic relationship since he'd lost his daughter. The subject came up again a few weeks back when a newer group member had started dating a short while after his wife's passing. Phil had advised against starting a relationship too soon and mentioned that he felt he had to be emotionally healthy before he would consider dating anyone.

"You're quiet all of a sudden," Mary Lou commented as they arrived at their destination.

"We both are."

"True," Mary Lou agreed. "I've mostly adjusted to widowhood. It's been over three years now, but even after all that time, it still feels like yesterday. The group has made a world of difference. And palling around with you and the others, too."

Joan felt the same. Her life was far better than it had been at any time since Jared's passing.

And to think it'd all started with a nasty letter from her HOA.

Chapter 31

The weather over Labor Day Weekend couldn't have been more perfect. The sun was out, and a warm breeze tempered the eighty-degree high predicted for Saturday afternoon.

Joan had everything set up for the barbecue with her friends. Within a few months, that's what each one had become—a treasured friend. They were the ones who'd showed her the path to new possibilities and the promise of the future.

Her sons, along with Maggie and Zoe, had left earlier in the afternoon and were headed to the Seattle Center for Bumbershoot, where an entire venue of events was lined up. Joan couldn't remember seeing Steve and Nick this happy. Her sons were both doing well in their selected careers, but, more important, in their personal lives, and that was all she'd ever wanted for them. In the years since losing their father, their bond had grown deeper, in part because of their concern for her. Joan enjoyed the banter between them, the inside jokes, the teasing, and the laughter. They were best friends along with being brothers.

Meeting Zoe highlighted the holiday weekend. Joan had instantly fallen in love with her son's fiancée. It didn't take her long to recognize that the young woman was a good match for her goal-driven son. Zoe brought balance into the relationship. She was bright and warm: exactly the kind of woman Steve needed to show him the fun side of life. The three of them had forged a deeper, more loving relationship in the last four months since she'd started on the road to acceptance and healing.

Maggie had made a big difference in her life, too. Joan's affection ran deep for her boarder. The two were kindred spirits. Joan considered Maggie the daughter of her heart.

Roy Herbert had finished his treatment and, from what Maggie told her, was doing great. He remained persnickety and didn't have a lot of good to say about the staff, the food, or his fellow addicts. None of it mattered, as long as he continued to follow his program and remained sober.

When the four left the house, piling into one car, Joan had stood on the porch, watching them go, her heart warmed by the sound of their laughter. She remained there long after they'd driven off, mulling over the changes since May. Jared would be pleased to know they had each, in their own way, come to terms with his passing.

Joan's friends arrived for the barbecue early in the afternoon. Edison was there to greet them, barking his welcome and then wagging his tail until each new arrival gave him the attention he craved.

Everything was ready. The picnic table was covered

with a red checkered tablecloth. Earlier Joan had arranged a large floral bouquet with the flowers from her own yard. The large vase graced the center of the table, abundant with white roses, chrysanthemums, and black-eyed Susans. The wicker lawn furniture that had been stored in the shed was dusted off and placed in the yard for the first time since COVID.

Mary Lou arrived with a huge bowl of her famous potato salad that Joan swore was enough to feed fifty. Phil had offered to man the barbecue. He contributed pork ribs to go along with the hamburgers Joan supplied. She had spent the morning baking a family favorite dessert, balsamic roasted fruit cobbler, making two pans to be sure there would be enough to feed the Bumbershoot kids once they returned.

Doug brought several varieties of drinks: sodas, beer, spritzers, and bottled water. Sally had a bean dip she swore everyone would love. Sherry brought her family-favorite baked beans, and Dr. O'Brien came loaded down with five different varieties of chips.

The newcomers to the group, Patty and Ely, who had both lost their partners, made a showing but didn't stay long. They mingled for a time, ate, and left soon thereafter, clearly feeling awkward just yet. Joan had been there once herself. The two were new and in various stages of their grief and loss. They appreciated the invitation and welcomed the excuse to socialize. At the same time, they felt out of their element, attuned as they were to socializing with their partners, not as a single person. The strangeness of it all wasn't an easy adjustment. Joan understood.

Doug sat next to Mary Lou on the lawn furniture, and

Sally and Dr. O'Brien were deep in conversation, which left Joan with Phil. Covered by the shade of the neighbor's madrona tree, they sat in padded wicker chairs, their feet crossed at the ankles on the ottomans, a cool drink in their hands.

"The ribs were a great addition," she told him, grateful he had thought to add them to the menu. He'd marinated the ribs overnight and partially baked them earlier before adding the long, thin slab to the grill to add the char and smoky flavor.

"Amanda loved my ribs," he said. "It was her favorite meal. It was what she asked me to make every year for her birthday dinner. My goodness, you should have seen her dig into those ribs. She'd have sauce smeared from one side of her face to the other with the biggest smile you can imagine. It's one of my happiest memories with her." He sighed with a smile. "I haven't barbecued even once since she died."

Surprise must have shown in Joan's expression, because Phil added, "No particular reason, other than Dad prefers to do all the cooking."

Joan appreciated that he would share the memory with her. "This is the first time I've had the barbecue out since Jared passed. It was too much work for me alone."

It came to Joan that she had reached the point where she could talk about Jared and not immediately experience the sharp pain of his loss. This was growth, she decided.

"We're each making strides forward, aren't we?" she said, sharing the insight.

"We are," he agreed. He set his drink down and nodded toward Doug and Mary Lou. "I think Doug is smitten."

Joan smiled and silently agreed. Mary Lou had been flattered and a little embarrassed by Doug's attention. On her own, Joan's friend admitted she might be ready for a relationship.

Dr. O'Brien was the first one to leave. She had plans with family later in the afternoon.

Joan got up from the chair and walked the counselor to the door. "I'm grateful you could come," she said.

"This was lovely," Dr. O'Brien said, briefly hugging Joan. "I want you to know how proud I am of you, Joan. When we first met you were fragile and unsure of yourself. It's been a blessing watching you find your inner strength. You've come a long way in a short amount of time."

"The group helped immensely. Looking back, I can't believe how stubborn I was, insisting those sessions weren't for me." It embarrassed her now, and she would always be grateful how the counselor had encouraged her to attend just one meeting before she made her final decision.

Dr. O'Brien squeezed Joan's forearm. "But it didn't take you long to recognize the benefit of these shared experiences."

"Journaling helped, too, and of course the workbook." Joan had faithfully read each week's notes and took the words to heart. It would have been easy to read the book alone, as each chapter had resonated with her. What had been instrumental in her progress was following through with the assignments suggested at the end.

"Your little Edison is a sweet puppy. How old is he?"

"As best I can tell, six months." She picked him up and he immediately licked her face.

Dr. O'Brien opened the screen door.

"Thank you for coming," Joan said, knowing the counselor had a busy life. That she'd been willing to share part of her holiday with the group was a compliment Joan didn't take lightly.

"Thanks again," Dr. O'Brien said, as she headed down the steps.

By the time Joan returned to the backyard, Sally was gathering up the last of her bean dip and preparing to head out.

"You don't have time for dessert?" Joan asked, a little surprised Sally would leave so soon.

"Did you count how many of those ribs I ate?" she asked, placing her hand over her stomach. "I wouldn't mind taking a piece with me, though."

"You got it."

Doug and Mary Lou decided it was time to leave, too. Joan wrapped up to-go plates with the cobbler and saw the three out the door.

That left her alone with Phil.

"I'll help with the cleanup," he said, when she returned from seeing her friends out the door.

"No need, Phil. There isn't a lot to do."

"Nonsense. I'm not leaving you alone with this." He started carrying in the leftover food, of which there wasn't much. The ribs had disappeared in quick order, and all that remained were a couple hamburger patties and a few buns.

Mary Lou left Joan with the potato salad, convinced Steve and Nick would finish it off, and she wasn't wrong.

Joan made room for the bowl in her refrigerator. Doug didn't want to worry about carting the leftover drinks home, so Phil brought those into the house. Standing side by side with Joan, he stored the cans on the bottom shelf.

Turning at the same time, Joan lost her footing and nearly stumbled. Phil caught her by the shoulders. She was about to make a joke about her lack of grace when her eyes met his. In that moment it felt as if the world went still. All sound faded, as something unspoken flowed between them. Joan didn't know when this had happened, all she knew was this incredible feeling that came over her unlike anything she had ever experienced before. They were friends and slowly it had grown into more. The night he'd stopped by when she'd missed a meeting, and then later working side by side, helping Maggie with the house. Their relationship had turned a corner. Joan found herself thinking about him more and more and enjoyed the time they'd spent together.

Neither spoke. Phil lifted his hand and brushed the hair away from the side of her face.

She covered his hand with her own and closed her eyes, leaning her face into his palm.

"You said Mary Lou and Doug might be ready for a relationship."

"Yes," she whispered, hardly able to find her voice.

"What about you? Are you ready?"

Nodding, she offered him a gentle smile. "I believe I am."

"Good," he said, his own voice gruff with emotion. He dropped his hand and leaned forward to kiss her.

Joan had often wondered how she would react to another man's touch. When Phil's mouth settled over hers, any doubt she'd feared instantly evaporated. They became fully involved in the kiss until they were both breathless.

With their foreheads touching, Joan smiled, and Phil did, too. "Are you ready for the rest of your life, Joan Sample?"

"Absolutely."

"Me, too," he whispered.

Epilogue

Joan sat back on her knees and wiped the perspiration from her brow. Edison was lazing on the lawn at her side, perfectly content to nap in the sunshine. Joan had been working, clearing out her front flower beds, getting them ready to plant the columbine and marigolds, two of her favorites. It was hard to believe that at this same time last year, she'd found it difficult to walk out the front door, let alone work outside in her yard.

What a difference a year can make! She still missed Jared and the life they'd once shared. She'd come to realize that revolving her entire life around him and his career had left her empty to enjoy her own pursuits. At the time she hadn't minded. They were partners, best friends, soulmates. Without him she had felt depleted, lost, and so terribly alone.

No longer. With the help of the grief therapy group, she'd found the wherewithal to move forward and take hold of life. A life she barely recognized now and that was, in some ways, better than the one she left behind.

Mary Lou had become a treasured friend, and Sally, too. Mary Lou had briefly dated Doug, but it hadn't taken her long to realize they were never meant to be more than friends.

Steve and Zoe had married in December. Her son faithfully called her every Sunday afternoon, and their conversations often weren't long but were always meaningful as they more openly shared details of their lives. More than once, he'd told her he didn't know why he'd waited as long as he had to marry Zoe. The two were building a future together. Zoe was full of life, laughter, and fun, spontaneous and joyful. Just hearing the happiness in her son's voice thrilled Joan. He'd taken over as manager of Dick's Sporting Goods' warehouse in the Phoenix area, and while he worked long hours, he made sure he was home for dinner every night and spent ample time with his wife.

Nick and Maggie were going strong, too, and that pleased Joan. It had been a blow to Maggie when her father died suddenly of a heart attack three months after he left the Turning Point Treatment Center. Maggie took his passing hard, as he was her only living relative. Thankfully, Roy Herbert hadn't taken a drink of alcohol in all that time. Another positive was the loving relationship that had developed between Maggie and her father. He was no Prince Charming, and his words were often peppered with grumbles and profanity, but he learned to show his love for Maggie in a dozen different ways. Before his sudden demise, Maggie had told Joan that for the first time since her mother died, she felt like she had a good relationship with her father.

Maggie had inherited the house, and with Nick's help

and the bank loan, she had managed to renovate it into the star of the neighborhood. Joan and Phil had helped as much as they could. The transformation in the front yard gave Joan pride, as the flower beds were full and abundant. Maggie had recently mentioned that people often stopped by to comment on how beautiful her yard was. Some had known her parents and had said how pleased they were to see the home come to life again.

Joan understood exactly what Maggie's neighbors had been saying. Like the flower beds at Maggie's and her own yard, she, too, had a renewed life. And it was a good life. One filled with such happy expectation. Joan Sample had found herself. Her days had purpose, and she felt she was giving to others instead of hiding behind locked doors, fearing whatever was on the other side.

Joan fully expected Nick and Maggie to marry as soon as Maggie finished her studies. Nick had stopped by earlier in the week to ask Joan's opinion on diamonds, which told her he was eager to get a ring on Maggie's finger.

Satisfied that her gardening was finished for the day, Joan stood and removed the gloves from her hands and dusted off her knees. At the sound of Phil's truck, Edison barked his welcome. Joan turned and watched as he parked in front of her home.

A smile came over her as soon as she saw him, and a light, happy sensation flowed through her. Phil was an instrumental figure in her new life. They each had suffered a significant loss and gathered the strength to find their way through the pain.

"Hey," she said, meeting him halfway up the walkway.

"Hey, yourself," he said, and placed a quick kiss on her lips. "I see you've been busy."

"I'm excited to get everything planted." The afternoon was perfect, and Joan didn't want to waste the sunshine.

"I don't know if I ever told you about the first time we met."

"Told me what?" she said, as she slipped her arm around his waist.

Edison demanded attention, and Phil bent down and patted his head. Content now, her puppy chased after a butterfly.

"Your message on the phone when you asked me to come to give you an estimate."

Even now, that call embarrassed her. She could already feel the heat coming into her cheeks. "What about it?"

"You said I must love flowers."

"Don't remind me," she said and groaned. "I can only imagine what you thought. I was so unsure, so scatterbrained, I found it hard to make a simple phone call."

"What you don't know, Joan, my love, is that in that moment, my heart knew."

"Knew what?"

"I know it sounds crazy. I had no idea if you were young or old, married or single, and yet I knew I was going to fall in love with you."

"You're making that up," she teased, and playfully elbowed him in the ribs.

The twinkle in his eyes left and he grew serious. "It's the truth, Joan Sample. Every word."

"Really?"

"Truly," he confirmed.

"That's . . ." Joan couldn't find the words.

Turning her in his arms, Phil kissed her again. "I knew then, and I know it now. I love you, Joan. I waited until I thought you were ready before I gave myself away. The fact is, you've had possession of my heart from the very first meeting."

Leaning her head against his shoulder, Joan sighed. "And you have mine."

"I know," he returned.

Raising her head, she huffed. "You did not."

He grinned, and instead of arguing, he kissed her again. Not a quick peck on the lips, but a full-blown kiss. One Joan felt all the way to the bottom of her soles. She tightened her arms around him and returned the fervor until, through the fog of desire, she heard the school bus in the distance.

"The kids," she whispered.

He kissed the top of her head. "You make me lose my head and feel like a teenager again," he admitted with a soft chuckle.

The thing was, Phil did that for her.

Taking hold of her hand, he asked, "You ready?"

She didn't know what he had in mind, but whatever it was, she was eager to find out.

2-in-1 collections from #1 *New York Times* bestselling author

DEBBIE MACOMBER

Sign up for Debbie's newsletter at
DebbieMacomber.com